THE MELODY THIEF

SHIRA ANTHONY

Dreamspinner Press

Published by
Dreamspinner Press
5032 Capital Circle SW
Ste 2, PMB# 279
Tallahassee, FL 32305-7886
USA
http://www.dreamspinnerpress.com/

The Melody Thief

Cover Art by Catt Ford

ISBN: 978-1-61372-694-5

Printed in the United States of America
First Edition
August 2012

eBook edition available
eBook ISBN: 978-1-61372-695-2

To my sister Rachel, with love.

God, grant me the serenity
To accept the things I cannot change….

Serenity Prayer
Reinhold Niebuhr

CHAPTER

THE MELODY THIEF

Tulsa, Oklahoma

HE SCREWED up his face, trying to ignore the bright lights at the edge of the stage, which burned his eyes and left multicolored imprints on his retinas. Cary Redding was barely fifteen years old, but he sat straight-backed, schooling his expression to reveal only calm resolve. Unlike some of the well-known performers he had watched on video, he did not move his body in time to the music, nor did he bend and sway. The cello became a physical extension of his body, and he had no need to move anything more than his fingers on the fingerboard and his bow over the strings.

When he played, he was transported to a place where it didn't matter that his face had begun to break out or that he seemed to grow out of his shoes every other month. When he played, he forgot his fear that he was *different*—that he was far more interested in Jerry Gabriel than in Jerry's sister Martha. When he played, he felt the kind of warmth he had horsing around with his brother in the backyard, chasing after a football.

For the past three years, he had studied the Elgar Cello Concerto, a soulful, intensely passionate composition, and one he adored. His cello teacher had explained that it had been composed at the end of World War I, and the music reflected the composer's grief and disillusionment. At the time, Cary hadn't been really sure what that meant, but he felt the music deep within his soul, in a place he hid from everyone. In that music, he could express what he could not express any other way, and somehow nobody ever seemed to understand that although the music was Elgar's, the sadness and the melancholy were his own.

At times he was terrified the audience would discover his secret: that he was unworthy of the music. But then his fingers would follow their well-worn path across the fingerboard, and his bow would move of its own accord. The music would rise and fall and engulf him entirely, and the audience would be on their feet to acknowledge the gangly, awkward teenager who had just moved them to tears.

Tonight was no exception. The Tulsa Performing Arts Center was packed with pillars of the community come to hear the young soloist the *Chicago Sun-Times* had proclaimed "one of the brightest new talents in classical music." Cries of "bravo" punctuated the applause, and a shy little girl in a white dress with white tights and white shoes climbed the steps to the stage with her mother's encouragement and handed him a single red rose.

He stood with his cello at his side and bowed as he had been taught not long after he learned to walk. The accompanist bowed as well, smiling at him with the same awed expression he had seen from pianists and conductors alike.

In that moment, he felt like a thief. A liar. The worst kind of cheat.

"Young man," the woman in the red cocktail dress with the double strand of pearls said as she laid her hand on his shoulder, "you are truly a wonder. You *must* come back soon and play for us again."

He knew how to respond; he'd been taught this, as well. "Thank you, ma'am." His voice cracked, as it had on and off for the past six months. His face burned. He was embarrassed he could not control this as well as he could his performance.

"He's booked through the next year," his mother told the woman, "but if there's an opening, we'll be sure to let you know." She would find an opening, no doubt, even if it meant sacrificing his one free weekend at home. His mother never passed up a chance to promote his career.

Back in the green room, his mother looked on as he wiped down the fingerboard of his instrument and gently replaced it in its fiberglass case, then carefully secured his bow in the lid. He'd barely looked at his mother since they'd left the small crowd of well-wishers who had gathered in the wings. He didn't need to see her face to know she was displeased. He didn't really want to know what he'd done wrong this time, so he started to hum a melody from a Mozart sonata he'd been studying. Humming helped take his mind off his guilt at letting her down again.

"You rushed through the *pizzicato* in the last movement," she said. "We've been over that section so many times, Cary Taylor Redding. You let your mind wander again."

He tried not to cringe; she only used his full name when she was *very* disappointed in him. "I'm sorry." His voice cracked again, and he inwardly winced. He didn't have to fight back the tears anymore. He'd stopped crying years ago.

"We'll just have to practice it some more."

He'd also long since stopped asking her why she always said "we" would practice something when he was the one doing the practicing. The one and only time he had pressed the issue, she had responded with a look of long-suffering patience. For days after, the guilt had pierced his gut and roiled around inside until he had apologized for several days running.

"Hurry up now," she told him. "We have a long drive back home."

"Did Justin call?" he asked with a hopeful expression.

"Why would your brother call?"

"He said he'd let me know if his team won tonight." He pulled on his thick winter jacket, grabbed the handle of the cello case, and dragged it across the floor on its roller-skate wheels.

"He can tell you all about it tomorrow."

He fell asleep in the front seat of the minivan as they headed back to Missouri. He did not dream, or at least, he didn't remember what he had dreamed about. He never did.

CHAPTER  2

BEST LAID PLANS

Milan, Italy—Thirteen years later

"OH FUCK, yeah!" Cary shouted in English as he pushed back against the other man's hips. The skinny Italian kid he'd picked up grunted and thrust harder, ratcheting up the pace, so Cary gripped the toilet to keep his balance. Sweat dripped down his neck. He never enjoyed kissing. He didn't need it. He liked it like this: rough, fast, and anonymous.

Someone in the next stall laughed, but Cary didn't give a shit. This was how it was supposed to be in a place like this, and someone else listening in only made it so much hotter. Here, he was just another nameless fuck, and that suited him just fine.

"That's it. Oh God, yes!" he cried as the kid nailed his gland again. He stroked himself in rhythm with the young man's thrusts, groaning as he came with a strangled gasp into his sweaty palm. The smell of come mingled with the faint scent of urine and toilet deodorizer. Years ago, the combination made him sick. Now, the seediness of it just made it more of a turn-on.

His partner grunted as he came hard, his body shuddering and his breaths coming in stutters. A minute later, the kid pulled out. Cary saw the used condom hit the water of the commode, and heard the sounds of a zipper and the latch being released on the stall door. He had already forgotten the kid's face. It was better this way. He didn't want anything but sex anyhow, and he didn't want to be forced to make small talk. In Italian, no less.

He leaned against the grimy wall and wiped himself with the cheap toilet paper, then added it to the condom in the water and flushed it down. His stomach rumbled—a few more drinks and he wouldn't remember he was hungry. He'd reheat something when he got back, or maybe he'd just sleep it off and grab something in the morning instead. It was usually better to nurse a hangover with an empty stomach. He knew from experience.

He walked back into the bar and sat at a table in the corner, making eye contact with the bartender. A minute or two later, he nursed a scotch and soda, his fourth that night, and leaned over to the man at the next table.

"*Sigaretta?*" Cary asked.

The man grunted and handed him a cigarette, then lit it for Cary as they leaned toward each other to span the short gap between tables.

Cary hated cigarettes. He only smoked in bars, and only after sex. At least that was what he told himself. He preferred the unfiltered variety—it gave him a more immediate buzz. They were easier to find here than in the States.

His hand shook slightly as he brought the cigarette to his lips and inhaled the acrid smoke. It was better than the drugs, right? He'd tried those too, but he'd given them up because they interfered with his playing. He could always sleep off the booze and the nicotine.

One of the regulars walked through the entrance, and their eyes met. Silvio. Nice ass. Terrific bottom.

It was turning out to be a great night.

AT NEARLY three in the morning, Cary stumbled out onto the empty Milan side street. His ass was sore and his thigh muscles were tight. He liked it that way. He needed to feel it in his bones the next morning or he hadn't gotten enough.

A light fog hung over the city, the fall air cool and damp. Cary shivered, his thin T-shirt little help against the chilly breeze. His housekeeper was right—curse Roberta, she was *always* right—he should have worn his leather jacket. He looked around for a cab, but there were none in sight. He'd walk over to the main avenue, via Padova, to catch one.

Fuck, he thought, tripping over the uneven pavement as he turned the corner onto another small street. He didn't notice the two men huddled in the doorway of a darkened building until one of them grabbed him by the neck. He caught the glint of a knife in his peripheral vision. *Fucking hell.*

"*I soldi*," hissed one of the thugs, the one standing in front of him smoking the remainder of a joint.

"I don't understand," Cary said in English. It was a lie. He was fluent in Italian. "I'm American."

"Money," the man repeated, in English this time. "Give."

"Don't have any." He didn't pull his wallet out and hand it over. Maybe it was the aftereffects of the alcohol. Or maybe it was the rough sex and the feeling of empowerment that still lingered at his frayed edges. Either way, he wasn't going to let these assholes push him around.

The man's response came in the form of a knee to his gut. Cary doubled over, coughing and spluttering. *Shit.* Was that blood he tasted on his tongue?

"Money. Now."

"You're fucking insistent, aren't you?" he blustered. The man behind him wrapped an arm around his neck and pulled him upright once more, pressing hard on his Adam's apple and making his vision swim with tiny specks of silver.

The man standing in front of him nodded. A hand reached into Cary's jeans pocket, pulled out the soft calfskin wallet, and held it up to the light. "Expensive," he told his partner in Italian.

"You come with us." The other thug's expression was one of triumphant glee. He pulled Cary's ATM card out of the wallet and waved it in his face. "Bank."

"No fucking way," Cary shouted. He wrenched himself free of the headlock and backed toward the curb.

The lights of via Padova were visible a scant block away. If he could just make it there, he might be able to get help or maybe scare them off. He turned to run, but something hard hit him in the kidneys, and he fell to his knees. He struggled back to his feet.

Before he could defend himself, one of the thugs' fists connected with his chin, and he staggered backward. He tried to maintain his balance but failed miserably. He hit the concrete hands first, and something in his left wrist snapped. He vomited up what little food was left in his stomach as a wave of intense pain washed over him.

"Asshole," he spat.

"Get away from him," someone warned in Italian. The voice came from nearby, but the pain in Cary's gut was still so bad he couldn't look up at the newcomer's face. He heard what sounded like a scuffle, a groan, and then footsteps running down the pavement.

"Are you all right?"

He pushed the hand on his shoulder away without thinking. The world spun and the pain in his wrist shot up his arm. "Oh shit," he groaned, clutching the wrist.

"I'm not going to hurt you," the man said, this time in lightly accented English. "You need help." The voice was calm, reassuring. "You need a hospital."

"No hospital," Cary gasped and tried to stay alert. "Leave me alone."

He got back to his feet, and the lights from the boulevard blurred at the edges. The last thing he remembered before he passed out was two strong arms as they caught him.

CARY awoke in an unfamiliar bed to the sound of muffled voices speaking in Italian. "... found him off via Padova. No identification. The man who brought him says he's an American."

He forced his eyes open and saw the metal sides of the hospital bed, the IV hanging from the pole, the needle taped to his hand, and the light-yellow curtains at the sides of the bed. The place smelled of disinfectant.

The last time he'd been in a hospital was when he'd watched his mother wither and die, her body wracked with pain from the chemo and radiation. He remembered his own guilt as he had sat by her bed, helpless to do anything. It had been the final insult, a coda, as it were, to their tumultuous relationship. He had never done anything right by her.

He reached for his right earlobe, jostling the IV, but not caring. The small diamond stud in his ear was still there, thank God. It had been a gift from his brother on his twenty-first birthday and was the only piece of jewelry he wore.

As he was getting his bearings, the shadows in the room shifted. No, not shadows—a man, seated in the corner. "How are you feeling?" he asked in English as he stood up and walked over to the bed.

Cary studied the newcomer through a haze of painkillers. Italian, judging by his accent, although his appearance was not classically Italian: blond hair, blue eyes, about the same height as Cary, early thirties, and hot as hell. Not that a man like that would ever look twice at Cary. Guys like him never did, and who could blame them?

"Do I know you?" Cary's voice was hoarse, and his mouth felt full of cotton.

The man looked back at him with a mixture of concern and humor. "You could say we've met."

"You... you're the man from the street." Cary recognized the voice. "How long have I been here?"

"A day," the Italian answered. "Perhaps I must introduce myself," he added. "I am Antonio Bianchi."

Cary hesitated. "Connor Taylor."

It was the name he used in the clubs. Or at least it had been since his agent had bailed him out of jail when a not-so-rainbow-friendly gendarme had caught him quite literally with his pants down outside a shithole of a Paris bar.

What you do with your life off the concert stage isn't my business, Georges Duhamel had told him after he'd bailed Cary out, *but you must at least use another name. I won't have you toss your career in the toilet.*

When all was said and done (and after he'd had a fake New York State driver's license made under the name "Connor L. Taylor"), Cary enjoyed being Connor. Nobody gave a shit if Connor liked to fuck men in the restrooms or alleyways behind rundown bars. Why would anyone care? After a few years, Connor had become Cary's excuse for the late nights and anonymous fucks—when he wasn't practicing or performing, Cary Redding *was* Connor Taylor.

"A pleasure to meet you," Antonio said.

"Thanks. For last night, I mean."

His wrist ached, throbbing to a dull beat like an insistent drum. His head felt like it was filled with jagged rocks. He looked down and saw the cast on his left arm. He vaguely remembered falling. Right, he had tried to catch himself before he hit the pavement.

Oh God.

"My wrist." He spoke the words aloud and his voice cracked. He tried to move his fingers, but the pain was so bad he gasped. A broken wrist meant he couldn't play. Without his cello, he was nothing. His stomach clenched and his eyes burned. In an effort to master his emotions, he turned away and bit his cheek.

"The doctor says your wrist will be fine," Antonio said, perhaps sensing Cary's distress.

This can't be real. I'm going to wake up and....

"I need to get out of here." The hospital room was suddenly too small. Panicked, Cary tried to sit up, but Antonio put a firm hand on his shoulder.

"The doctor… he says you may leave when you are ready, but you have this—" He struggled to find the word. "—*commozione cerebrale*," he finally said. He pointed to his head. "You know, from falling?"

"A concussion?" It explained the killer headache. Cary lay back in the bed. He felt overwhelmed, defeated. He lifted his hand to his face, and the IV line caught on the edge of the bed.

"*Sì*. A concussion," Antonio said as he freed the line for Cary. "He says you must not be alone tonight. Is there somewhere I can take you? A person who can look by you, then?"

There was no one. No family or close friends. He had no one, really, except his housekeeper, Roberta.

"If you wish, you may stay with me."

Cary realized Antonio had guessed, correctly, that Cary had no one to stay with him.

You shouldn't be surprised. You look like street trash.

He wasn't sure how he felt about that. He knew he looked like one of the hustlers he sometimes paid for sex, and he wondered what kind of man would willingly take someone like that in, knowing nothing about them.

But then again, it's not like someone with a broken wrist and a concussion would be a danger to a big guy like him.

He considered the offer for a moment. It wasn't as if he had anything to fear from Antonio, either. The guy had taken him to the hospital, after all. The offer was far more tempting—no, make that *Antonio* was far more tempting—than asking his housekeeper to play nurse and mother.

He looked away from Antonio. He hoped it would come across as though he were thinking things through, but the truth was that the realization that he was entirely alone hit him harder than he'd expected. He'd never been weak. He'd been on his own for years. He hadn't needed anybody's help. And yet now, he felt vulnerable. He *hated* feeling vulnerable.

He took a slow breath, doing his best to hide his emotional turmoil. "I wouldn't want to impose," he said, trying to sound casual, confident.

"Not at all, signor Taylor. It would be my pleasure."

"Are you sure?"

"I'm sure," Antonio said. Then, as if realizing why Cary might hesitate to accept the invitation of a complete stranger, he added, "But if you are not *confortevole*—ah, what is it?—comfortable with this, I think you can stay here longer. I will not be insulted."

Was it any different to go home with a stranger for a night of fucking? *Guys who come charging in on white horses don't usually rape you the next day.*

He closed his eyes and saw his mother's face. She had predicted this. *You won't be happy living that way, Cary*, she said when he came out to her. *It's not natural. It's a sexual... perversion. It's sinful. An addiction.*

He had defended himself. *I'm not a pervert, Mom. This is me. This is what I am.*

How can you say that, Cary Taylor Redding? How can you risk everything we've worked so hard for?

Funny, how he'd started cruising the bars to show her he didn't give a shit about what she thought. But he'd come to crave the sex, booze, and smokes. They satisfied a hunger his music could not. She hadn't wanted to listen, and in the end he'd just proved her right. He had lost the only thing that really mattered to him: his music.

It's not forever. It'll heal. The thought did little to allay his fear, and he moaned softly.

"Are you all right?" That voice again. Right. Antonio.

"Sorry," Cary said, embarrassed. "I guess I'm still a little sleepy."

"It's okay. I will ask about getting you to leave this place and perhaps something for the pain. You must rest now."

"Thank you." Cary watched as Antonio pulled the covers back over him and walked out of the room. His white knight.

And you're about as far from a princess as they come.

A FEW hours later, having spoken with the doctor, Cary was released from the hospital with a bottle of painkillers and instructions to come back in six weeks to have the cast removed and begin physical therapy. While Antonio went to retrieve his car, Cary quickly provided the hospital staff with his home address. He was grateful the police had taken him to a public hospital—there was no bill to speak of for emergency patients. He wasn't sure how he'd have felt if Antonio had insisted on paying for his stay.

Cary said little as they rode the elevator down to the ground floor. The painkillers had begun to wear off, and he was feeling anxious, tense.

"This broken wrist," Antonio said, perhaps sensing Cary's dark mood, "it will make it difficult for your work, no?"

"You could say that." *Impossible, really.* He pushed the thought from his mind. He would get through this. He reminded himself again that the doctor had said his wrist would be fine in a few months.

"What kind of work do you do?"

"I'm between jobs now." The truth, although not the entire truth. It was late October, and his next gig was in Rome in four weeks. He had also been scheduled to teach a series of master classes in early December.

It could have been worse, he reminded himself as he climbed into Antonio's car a few minutes later. *A hell of a lot worse.*

So why was his gut tense? He tried to focus on something else. It wasn't that difficult. Antonio's broad shoulders were an easy distraction.

ANTONIO'S apartment was nearly as big as Cary's own. The high-ceilinged rooms were tastefully decorated in an eclectic mixture of modern Italian furniture and antiques. Photographs of smiling children and adults adorned the tabletops and bookshelves. From the abundance of blue eyes and blond hair, Cary guessed these were Antonio's family.

"You look tired," Antonio said as he shut the door behind them. "Perhaps I make dinner while you sleep?"

"Thanks." Cary caught a glimpse of a large bed through a doorway to their right. He rubbed his arm above his broken wrist without thinking and winced. The dull ache had now become an angry throb.

"May I get you some pills? For your arm?" Antonio held up the doggie bag of chemicals the hospital had sent home with Cary.

"That would be great."

"Perhaps you like to use the telephone while I get it for you?"

Cary stared blankly at Antonio.

"You know," Antonio continued, "if there is a person who might... ah—" He struggled to find the word. "—worry for you?"

"No," Cary answered as understanding came. "I'm fine. There's nobody."

Worry about me? Other than a geezer of an agent and a brother halfway around the world?

Justin would care. In fact, he would worry a lot. They were brothers, after all. But Cary didn't want to bother him and his family. And Georges, Cary's agent, would have a cow when he learned Cary had broken his wrist, but only because he'd need to cancel a few months of gigs while it healed. Yeah, he'd have to tell the idiot at some point, but why rush it?

He thought briefly of Roberta. *She's your housekeeper. What does she care if you stay away for a few nights? It's not like you haven't before.* But he knew he was lying to himself. Roberta was far more than an employee. He'd call her after he'd had a chance to rest. He'd tell her he was spending the night out so she wouldn't worry.

Something akin to compassion or maybe pity flashed through Antonio's eyes, but he said only, "Please. Use the bed. I will bring you the medicine."

Cary was almost asleep when Antonio came back into the room with a glass of water and a few pills. "This will help with pain," he told Cary. "I will arouse you when dinner is ready."

"Mmm," Cary murmured, repressing a grin in response to Antonio's faulty turn of phrase. It wasn't all that difficult to control himself, since he was damn near asleep already and his wrist hurt like hell. Still, the thought made for some very sweet dreams.

CHAPTER 3

TRUTH IS

"SIGNOR TAYLOR? Connor?" The voice was like chocolate. Better, maybe. Deep and sexy.

Cary kept his eyes closed. He wanted Antonio to say it again. Something like "Coh-noor," only hotter. If his wrist didn't hurt so fuck-shit-damn much, he'd definitely have flirted with the guy by now. Or at least attempted it.

As if he'd be interested.

"Signor Taylor? Dinner is prepared. Are you well enough to come to the table?"

Cary decided what he wanted, what he *needed*, was to hear Antonio speaking Italian. Not that the guy's English wasn't good, but he could just imagine that sinful bass-baritone voice speaking the world's sexiest language. It would mean tipping his hand a little, but he had a few cover stories he used at the bars, along with the phony name. He hadn't planned on sharing more about himself than was absolutely necessary, but hearing Antonio speak to him in Italian was more than worth a bit of the truth.

"*Mille grazie.* But I'm fine. Is there something I can help you with?" Cary answered in nearly flawless Italian.

Antonio's eyebrows shot up in surprise, and he responded in kind. "I didn't know you spoke Italian. And you speak it so well."

Oh so worth it.

"My mom's family was Italian, so I decided to come here after graduate school," Cary said. "I liked it so much I decided to stay. I've been in Milan about five years now."

It wasn't that far from the truth. He had come here to study at twenty-four, the year his trust account had become his own, free from his attorneys' control. The profits from several recordings had been enough to buy the apartment, and he earned enough from his performing gigs to pay for living expenses and Roberta's salary and still put some money away for a rainy day. And with a broken wrist, he figured it was pouring right about now.

The thought made Cary's stomach turn. He didn't want to think about reality. Not yet, at least. He decided instead to focus on the attractive man standing by the bed, looking at him with concern.

Antonio offered him a hand as he sat up. There was nothing overtly sexual in the touch, but Cary liked the contact. His gaze tracked a line from Antonio's hand to his bicep, visible beneath his silk shirt, and his mind wandered. He imagined trailing his lips over the taut skin and inhaling Antonio's scent.

Stop it. You don't even know if the guy's gay, let alone interested.

A quick inventory of his aches and pains and Cary decided he felt pretty good, all things considered. The meds had tamed the pain beast in his arm, as well as his chin and back, where he had been kicked. Using the bed for support, he stood up. His head spun, and he instinctively reached for Antonio's arm.

"Better?" Antonio asked after a moment.

"Better. Just a little dizzy."

He continued to grip Antonio's arm until he regained his bearings. This close, he could smell Antonio's scent on the air. He breathed it in as he tried to place it. Fresh. Citrusy.

A small picture frame by the bed caught Cary's eye. Antonio and another man, dark-haired, attractive, with a neatly trimmed beard. Arm in arm, smiling. Antonio looked very young—Cary guessed he couldn't have been more than twenty-five in the photograph. In the background were colorful houses and water that looked almost green. The Mediterranean. Cary knew of no other place that looked quite like that.

"So," Cary asked as he took a few more deep breaths, "were you coming from a bar when you found me the other night?" He knew full well the only places open in the area at three in the morning were gay bars.

Real subtle. Might as well ask him if he's queer and just be done with it.

Antonio chuckled, and Cary felt his cheeks warm. "I was having drinks with friends at Uno. You know the place?"

Did he know the place? Of course he did. High-end gay bar. Expensive drinks. Good music.

"Sure. I've been there a few times. It's a nice place."

Just not for bathroom fucks.

"Yes," Antonio said. "It's a nice place."

"I'm glad you were there." Cary released Antonio's arm. He didn't really want to, but he wasn't sure he could fight his body's physical response if he stayed this close.

Antonio eyed Cary with concern, then asked, "Would you like to wash up before dinner? There's soap and towels in the bathroom."

"That'd be great, thanks."

"If you'd like, I could go over to your apartment and pick up some clean clothing for you after we eat." Antonio put his arm around Cary's shoulder to steady him and switched on the bathroom light.

"That's really not necessary." Cary wasn't sure how he'd explain the expensive apartment to Antonio, and he knew he wasn't ready to face the new reality of his life. "I'm just going to be sleeping, anyhow. I'll get some clean clothes tomorrow. Thanks, though."

Antonio's arm felt so good around him that Cary leaned into the broad chest without thinking. *God, he smells nice*, Cary thought again as Antonio helped him into the bathroom.

For a moment they just stood there in the doorway, Antonio clearly worried that Cary might pass out. "Are you sure you're all right?"

"I'm fine, really. The dizziness is gone. I'm just a little tired, that's all."

"I'll wait just outside. Let me know if you need me," Antonio told him as he closed the door. He still spoke in Italian. Cary smiled at the realization that his Italian must have passed muster.

Cary walked over to the sink and caught a brief look at himself in the mirror above. He looked as bad, maybe worse than he had expected. His light-brown hair was greasy and his hazel eyes were bloodshot. He hummed to himself as he ran tentative fingers over the rainbow-colored bruise on his jaw, feeling a lump the size of his thumb.

He filled the sink with warm water and splashed it on his cheeks, then washed his face, a process made far more difficult with only one viable hand. (The doctor had given him strict orders not to get the cast wet.) Cary did his best to avoid his jaw, but it still hurt when he patted it with a towel a few minutes later. The soap smelled faintly of lime. Simple, understated. Much like the clothes Antonio wore—jeans with a powder-blue shirt.

Curious, he opened the mirrored cabinet. No fancy aftershaves, no medicine aside from a bottle of aspirin, a straight-edge razor and a package of blades, a badger-hair shaving brush, and a small container of shaving soap.

No-frills guy. Nice.

He liked his men that way: simple, straightforward, masculine. At least, when there *was* a choice. Lately, the pickings had been slim. He imagined wetting the brush and smearing soap all over Antonio's jaw. He had never used an old-fashioned razor, but he pictured himself holding Antonio's chin in one hand, the blade gliding over Antonio's skin, the smell of lime in the air.

He emerged a few minutes later. Antonio stood up from the bed and offered him a clean shirt. "I thought you might like to change anyhow."

"Thanks. I appreciate that. I'm not sure if I can manage it, though…." It would have been a great pickup line, but it was the truth—he really wasn't sure he could pull his own close-fitting T-shirt off over the cast. It had been difficult enough for the nurse to help him put it back on at the hospital.

"Let me help you." Antonio tossed the shirt onto his shoulder and helped Cary pull off the stained T-shirt. He held out a loose-fitting short-sleeved camp shirt much like the one he himself wore. "I thought this might be easier."

The shirt was a bit large in the chest—Cary was leaner than Antonio, but at nearly six foot three, he was about the same height as Antonio—and the length was perfect. There was no doubt it was a better choice than a T-shirt, as it slid over the cast with ease. Cary allowed Antonio to button it closed. He couldn't have done it anyhow, and the feel of Antonio's fingers as they brushed his skin through the filmy fabric was wonderfully sensual.

Cary imagined those fingers on his chest, imagined Antonio taking one of his nipples between his thumb and forefinger and rolling it around. He shivered and looked up at Antonio's face. Antonio's jaw tightened, and Cary felt him pull abruptly away. He wondered if Antonio was feeling the same heat between them. But before Cary could respond, Antonio went to open the bedroom door and said, "Time for dinner."

Dinner was a simple meal of pasta and chicken. "I love to cook," Antonio admitted a bit sheepishly, "but I'm still learning. My mamma taught me the basics, but I'm nothing like she is."

Cary watched as Antonio leaned over his plate and cut the chicken for him. For the second time that night, he felt the heat rise in his cheeks as he caught himself staring at the gap in the fabric of Antonio's shirt in an effort to catch a glimpse of the skin beneath.

A broken wrist and you turn into a blushing Disney princess?

Antonio sat back down and waited for him to spear a piece of the meat. "Good?" he asked as Cary chewed.

It was horrible. Cary imagined how a bicycle tire might taste if it were doused in salt and butter and drowned in white wine. He did his best not to meet Antonio's eager eyes and laughed to himself. The first Italian he had met who couldn't cook.

So Mr. Perfect has an Achilles heel, after all.

"Delicious." He tried to chew the rubbery meat without being too obvious. He was hardly going to complain, though. He was hungrier than he remembered having been in years.

"Really?" Antonio grinned.

"Really."

Cary swallowed an overcooked pasta noodle, repressed a lust-inspired laugh, and hoped Antonio was better in bed than in the kitchen.

Now you're really dreaming.

"So, Signor Taylor—"

"Please, call me Connor."

"Connor, then," Antonio said between sips of wine, "what do you do for a living?"

"Waiter. Not much else available for an unemployed musician to do in Milan." Well, it was mostly true, Cary reasoned. He was definitely unemployed now. The thought scared him more than he'd admit.

Funny, Cary's music had never been part of Connor. But Cary wanted Antonio to know about it. Of course, Connor had also never had a comfortable conversation with another man that didn't revolve around sex.

"Music? Really? What instrument do you play?" Antonio's interest seemed quite genuine.

"I studied composition." This was true. Cary had majored in cello performance and minored in composition at New England Conservatory of Music, although he had never considered a career as a composer. He loved playing the cello too much.

The thought of the cello sitting in his apartment practice studio made Cary's throat tighten. He wished he had some wine, but Antonio must have heard the doctor's warnings about mixing the painkillers with alcohol, and had filled Cary's glass with sparkling water instead.

"Do you like modern music, then?"

"Love it," Cary answered. "Although I like the late romantic stuff just as much. I didn't really discover modern music until I was in school. I love the challenge of it. You know, how it pushes the limits of what we're used to hearing?"

This was also true. Cary's friend and mentor, David Somers, had introduced Cary to modern music in his first year of college when he'd asked Cary to fill in on a new music program for the Chicago Symphony.

"I sat through a performance of John Cage's piano music once," Antonio said with a chuckle. "It mostly pushed the limits of my patience. I wanted to laugh."

"You mean 'Four Minutes, Thirty-Three Seconds'?" Cary snorted. "The one where the pianist just sits at a closed piano for four minutes and does nothing?"

Antonio nodded.

"But that's the point. I mean, Cage knew what he was doing. He was trying to make people think."

"I think I fell asleep."

This time, Cary laughed and leaned over the table with his chin in his good hand. "Well… I probably did too. Just don't tell anybody. But the concept—*that* was cool. Daring, really."

"You love music, don't you?"

"Yeah." The question reminded Cary of his broken wrist, and his face fell. He had been enjoying Antonio's company so much, he had nearly forgotten about his wrist.

Antonio seemed to sense Cary's discomfort. "I love music too. But I'm a terrible musician. My mother gave me piano lessons when I was a kid. The teacher fired me." He laughed, but Cary saw a hint of pain in Antonio's eyes at the admission.

Apparently his mother's cooking lessons were about as successful.

"What do you do for a living, Antonio?"

Antonio sipped his wine again, taking his time to answer, as if he were considering something. "I'm a lawyer," he said eventually. "I advise businesses."

Gorgeous man, boring job, Cary concluded. "That's interesting," he said, trying to look as if he meant it.

"Not really. But I get to travel. That's the only really interesting part of the work."

Antonio picked up Cary's glass to refill it, and his hand lightly touched Cary's forearm. Their eyes met, and Cary wished he were drinking something stronger. A *lot* stronger. Why the hell was he hesitating at all? The worst that could happen would be for Antonio to reject his advance, right?

Antonio looked momentarily ill at ease. "Time for dessert," he said as he stood up. He gave Cary a warm smile.

A snappy comeback—a come-on, really—crossed Cary's mind, but he said nothing. It just didn't seem right. Instead, he stood and picked up his plate. Pain shot up his broken wrist, and he winced.

"You sit. I'll take it. I don't make invalids work."

And a gentleman too.

"Thanks. And thanks for dinner, Antonio."

"You're welcome."

Antonio returned a few minutes later with espresso and a flaky pear tartlet cut in half. "I'm sorry we have to share. I hadn't expected company tonight." He smiled warmly.

"Don't apologize," Cary told him. "It looks delicious."

"I didn't make the pastry," Antonio admitted when Cary rumbled his approval a moment later. "I'm a horrible baker. Consider yourself fortunate."

"I do," Cary answered. But he wasn't thinking about Antonio's baking.

Antonio shot him a strange look but said nothing, and the words hung in the air as they ate their pastries.

CHAPTER  4

LITTLE STINKERS

"WOULD you like to take a bath before bed?" Antonio put the last of the dishes away in the kitchen as Cary leaned against the counter and watched.

They'd been discussing the soccer season and Italy's prospects for the World Cup. It had been a comfortable, relaxed conversation, and Cary realized he'd actually been flirting with Antonio.

"Is that a hint?" Cary said with a playful grin.

"I hadn't meant it that way. Although since you put it like that… yes. You smell bad." Antonio's grin belied his words, and Cary realized he too was flirting.

"I'm hurt that you'd say that." Cary put his good hand against his chest and tried to look insulted. He knew he smelled like stale cigarettes, sweat, and worse, even.

Antonio laughed. "No, you're not hurt. And you *do* need a bath."

"Does that mean you're willing to help me?" He needed the help, he reminded himself with a wry grin. The doctor told him not to get the cast wet, hadn't he? He was pretty sure he wasn't imagining Antonio's interest.

Antonio smiled, closed his eyes briefly, and let out a long breath. "I suppose it does."

Cary did his best to appear just appreciative of Antonio's assistance, although judging by Antonio's wary look, Cary realized he wasn't that convincing.

When Antonio emerged from the bathroom a few minutes later, Cary waited in the bedroom, naked. (Unbuttoning a shirt one-handed was far easier than buttoning it). If this surprised Antonio, he didn't show it. Still, he kept his gaze fixed on Cary's face with obvious effort, something Cary noticed with smug satisfaction.

Cary didn't consider himself classically handsome, but he knew he was attractive in a comfortable guy-next-door way. Years of faithful trips to the gym had transformed his gangly body into a more muscular one. He prided himself on his flat stomach and narrow waist and on the hint of definition in his arms. He had never been shy about showing his body, and he sure as hell wasn't going to start now. He was having too much fun. And, he realized, he wanted Antonio.

"The bruising looks painful," said Antonio as Cary climbed gingerly into the bathtub.

"It's not that bad. The medicine helped."

Antonio dipped a washcloth in the warm water and began to wash Cary with clinical detachment. "Keep your wrist on the side. You don't want to get the plaster wet."

"Feels good." Cary closed his eyes and leaned back against the tub.

Antonio snorted.

"What? Can't a guy enjoy himself?"

"You're trying too hard." Antonio ran the cloth down Cary's chest.

"Does that mean you're going to join me in here?" Well, a guy could dream, couldn't he?

"Definitely not."

Antonio finished up with the washcloth, then took the sprayer and proceeded to wet and wash Cary's hair.

"Here," Antonio said a few minutes later, handing Cary the washcloth. "*You* can get the last spot." Cary noticed the hint of blush that stained Antonio's pale cheeks.

"About tonight," Cary began, determined to make the most of the situation. "We can sleep—"

"I'll be sleeping on the couch," Antonio interrupted with calm resolve, having clearly anticipated the question.

Cary frowned. "But it'd be a lot more comfortable if you slept with me in the bed." He stood up and faced Antonio, knowing his arousal was as obvious as the come-on. "You could dry me off and then—"

"It's quite comfortable," Antonio interrupted again. "You can take my word for it."

And with that pronouncement, he offered Cary a hand out of the tub and wrapped the towel around him as fast as he could.

"SURE you don't want to join me in the bed?" Cary asked a few minutes later, as Antonio came out of the bathroom in sweatpants and a T-shirt. He carried a glass of water and more pain pills. "I could warm you up, you know."

"That's very kind of you, Connor, but I'll be quite all right on the couch."

Cary swallowed the pills in silence. He knew the pain in his wrist made sex pretty much a nonstarter anyway. Still, he had enjoyed messing with his scrupulously polite host. And when he was feeling better, who knew? What difference would another twenty-four hours make in the grand scheme of things?

Cary expected Antonio would head back to the living room, but as he picked up a pillow from the bed, he stopped. For a moment, Cary thought Antonio might touch him, but then he sat down on the edge of the bed.

"How are you feeling?" Antonio asked.

"I'm fine." Well it was true, wasn't it?

"I...." Antonio hesitated as if he were trying to say something but thought better of it. "It's just that it must be hard for you. The broken wrist. The bruises. It'll make things difficult for your... work."

Cary glanced at the cast and shrugged. "I'll be okay. I'm sure."

At that moment, though, Cary wasn't so sure. A wave of fear rose within him, and he reminded himself that the doctor had said he'd be fine. He would play again. There wasn't another option, was there? It was everything to him, his music. Without it, what was he? Cary brushed the thought away, as he had done earlier.

"If there is something I can do for you, please let me know." Antonio looked genuinely concerned.

"I'll be fine. Really." Antonio squeezed his shoulder, and Cary wished he could fall into those powerful arms. He imagined what it might feel like to bury his face in Antonio's chest, to feel that body pressed against his own....

Antonio pulled his hand away far sooner than Cary wanted, and stood up again, pillow in hand. "You need to get some rest," he said.

"Good night, Antonio. And thanks," Cary added in a serious tone, "for saving my ass."

"*Sogni d'oro*, Connor." Antonio closed the door behind him.

"ZUMMM, zummm, zummm...." The sound grated on Cary's ears, and he pulled an extra pillow over his head. He had been dreaming about something really nice, and.... He felt the sharp pain in his wrist and realized he had completely forgotten about the events of two nights before.

"Zummm, zummm, zummm...."

"What the hell?" he snapped in English as he threw the pillow off the bed with his good arm.

From under heavy eyelids, he focused on a small metal airplane about three inches from his nose. The eyes that met his were a vivid blue—not Antonio's, although the similarity in color was quite remarkable—and belonged to a child of four or five.

"Who are you?" Cary demanded in Italian. He hated kids almost as much as he hated being woken up from a good dream, and this particular dream had prominently featured a certain blond Italian.

The hand began to move again, making the toy airplane glide and bank. "Zummm, zummm, zummm...." The little boy, whose long blond curls ended at his shoulders, smiled at him.

"Who are you?" Cary repeated, long past the end of his patience.

"Who are *you*?" the boy countered. Then, as if putting the pieces of a particularly complicated puzzle together, he said, "Oh. You're Papà's *guest*!"

Papà?

The kid was giggling now. "Is your name Corrie? No," he said as he chewed his bottom lip. "Papà told me, but I forgot—"

"Connor," Cary supplied. Anything to get that high, squeaky voice out of his I'm-grumpy-don't-mess-with-me-in-the-morning ears.

"Connore! That's it! Connore!"

"Connor."

"Connore," the boy repeated, again adding the final *e*. His face was screwed up in a frown, as if he were challenging Cary to correct him one more time.

"Fine." Who was he to argue with a bratty kid at eight in the morning?

"I'm Massimo," he announced with his chin held high. "Massimo Bianchi. I'm five years old. Almost six."

"Nice to meet you," Cary answered, more out of resignation than politeness.

"Daddy said you spoke Italian." Massimo didn't seem convinced. "He said you were American. I don't think they speak Italian in America." The expression on his face was defiant.

"They don't. I learned to speak it here, in Italy."

This seemed to appease Massimo. He shrugged and went back to buzzing Cary's head again with the airplane.

"Would you stop that?"

"You didn't say 'please'," Massimo said with an expression of calm irritation that immediately called to mind Antonio.

"Would you *please* stop that?" *Little brat.*

Massimo appeared to consider the question. Then, apparently deciding he was having too much fun to stop, he dive-bombed Cary's face.

"Massimo?" a woman's voice called from outside the bedroom.

"Don't tell her I woke you up." Massimo raised his eyebrows and bit his lip.

"You didn't say 'please'," Cary said with satisfaction. *Chalk one up for the grown-up!*

"*Please*, Connore, don't tell her I woke you up."

The door to the bedroom opened, and a woman peered inside. "Oh," she gasped, shooting a look of reproach at the little boy, "he woke you up, didn't he?"

"No," Cary lied. "I was already awake when he came in."

"Massimo," the woman said with narrowed eyes, "go back into the living room. Let Signor Taylor sleep." She kissed Massimo on the top of his head and sighed theatrically.

"Yes, Mamma." Massimo flashed Cary a bright grin as though they were now best friends, then scampered off the bed and out the door.

"I am so sorry," the woman said as she pushed her long brown hair from her face. "I was making breakfast, and I didn't realize he had come in here. Massimo is just so curious."

"Don't worry about it," Cary told her. "It's fine, really."

"He's a lot like his father, always curious about things."

"So Antonio is his father?"

Great. Mr. Perfect has a kid. Way too complicated. His hope for a mind-blowing one-night stand was fading fast.

"Oh, yes." She smiled and shook her head. "They're very much alike." Then, as if suddenly realizing something, she clapped a hand over her mouth and said, "Oh! I'm being so rude! I didn't even introduce myself. I'm Francesca Fratelli."

"Connor Taylor." Cary's heart did a nosedive for his stomach. Francesca wore a wedding band on her right hand in the European custom.

No wonder he wasn't interested.

"So you're Antonio's wife?"

She laughed, a light, musical laugh that rang about the bedroom. "Oh!" she exclaimed. "No, no. We've been friends since we were children—he's like my brother."

The extent to which it relieved Cary to hear this surprised him. *Why would you care, anyhow? You only wanted to sleep with the guy, not marry him.*

"I see" was all he said.

"Speaking of work," she continued, "Tonino asked me to make you some breakfast. He left for the office about an hour ago."

That's right. Today is Monday, isn't it? He really needed to call Georges and let him know about canceling the upcoming gigs.

"That's very kind of you."

"Antonio and I grew up together near Stradella, not far from here," Francesca explained as they sat down for a breakfast comprised of a variety of fruit, cheese, and bread. "His family still lives there."

The apartment was quiet, for which Cary was more than grateful. Massimo was now lying on his stomach on the couch, feet up in the air, reading a book.

"So you live in Milan?"

"Yes. I moved here a few years ago with my partner, Marissa. I'm a painter." She filled his coffee cup and passed him a tray of cheese and prosciutto. "I've had a few shows in Milan and Rome. I work at a gallery in the city." She gestured to a painting hanging on the wall.

"Interesting piece," he said, noting the splashes of bright colors on the mostly dark background and the hint of a human shape they combined to create. It was a sensual, unusual work. Something he could see hanging on a wall in his own apartment. "I like it."

She blushed charmingly. "Thank you, signore."

"Please, call me Connor."

"Connor. Your Italian is very good," she added as she offered him some more bread.

"I've got a pretty good ear. And I love the sound of the language."

"I'm so sorry about what happened to you. Tonino told me about those horrible men. Does it hurt much?" she asked.

"Just the wrist. But it's better today. I just look worse." He touched two fingers to his jaw.

"So I hear you're a waiter."

Cary nodded as he sipped his coffee.

"What restaurant do you work at?"

Cary tried not to choke. Lies were easier to stomach if you didn't have to go into a lot of detail. They were also easier when you were drunk. "I sort of fill in at a few places."

He felt like a total shit now. He needed to go home.

"Tonino left you some clothing." She pointed to a chair by the front door. A pair of pants hung over the back, along with a neatly folded shirt and socks. "He was sorry he couldn't stay. He'll be back at lunch."

"He's already done a lot for me. And I really should be going. The doctor was just worried about last night."

Her expression was almost wistful, as if she were disappointed to hear this. "I'm sure he would want you to stay," she said. "At least until he comes home."

"That's really nice, but I'll leave him my number. I'd like to thank him."

And I have some great ideas about how I can do that, if he'll let me.

CHAPTER 5

OLD HABITS, OLD HAUNTS

IN THE end, Francesca insisted he take a cab back "home." She sent him off with more Euros than he needed to pay for it, in part because Cary lied about living much further out of the city, in a less expensive neighborhood. He would pay it back as soon as he saw Antonio again—and he had every intention of seeing Antonio again—so he brushed off his guilt and took the money.

Roberta met him in the doorway of his apartment, her palpable relief replaced a split second later with a look of horror as she took in his bruised face and the cast on his left wrist. "Oh, Signor Redding! What will you do?"

Her genuine and unexpected concern had him shifting awkwardly on his feet. He was even more surprised when she launched herself at him, taking him in her arms like he was a wayward child who had finally come home.

He winced as she hugged him tight. "It's nothing. I'm fine, and the cast will come off in six weeks. The doctor said I might need a little physical therapy, but it'll be fine."

"I was worried about you." She frowned at him, and he managed a wan smile.

"Thanks." He loved that she thought of him as a surrogate son, but it also made him uncomfortable. He felt undeserving.

"Signor Duhamel called this morning," she said as she shooed him inside the apartment. "He says you should call him. Maestro Somers had a cancellation on this season's schedule, and he needs to know by tomorrow if you're interested."

"Thanks, Roberta. I'll call him."

She raised an eyebrow and said, "You haven't told him yet, have you? About what happened?" He scowled at her as she clucked like a mother hen. "And you haven't been eating enough, have you, *stangone*?" He opened his mouth to protest the nickname—"beanpole"—but she just laughed and headed for the kitchen.

The apartment was, as always, immaculate. Roberta wouldn't have it any other way. The simple linen curtains were open to the bright sunlight, the colorful Japanese silk pillows lined up in a neat row on the sofa. Like the pillows, Cary had bought most of the artwork that adorned the walls and tabletops on his trips abroad. A Thai silk weaving hung above a collection of three Hopi kachina dolls he'd found in New Mexico. Two abstract paintings he'd discovered in Paris were strategically placed over the couch, and the rest of the surfaces sported glass bowls, wood carvings, and other objects that had caught Cary's eye.

He walked into the living room and past the open doorway to his practice studio. It was a brightly lit room with a baby grand piano and his favorite chair to play in. In the corner was his cello, safe in its white fiberglass case. As with the rest of the apartment, the walls here were also covered in artwork. His favorite artwork. A collection of masks in various sizes and materials, each unique.

Cary didn't step inside the room but just stood in the doorway and forced himself to breathe. He had expected this would be difficult, seeing this place and knowing he couldn't play. He just hadn't realized *how* difficult it would be.

Cary Taylor Redding, his mother's voice echoed in his mind, *you must practice every day. Even if it's just for an hour or two. Music isn't like a book that you put down and forget about. It's part of you. Always.*

This time, it wasn't just an ache that stirred in his soul. It was something else. Guilt. He knew the feeling well, although it had been years since he'd felt it quite so keenly. He closed the door to the studio, went back into the living room, and poured himself a drink. He'd skip the painkiller. He decided he needed the alcohol more.

When he settled on the couch a few minutes later, the heat of the cognac warmed his chest. With a deep breath, he picked up the telephone and hit one of the speed dial numbers. He wasn't looking forward to this call.

"YOU what?" Georges Duhamel shouted through the phone.

"I got mugged," Cary repeated, holding the handset between his chin and shoulder and rubbing his face with his right hand. "I broke my wrist. *Mon poignet.*" He figured the guy probably had understood the first time—his English was far better than he let on—but he thought he'd make sure.

"*Espèce de con,*" his agent cursed under his breath.

"I heard that, Georges," Cary said in French. He took another deep swallow of his drink.

"Good, you stupid boy. I will not ask what you were doing. *Tu me fais chier, avec ton*—"

"I know I piss you off," Cary interrupted, shifting back to English again and chuckling. "But you still love me, don't you?"

"As if."

"You'll need to cancel the Rome gig next month, but I should be able to do the master classes, even if I can't play yet."

"What about Florence in January?"

"The doctor says I should be good to go by December. January should be fine."

There was silence on the other end of the phone, then a resigned "Fine. I take care of it."

"Thanks, Georges."

"Oh, I almost forgot. Maestro Somers is in Milan conducting. He said to call him so you might have dinner while he's here. He tried to call you, but you didn't answer your phone." There was a soft huffing sound on the other end of the call, but when Cary said nothing, Georges continued, "He also says there's a cancellation on the Chicago Symphony schedule in March. He wanted to know if you could substitute. The Elgar or the Dvořák B Minor. Your choice."

"Dvořák," Cary said without hesitation. "The Elgar's too gloomy for Chicago in the winter."

Georges laughed. "March is spring."

"Not in Chicago. Too damn cold." Cary hesitated a moment, then added, "I'm sorry to put you out like this." He meant it too.

"You are going to kill me. If you don't kill yourself first."

"I'll try to behave."

"Perhaps you find some nice man and make a home."

"Not anytime soon. Not if I can help it."

"I will send you e-mail when I get confirmation from Somers's assistant. For now, you let Roberta make you eat well, and you sleep. No late nights, *comprends?*"

"You know I don't speak French worth a damn," Cary teased, reverting to French once more.

"*Ta gueule,*" he heard Georges swear as he hung up the phone.

BY FOUR o'clock that afternoon, Cary was full of nervous energy, restless. He paced about the apartment, trying to find something to do with himself. He couldn't remember when he'd spent an entire day without practicing, and the list of things he needed to do that didn't require two good arms was far too short.

His wrist ached too much for sit-ups, and lifting weights with one arm got old very quickly. He turned on the TV and watched reruns of *CSI: Miami* dubbed in Italian. The episodes were at least three years behind those in the States, he guessed. During the second episode, he fell asleep and awoke to find a message on his cell phone.

I just wanted to check to see that you were feeling better, Antonio had said. *I'll call you in the morning.*

Morning. I guess that's all she wrote. Apparently Antonio wasn't all that interested in what he had to offer. Why would he be, anyhow? He had just been kind. Cary smiled sadly; he had honestly liked the man.

Around eight that evening, Cary dragged himself to the kitchen and sat down at the table to pick at the food Roberta had left for him. It was, as always, delicious, and he was reminded of Antonio's failed attempt at dinner the night before. Still, he would have been happy to eat more of Antonio's food, as awful as it had been, if only to have another shot at the man.

After giving up on his dinner, Cary decided to give practicing a try. He had barely managed to tighten the bow when his wrist started to ache. For an hour, he did exercises for his bow arm, then finally gave up and put the instrument away.

"THIS is Aiden Lind. I can't talk right now. Leave me a message, and I'll get back to you."

"Hey, Aiden. It's Cary. You in town anytime soon?" He didn't want to sound desperate, but he was pretty sure he would go stir crazy without being able to practice. At least with Aiden in town, he'd have some company for his misery. "Georges said David's in town, and I remember you saying you had a gig at La Scala for the opening in December. So I thought maybe—"

The phone beeped, cutting him off.

"Shit." Cary sat back down on the couch, wishing Aiden had moved to Milan, as he had once threatened to do.

Aiden had been Cary's best friend ever since David Somers, the music director of the Chicago Symphony, had introduced them five years before. Back then, Cary was pretty sure David had hoped Aiden and Cary might become more than friends and that Aiden might help Cary find some stability in his life. But between Aiden's traveling for his operatic career and Cary's lack of interest in a long-term relationship, the two men had instead settled into a comfortable friendship.

Cary glanced up at the clock. Thirty minutes had passed since he'd last checked it.

Fuck.

On a normal Monday, he'd have spent the entire day practicing, taking breaks to lift weights and do a few hundred sit-ups. If he didn't have a rehearsal the next morning, he'd head for the bars. Even now, he felt it: the overwhelming urge to leave the confines of the apartment, have a few more drinks, and find a partner to satisfy his need. Get fucked, maybe. Or maybe just get off. It didn't really matter. Either one would do.

He needed to get out and blow off steam. He didn't have the energy for via Padova and the bar scene tonight, but he knew a park only a few subway stops away that would do just as well. After downing another drink, his fourth that day, he stopped fighting the urge. He didn't even bother to change his clothes—Antonio's clothes, really. He just shoved a few condoms into his pocket, threw on his jacket, grabbed his keys and some cash, and he was out the door.

It was far colder than three nights before, but the frigid air did nothing to dampen Cary's anticipation. The subway was bright and relatively clean, in stark contrast to the dimly lit and slightly seedy park. It always struck Cary as ironic that the park abutted a tiny church. By day, children played as their parents looked on. At night, hustlers did a brisk business.

The last time he'd come here, he fucked a pretty kid behind a large tree. Tonight, he just wanted to get fucked. His body thrummed with need: the raw, demanding kind that could only be satisfied by having a hard dick in his ass. No lube—he needed to feel the burn. He was half-hard already, just in anticipation.

He thought of Antonio and just as quickly pushed the image away. He didn't need a perfect man, just someone to satisfy him. And it was a hell of a lot easier like that, wasn't it?

"Can I help you, signore?" The kid was young, but not too young. Twenty-three, he guessed. Tall, attractive, with wavy dark hair, he wore a T-shirt at least a size too small, his jacket open so Cary could see the outline of the kid's nipples through the fabric.

When Cary didn't answer, the newcomer licked his lips suggestively and indicated the small maintenance shed a few yards away, then sauntered over to it. Cary followed as he watched the too-tight jeans and the tempting ass they outlined.

Oh yeah, this was what he needed. Forget the uptight lawyer with the perfect life, his perfect apartment, and his perfect kid. Antonio didn't want him, anyhow, so why try to fool himself?

CHAPTER  6

WHO'S THE CLOWN?

HE AWOKE to the angry buzz of his cell phone on the table by his bed. His ass ached, but his head hurt more. The pain in his wrist had returned with a vengeance. He had forgotten to take his meds the night before, and the alcoholic buzz was long gone, replaced by a sour taste in his mouth and a killer hangover. He smelled cigarette smoke on himself. He remembered now—the kid hadn't had any smokes, so he had bought a pack at the *tabaccheria* down the street. It lay, half-empty, on the nightstand.

"Yeah?" Cary grumbled as he tapped the phone in irritation. He closed his eyes to block out the sunlight. He should have shut the stupid phone off when he stumbled in at three in the morning.

"You must get lots of compliments about your phone persona," said the voice on the other end.

"Antonio?" Cary reminded himself that Antonio had said he was going to call to check on him in the morning, and tried not to get his hopes up.

"Good morning to you too, Connor. Are you always so agreeable in the mornings?" There was a trace of humor in Antonio's voice.

"Sorry," Cary said. "Late night." He closed his eyes again and imagined Antonio, dressed for work in an expensive suit that skimmed the muscular planes of his body. A starched white shirt, open at the collar. Antonio's Adam's apple and the indentation below, at his throat.

"I woke you up, didn't I?"

"It's okay. I needed to get up." Normally, Cary would have been up hours ago, even after a late night. He always got more practicing done first thing in the morning, even with a hangover. "What's up?"

"I just spent an hour listening to my son go on about the 'funny American'. Says you're his new best friend. Something about an airplane?"

Little stinker wakes me up and now I'm his hero?

"I managed to get dive-bombed a few times."

"Francesca says you two get along well."

"I hate kids."

"That's not what I hear. Francesca said you were really good with Massi, and he's not always the easiest to please."

"Must be my stellar personality."

"Of course."

A moment of uncomfortable silence passed as Cary struggled to find another snappy comeback and came up empty. He didn't think well hungover.

"Listen, Connor," Antonio said. "I was going to come over and check on you, but you didn't leave an address."

"Nothing to worry about here. I'm fine." Cary ignored the implied question. "There's someone here to help, if I need it."

"Oh."

There was a hint of disappointment in Antonio's voice Cary couldn't help but notice.

Maybe he's more interested than he lets on. The thought made Cary shiver, and he imagined himself on that big bed, Antonio's cock in his ass and those big hands on his waist, the sound of their skin slapping…. Or maybe the other way around? For Antonio, he'd gladly top.

"Connor?"

"Hmm?" Cary hadn't heard a word of what Antonio said. "Sorry, Antonio," he said, adjusting himself in his briefs. "I didn't catch that."

"I… I've gotten myself into a little bit of a jam."

"I thought that's what people hire lawyers for."

"Thanks for the help." Antonio chuckled. "No, this jam comes just about up to my waist and likes metal airplanes."

"I told you I hate kids."

"Funny thing about dogs, cats, and kids," Antonio replied, "they always seem to want to be with the people who hate them the most."

"No kidding. So what did you do? Rent me out for babysitting?"

"Not exactly. But Francesca just happened to mention to Massimo that there's a circus downtown this weekend, and I was thinking of taking Massi on Saturday—"

"You mean with clowns?" It was the only thing Cary's sleep-deprived brain could think of.

"They usually have clowns," Antonio said with a gentle chuckle.

"And candy apples?" The vague memory of his mother buying him and Justin bright-red candy apples on sticks made Cary's mouth water.

"Apples? Why would there be apples at a circus? Circuses have clowns and animals and people flying about in the air."

"So what do I have to do with the circus?" Cary wasn't going to try to explain the apples. Apparently the tradition was not an Italian one.

"It seems Massi has gotten it into his head that clowns are American."

Cary laughed. "Maybe he's been watching too much CNN reporting about things in Washington."

"Those clowns aren't very funny. I think it has more to do with the bruises on your face and something Francesca told him about clown makeup."

"You're joking."

"Hardly."

"I still don't see where this is going," Cary put in. He was enjoying the banter, but he was now completely lost.

Another reason to hate kids.

"I tried to explain to him that the clowns in Italy are Italian," Antonio replied. "I think, in the end, he finally understood."

Good. A tiny island of clarity in a sea of otherwise incomprehensible explanations.

"I still don't understand."

"He wants you to come along."

"To the circus?"

"That was the general idea." Antonio laughed and then sighed into the receiver. "I told him you weren't feeling well and you needed your rest, so I'm sure he'll understand if you can't come."

Cary realized with sudden clarity that it wasn't the kid who wanted him to come. *Antonio* wanted him to come.

Maybe the entire fucked-up weekend wasn't such a waste of time, after all.

"Tell him the American clown would love to come along."

"Really?"

"Really. It sounds like fun. I can't remember the last time I went to a circus." Cary thought the older Bianchi sounded at least as happy as Massimo might be.

"Then we'll pick you up at your place around two on Saturday, if that works for you."

Shit. Cary had forgotten *that* little complication. "No need to do that." He tried to sound casual. "I've got a few errands to run near your apartment. Why don't I just meet you there?"

"Sure. That's fine."

"I'll see you then."

"I'm... I mean 'we' are looking forward to it."

Cary tapped the cell phone and leaned back on the pillows with a knowing smile. *He definitely wants to see me again.* The thought both scared and excited him.

"CONNORE!" A pint-sized flurry of blond curls flew at him as he stood in the doorway of Antonio's apartment. "Papà said you were coming!"

Cary winced as Massimo grabbed onto his left arm to drag him inside.

"Massimo," came Antonio's stern voice from behind the boy, "remember how I told you Signor Taylor got hurt last week? You have to be gentle with him."

"I'm sorry, Connore." Massimo's big blue eyes were full of shame. "I didn't mean to hurt you."

"It's okay," Cary lied and thought he should take another pain pill before they got going, or he'd be in agony by the end of the day. Why had he agreed to this again? Oh yeah. The gorgeous guy standing behind the bratty kid, watching him with something like... *interest*? Cary wore a fitted shirt and snug jeans. Had Antonio noticed?

Don't you dare *blush!*

Cary looked down at Massimo and smiled mechanically as he struggled to maintain his composure. When he caught Antonio's expression again, he saw only friendship there.

"Good to see you, Connor." Antonio swept Massimo up into his arms and flung him over one shoulder to the sound of squeals and giggles. "I apologize for this one," he added as he tickled the squirming five-year-old. "He's just a little excited about this afternoon."

Cary tried to look nonplussed as Antonio set Massimo down. "Now go to the bathroom and then put your shoes on. We'll be going in a few minutes."

"I'm really not good with kids." *Or their hot-as-hell fathers.*

"You're doing great," Antonio told him, and Cary sincerely hoped he was, on both accounts. "I appreciate your coming with us today. Francesca is working on a show this afternoon, and I told her I'd keep Massi busy."

"She's lucky she has you to help."

Antonio gestured Cary inside the apartment. "No," Antonio said, his eyes full of warmth, "I'm the lucky one. When she asked me to have a child with her, I never realized how much I would enjoy being a father."

Cary was beginning to understand. Italy wasn't exactly the most progressive country when it came to homosexuality. Francesca and Marissa would never have been able to adopt a child here.

"It was very nice of Francesca to feed me breakfast the other day," Cary said. He reached into his pocket and pulled out some bills. "Would you mind giving this to her? She gave me money for the cab home, and I wanted to pay her back."

"Of course." Antonio took the money, his fingers brushing Cary's. Cary repressed a shiver at the touch. Antonio turned and walked over to the side table, putting the bills down there.

"How does your family feel about your being a father?" Cary did his best to distract himself from his view of the back of Antonio's neck. From this angle, Cary saw the muscles that ran from below his ears to his shoulders, and the outline of Antonio's spine beneath the smooth skin. He imagined himself biting and licking at that skin. He was thankful he had worn his shirt outside of his jeans; he got hard just with the thought.

"My mother was beside herself when I told her," Antonio said as he joined Cary by the door once more. "She had pretty much given up on me ever having children, although she has plenty of grandchildren. But I'm the only son."

"Are you out to your family?"

"Since *scuola superiore*, your high school," Antonio explained. "I am fortunate in that, as well."

"Really? I mean, even in the States...."

"My mother was born in Italy, but her family was German and very open-minded. My father wasn't as accepting, but he loved my mother."

Antonio laughed. "She's a stubborn woman. He had no choice but to tolerate me. Eventually, I think he even came to terms with it."

"That's good." Cary swallowed and looked briefly at the floor. He was surprised to realize that he envied Antonio. His own experience with his mother hadn't gone nearly as well. At the thought of his mother, Cary tensed his jaw, and forced the memory away.

That was a long time ago.

"SO," ANTONIO said as they stood at the line for the concession counter an hour later, "do you have family in the States?"

"A brother," Cary explained. "He lives in St. Louis, Missouri. Married with three kids. All boys. I get to see them from time to time. My dad died when I was a baby, and my mom died when I was in college."

"That must have been difficult, losing both your parents when you were young."

"I guess." Cary didn't think much about it. Or he hadn't, at least not recently. "I never knew my dad, so I didn't really have anything to miss."

"Papà!" Massimo shouted happily as he pulled his father up to the counter. "It's our turn."

Cary was secretly relieved at the interruption—he didn't want to discuss his parents. The broken wrist had done nothing to keep the painful childhood memories at bay. In fact, it seemed to have reawakened them.

They ordered sodas and *ciambelle,* Italian doughnuts dusted with powdered sugar, before finding their seats. The smell of animals and manure hung in the air in the large arena, mingling with the smell of buttered popcorn and the sweet, greasy scent of the *ciambelle.* Cary felt like a kid again as he inhaled the mixture of smells. And although it was a smaller circus than the huge spectacles he had come to expect in the US, something akin to excitement stirred in his own heart as he took in the stadium filled with parents and children.

A family of eight filed in past them, all chattering excitedly about the circus. Below, a parade of animals entered from a large doorway, and acrobats swung by their knees on trapezes hung from the rafters.

"So I'm guessing from the photos in your apartment that you have a pretty large family," Cary said after they had gotten Massimo settled. He leaned closer to make himself heard over the din of the crowd and the announcements over the PA.

"You could say that." Antonio's face lit up at the mention of his family. "Four sisters, ten nieces and nephews. Most of us live in or near Milan, so we see each other at least once a month at the vineyard."

"Vineyard?"

"Yes. In the Lombardy wine region. After my father died a few years ago, my mother hired people to run it for her, but she still lives on the property. It's a very large house. Perfect for family get-togethers. The kids can run around and the adults sit, eat, and drink. Remind me to have you try the wine—it's excellent."

"Papà! Connore! Look! Clowns!" Massimo stood up and nearly spilled his drink in his excitement, but Cary grabbed it at the last second.

"See, I told you, they're Italian clowns," Antonio pointed out.

"How do you know that?" Massimo demanded with a frown. "You can't hear them speak."

"Smart kid. He has a point, though." Cary grinned at Antonio, who laughed. Massimo, seeing this interaction, flashed Cary a bright smile and then looked pointedly at his father as if to say, *See... Connore agrees with me!*

A group of children from the audience had gathered down on the floor of the arena, and the clowns came over to greet them.

"Would you like to find out if the clowns are Italian?" Cary heard himself ask.

He was still trying to figure out why he had even offered when Massimo responded with an energetic "Will you take me, Connore? Please, please!"

"Sure." Cary ignored Antonio's look of approval and hoped he didn't look half as nervous as he felt. He still hated kids, he told himself as he and Massimo descended the sticky concrete steps and joined the parents and children near the ring.

Massimo watched in fascination as one of the clowns made a balloon dog and handed it to a little girl, who jumped up and down in excitement when she showed it to her mother.

"Would you like one too?" Cary asked as they moved closer.

"Sì, sì!" Massimo shouted. The clown smiled at them and put his hands up in the air. "What does he want, Connore?"

"He wants to know what you want him to make for you."

"I want... I want...," Massimo repeated, his face screwed up in concentration.

"I think I have an idea," Cary said. "Do you trust me?"

The little boy appeared to consider this question, then nodded.

Cary winked at Massimo and approached the clown, covered his mouth with his hand, and whispered something into the clown's ear. The clown nodded and got to work.

"What's he making?" Massimo was wide-eyed as he watched the clown's quick movements with fascination.

"I won't tell. That would spoil the surprise, wouldn't it?"

The twinkle in Massimo's eyes belied his studious frown, and he burst out laughing a moment later when the clown handed him the balloon creation. "It's an airplane!" he shouted happily, dancing about and pretending to make it fly.

"*Grazie.*" Cary nodded to the clown as they turned to head back up the steps so Massimo could show his father. The clown waved his arm with a flourish and bowed.

"Papà was wrong," Massimo said as they headed back up to their seats, weaving in and out of other parents and children descending the steep steps. Massimo clasped Cary's good hand and held the airplane against his chest to protect it.

"About what?"

"About the clowns."

"How's that?" Cary asked.

"They don't speak Italian."

"And they don't speak English, either, do they?"

"Nope," laughed Massimo. "They just don't *speak* at all!" Then, a moment later, he announced, "I like you, Connore. My papà likes you too."

"Is that so?" Cary countered. Was he getting the hang of this talking-to-a-kid thing?

"My papà used to live with a boy he liked. His name was Massimo, just like mine."

"Really?" So Antonio wasn't a monk, after all. *Interesting.*

"He died."

"Oh." Cary wasn't sure what to say to that.

Massimo, however, was unfazed. "You like boys, don't you? I mean, grown-up boys." Massimo lowered his voice and went on to explain, "Like Papà does? You know, better than girls."

"Yes," Cary admitted, surprised at how much the child understood about sexual orientation, "but—"

"Are you going to stay with us, then? Like Massimo stayed with Papà, before I was born?"

Crap. How the hell do you answer that? "No, kid, I hadn't planned on it?" Or maybe "Just long enough so he can fuck me into the bed?" It wasn't as if he expected much more, anyhow. He didn't *want* any more than that, right?

"I don't think so, Massi. We're just friends," Cary finally said. "I don't think—"

"It's good you're friends," Massimo interrupted, looking quite pleased. "So Papà and I will just have to make you stay."

And what, thought Cary with a sigh, *can you possibly say to that?*

But as they arrived back at their seats, Cary wondered what Antonio would say when he realized Connor was a lie. *Then again, so much of my life is a lie anyhow.* What was one more whopper piled on top of the others?

CHAPTER  7

THE ELEPHANT IN THE LIVING ROOM

THEY arrived back at Antonio's apartment four hours later. Massimo fell asleep in the cab, and Antonio carried him to the big bed, where he tucked the boy in as Cary watched.

"Thank goodness," Antonio said a moment later, closing the door to the bedroom. "If I have to hear about the elephants one more time...." He covered his mouth with his hand and yawned. "Sometimes he even makes *me* tired."

"You're really good with him." Cary knew he shouldn't care, but he was even *more* attracted to Antonio after watching him with Massimo. It was a strange realization, and one that left Cary ill at ease.

Next thing you know, you'll be offering to help him wipe the kid's nose. Or worse....

"Thanks."

When Massimo started to get cranky as the day wore on, Antonio had been nothing but patient. Well, almost. At one point, Cary had seen the frustration in Antonio's usually calm features when Massimo, for the second time, dropped his lollipop onto the filthy floor. Still, Antonio hadn't given in to Massimo's demands for more candy.

"I'm pretty sure I'd have bought him the lollipop when he started to whine," Cary admitted.

This statement was rewarded with a rumbled laugh. "What you don't know is that I *did* give in to the whining. About a hundred times. And every time I did, Massi ended up with a sugar tantrum that would have put Attila the Hun to shame. It just took me a while to learn my lesson." Antonio grinned and walked over to the kitchen. "More coffee?"

"Please." In spite of the espresso they had stopped for on their way home, Cary was nearly as tired as Massimo. More caffeine would do him good. That, and he was enjoying Antonio's company too much to go home so soon.

"It's like anything," Antonio continued as he worked the espresso maker. "You get better at it with practice."

They settled down on the couch and sipped their coffee. This close, Cary could see the tiny lines at the corners of Antonio's mouth. He couldn't help but be amazed at how Antonio's blue eyes appeared almost turquoise in the fading light filtering in through the windows. And that hair... Cary could see strands of red woven throughout. It was cropped close at the back of his neck, but the top was longer, tumbling over his ears and forehead. Cary longed to run his fingers through those curls and feel the short hairs tickle his upper lip as he licked the skin at the nape of his companion's neck.

"I had fun today," Cary said as he brought the tiny cup of fragrant coffee to his lips.

"You sound surprised."

Cary saw the challenge in Antonio's eyes and offered a conciliatory smile. "I guess I am."

"You don't get to visit your nephews often?"

"Not as often as I'd like. And when I'm there, I don't spend much time with them. Like I said, I hate kids."

The truth was that Cary had always been a little afraid of his three boisterous nephews—afraid he'd bore them, or not like what they wanted to do and be bored himself. He'd never played much as a child since he'd always been too busy practicing, and he honestly wasn't sure what kids liked to do. He'd never watched much TV, and he hadn't owned a single video or computer game. The only reason he knew anything about games at all was from watching his brother play.

"Besides," Cary added, "they'd probably think I was about as far from cool as you could get."

"You'd be surprised. Kids mostly just want someone to pay attention to them. Massi thinks you're great. Are you any more cool around him? He thinks you're a nice guy. And so does his papà," he added.

Cary's cheeks warmed at the compliment, and without really thinking, he reached for Antonio's jaw. God, but he wanted to kiss Antonio, to taste him!

Antonio did not pull away but searched Cary's face as if he were expecting to see something there, then put his own hand over Cary's as the corners of his mouth edged oh-so-faintly upward. But he did not kiss Cary, nor did he move closer.

Cary's hunger now clawed at the back of his brain, urging him to do something, anything, to claim those full lips. He leaned forward with a questioning look in his eyes.

Oh God... I want this....

Antonio's cell phone rang. Through his lust-clouded mind, Cary recognized the ring: Bach's "Jesu, Joy of Man's Desiring." Cary had to smile. He had always loved that melody. It was one of the first pieces he had ever played.

"*Scusi,*" Antonio told Cary as he stood up. "That's Francesca."

Cary yawned and settled back on the couch, closing his eyes as he listened to Antonio recount their afternoon at the circus and make plans for Massimo's weekend. He must have fallen asleep, because the next thing he heard was the sound of little feet trotting across the wood floor and a very loudly whispered, "Is he sleeping?"

"I think so," came Antonio's reply.

Apparently, for a five-year-old, a grown man falling asleep on the couch was just about the funniest thing imaginable.

Just wait until you're a teenager, Cary thought as he repressed a laugh.

"Are you sleeping?" This time, the words were whispered directly into his ear.

"No!" Cary shouted, grabbing Massimo around the waist with his good arm and tickling him mercilessly. They rolled around for a minute or two, laughing, until Cary saw Antonio standing over them, holding Massimo's coat.

"I hate to have to stop you two children," Antonio said, "but I need to take Massi to my mother's for the weekend. I have a client in town I need to meet, so he can't stay with me." Massimo climbed off Cary and made a disappointed face. "I can drop you off at your place, if you'd like, Connor."

"Thanks," Cary said, "but I thought I'd stop by a friend's on my way home." When had he gotten so smooth with the lies?

"Are you coming back to see me and Papà soon?" Massimo asked as they walked out of the building a few minutes later.

"I'll do my best," Cary promised. In spite of everything, Massimo had grown on him. And his father.... He had thought he had seen desire in Antonio's gaze more than once that day, and yet here he was, facing the unsatisfying prospect of yet another night spent alone in his own bed. He felt only slightly guilty to find himself hoping the next time he saw Antonio, Massimo might be spending the night with his mother.

If the guy's even remotely interested. The way things were going, he figured he'd have better luck at a monastery.

"JUSTIN?" Cary sat on the couch, his feet on the coffee table, cell phone against his ear.

"Cary? Is that you?"

"Yep."

"It's been three weeks since you called. I left several messages on your cell, but you never called me back. Damn, you had me worried. I was just about to call Roberta and check on you." Cary heard the concern in his brother's voice, even with the lousy connection, and he ignored the spasm of guilt in his gut.

He's right. You should have called him. Justin worried about him. He always had.

"Sorry. It's been a rough few weeks."

"What happened?"

"Got mugged," Cary explained. "Broke my wrist and—"

"Your wrist? Oh crap, Cary. Is it going to be okay? I mean, are you going to be able to play again?"

"Yeah. Doctor says I'll be fine. Maybe a little physical therapy, but I should be back to work in another month or so."

"Shit, Cary. That was a close call."

"I'm fine. Really. I'm a big boy now, remember?"

There was a hissing sound through the phone, and Cary pictured his brother releasing air from between his lips like a steam pipe. "Right. Tell me it wasn't two in the morning when you got mugged, and maybe I'll buy that."

"It wasn't two in the morning," Cary said with a laugh. "It was three. But really, bro, I'm fine. You don't need to worry. Okay?"

"Okay."

Cary knew Justin was unconvinced, and he made a point of changing the subject. "So how are Vicki and the kids?"

"Great. Vick got a raise. Clayton, Caleb, and Jackson are doing great. Clay's playing Little League ball this year, and Caleb will probably go out for the team next year. Jackie's watching and waiting. It's hard, being four and watching your big brothers do things you'd like to do."

Cary's thoughts wandered to Massi and the circus. Which, of course, made him think of Antonio and the near-kiss of three hours before. He fought his body's response. "Glad to hear it. Send me some photos when you have a chance. I'm sure I'll barely recognize them now."

Justin chuckled. "No joke. At this rate, Clay's going to be taller than both of us."

"Call you next weekend?"

"You damn well better," Justin warned, "or I *will* call Roberta."

"I will. Promise."

"All right. You coming for Christmas?"

"I'm not sure. Maybe."

"The boys'd be happy to see their uncle. I'd like to see you too. I miss you."

Cary's jaw tightened. He'd been avoiding St. Louis like the plague since his mother died. The few trips he had made in the past five years had been more difficult than he had expected—it didn't matter that his mother had been dead nearly ten years now. The memories were still raw, painful. "I'll take a look at the flights and check my schedule," he said. He knew he'd do neither.

"That'd be great."

"Talk to you later, Justin."

"Take care of yourself, Cary. Love you."

"Thanks." Cary tapped the phone and laid it on the table, leaning back against the cushions and closing his eyes. Justin had been more of a father to him than an older brother, and Cary adored him. Why was it so hard for him to say the words?

You really should visit before the boys are in college. He resolved to have his US agent book him a gig in St. Louis. The thought made him uneasy, and he tried to ignore the surge of adrenaline that accompanied the possibility of a visit back to his old home, with little success.

Justin had always been the grown-up and Cary the little kid. Necessity, maybe, given that their only parent had been so focused on Cary that Justin had been forced to grow up faster.

Funny, Cary thought, *how different we are.*

His nephews were lucky to have such a loving, attentive father. The kind of father Cary had always longed for.

His thoughts veered unexpectedly back to Antonio. How good he was with Massimo. So patient. Affectionate. Fun. Cary smiled and imagined

Antonio's laughter. The way he pushed the hair out of his face when he spoke animatedly. The low rumble of his voice.

At this, Cary's cock happily asserted itself. *Shit.* The idea of hanging out at the apartment and jerking off was almost unappealing enough to subdue his traitorous erection. Almost, but not quite. He needed to get out of the apartment and do something with the nervous energy.

TWO hours later, he was bent over a toilet in the bathroom of a dive near via Padova, only a few blocks away from where he'd gotten mugged, and getting fucked to within an inch of his life. He closed his eyes and tried to settle into the rhythm of it, to savor the burn. It wasn't working. He hated these toilets, glorified holes in the ground where you stood on porcelain footrests. There was nothing to hang on to except the sink to his left, but the cast made it difficult, and he had to press his good hand against the filthy tile wall. He kept slipping on the wet porcelain floor, and his partner finally grabbed him at the waist to keep him from falling.

Even the buzz of too much alcohol didn't help him focus on the sex. He tried to relax into the movements, even tried to imagine his partner was Antonio. But Antonio wouldn't be fucking him in a dive like this, would he?

Taking a chance that his partner wouldn't let him fall, Cary took his hand off the wall and pulled and stroked his own cock. But he couldn't keep himself hard, and the smell of urine made him queasy. His companion climaxed with a grunt, muttering something like "thanks" before he tossed the condom and left Cary alone, oblivious to the fact that Cary hadn't come. It didn't really matter; Cary wasn't going to get off. He knew it.

A roach scampered across the floor about a foot away from his shoe. For the first time in years, Cary noticed the filth, and it bothered him. The walls were a dingy yellow, and Cary didn't even want to think about what was stuck to the painted surface. He noticed a used condom in the corner, overlooked by whoever had cleaned the bathroom, if it had been cleaned at all, and his stomach protested.

He closed his eyes to gather his thoughts, but he saw his mother's face in his mind's eye. He heard her voice reminding him of what a disappointment he was. He was fifteen again, and he saw himself standing on stage, bowing to the applause from yet another adoring audience. He didn't deserve their praise. He had only ever wanted *hers*, anyhow.

You have to earn the applause, Cary Taylor Redding. Nothing in this life is free.

He wondered what his mother would think of him if she could see him now, bare-assed and bent over a filthy toilet, reeking of alcohol and cigarettes. He laughed, and the bitterness of the sound hung in the air.

No wonder Antonio didn't want to touch him. Who would want to?

Oh shit.

He leaned over the water and vomited. He took a few deep breaths and shivered, then pulled his pants up from around his ankles and zipped the fly of his jeans. He felt cold and sweaty under his clothes. Another wave of nausea and he was coughing and spluttering, a sour taste in his mouth, the back of his throat burning.

He splashed some water on his face, trying to avoid his reflection in the mirror. He caught only his bloodshot eyes in the dirty glass, but it was enough to make him pause and look.

Fuck this.

He would cut his losses and go home. Sleep it off.

TWO blocks from via Padova, he heard the footsteps behind him. He was a block away from where he had gotten mugged, and it was nearly the same time of night. He picked up his pace, his heart beating so fast it felt as though it might jump right out of his chest.

Now he wasn't just sick, he was scared. Terrified. He'd never considered carrying a weapon, but now he wished he'd thought of it. Sure, he was a tall man, far taller than the average Italian, but what had that gotten him before? A broken wrist and a shitload of bruises.

One more block and he'd be on the busy street. Every doorway seemed to cast shadows, and he imagined someone in each, waiting to jump out at him. Maybe this time they'd have a gun.

He was sure someone was following him now. He wasn't going to let them beat the crap out of him again. He'd beat the crap out of them first.

He whirled around. "Stay the hell away from me!" he shouted in Italian.

The man and woman behind him—obviously drunk—laughed, then quickly headed off in the other direction. He just stood there, panting, his heart still racing. His hands were shaking. *He* was shaking.

Safe inside a taxi a few minutes later, he relaxed back into the seat, staring out the window at the buildings as they whizzed by. He felt like shit. Worse. He felt like an idiot. When had he become so afraid?

The driver let him out in front of his building. Cary already had his keys in his hand as he punched the pass code into the outer door. He scanned the area around the vestibule and entrance, fearful that someone had followed him.

Get your shit together, he thought as he rode the elevator up to his apartment. Once inside, he latched the deadbolt and tossed his jacket on the couch. He kicked off his shoes and poured himself a double shot of tequila. He downed the drink in one gulp and refilled the glass.

His gaze wandered to his studio, and he eyed the cello case in the corner of the room. He put his glass down on the piano and walked over to the cello. He ran his good hand over the smooth fiberglass case and inhaled a slow, deep breath.

Oh, how he longed to play! How ironic, that as a teenager he dreamed of taking even a day off from practicing. And now it would be weeks before he'd be able to do anything but run the bow over the strings, and he was miserable. When had his life become music all day and anonymous sex at night?

You need to ditch the drinking and the bars.

How many times had he told himself that? He'd tried to stop. He really had. But each time, he'd gone back. How could he stop when there was nothing else in his life but his music? But now…. He blinked away tears and took a deep breath.

What the fuck is wrong with you?

He pulled the instrument out of its case and inhaled the scent of the wood and lacquer. He plucked a few strings, then replaced the cello and latched the case. After retrieving his drink, he sat down at the piano and closed his eyes. His arms depressed the keys, and the instrument responded with a jumble of notes.

He imagined Antonio, with his sandy blond hair and his face rough with stubble. For just a moment, Cary wished for more than just a one-night stand. He thought about Massimo, not the child this time, but the man he was named for. What kind of a man had he been?

A better man than you. Someone who doesn't lie. Someone who deserves Antonio.

"Fuck you, Cary Taylor Redding," he said under his breath. "This is all you are."

CARY didn't sleep well after his failed evening at the bar. Still, the next morning was bright and relatively warm for November, and he was glad to have something to do for a change.

"Aiden!" Cary caught a glimpse of the lanky opera singer as he made his way through the *paninoteca*. The small restaurant looked out over a large piazza near the train station, and was hardly memorable with its utilitarian glass windows, tiny metal tables, and tile floor. Still, it was one of the best places in Milan for panini sandwiches, and at the height of the lunch hour, it was filled to capacity with a lively crowd.

It took Cary a bit of wrangling to get past the tightly packed tables and over to where Aiden waited. "It's great to see you, man."

The two men embraced. It had been nearly six months since Cary had last seen his best friend, and he realized now how much he had missed him.

"Cary." Aiden Lind paled as he took in the cast on Cary's arm. "Damn. What happened? How'd you get hurt?"

"Minding my own business on a Milan street?" Cary did his best to sound casual. He was pretty sure Aiden wouldn't buy his bullshit.

Aiden frowned as they ordered their paninis at the counter, picked up their drinks, and took their seats. "So," he said, facing Cary across the table, "gonna come clean?"

"Not much to tell." Cary really wasn't up for a lecture. He was hungover and sleep deprived. He adored Aiden but didn't need a mother hen; his brother was doing just fine in that department.

"Cruising again?" Aiden leaned over his coffee and glared at him.

"None of your business, Mr. Happily-Ever-After," Cary shot back in his snarkiest voice. "Not all of us are pining for domestic bliss."

"Since when is it a bad thing to spread some of the happiness around?"

The waitress came by with their sandwiches. "How's Sam?" Cary asked, happily taking advantage of the interruption to change the subject.

Aiden's face lit up at the mention of his partner. Cary thought it was kind of cute. "He's great. Nice thing, being the boss. You can take off and nobody can complain. He'll be here for Thanksgiving since I can't go home to Philly."

"David invited you too?"

"Yeah. Nothing like Thanksgiving at an Italian villa." He grinned. "So what about you? Other than getting beaten up, I mean."

Cary raised an eyebrow as he bit into his sandwich, which promptly fell apart. Eating panini, like just about everything else, was easier with two hands. As he picked up a fork and began to salvage the mess on his plate, he realized the distraction was a good thing—he wasn't sure how he wanted to answer Aiden's question. In the end, he just shrugged.

"Relationships? Dates?"

For nearly a minute, Cary just chewed his sandwich and considered the question. He was beginning to enjoy the look of frustration on his companion's face. "Maybe," he said at last.

"Really? Bang-Me-in-the-Bathroom Redding?" Aiden put his hands to his cheeks in feigned shock.

"You really are a cruel bastard."

"I only calls 'em as I sees 'em, man. But do tell."

"Not much to tell. He chased away the muggers. Nice guy. Maybe *too* nice. Doesn't hurt that he's easy on the eyes, either."

"Screwed him yet?" Aiden innocently wiped his mouth with his napkin.

"Shit, Lind, you're the worst. Implying that I—"

"Oh shut up, idiot. Don't tell me you're not thinking about that. It's me, remember?"

"No," Cary said with a growl, "I haven't fucked him yet." His best evil grin didn't seem to do the trick. Aiden wasn't buying any of it. "It's not for lack of trying."

"You mean you haven't slept with him and you're still hanging around? What's up with that? Decided to try dating instead of slumming it?"

Cary opted for a bit of the truth. "We went to the circus together the other day with his son, and—"

"Whoa, whoa, whoa! His *son*? The guy has a kid?"

Cary took another bite of his sandwich and chewed it slowly, knowing full well Aiden was about to explode. "Yeah." He took a gulp of his soda and set it back on the table, causing the table to wobble a bit on the uneven tile floor. "He's good with him too."

"Doesn't really sound like your type," Aiden observed. "Does he like music?"

"I guess. He says so, anyhow."

"What does he think about your career?"

"Well," Cary said, pretending he didn't care, "he doesn't... ah... really know about what I do for a living."

"You're shitting me." Now Aiden really *was* surprised.

"It's a long story. I sort of told him I was an unemployed musician."

"Cary...."

"I never thought I'd see him again. It just seemed like the right thing to say. Cary Redding is more complicated."

"But if he likes music, didn't he recognize your name?" Aiden had stopped eating and had both elbows on the table, supporting his chin in his hands and just staring at Cary as though he had lost his mind.

"Well... no... not really...."

"You used that fake name? What is it?"

"Connor." Cary looked down at the mangled panini on his plate so Aiden wouldn't see him squirm.

"Shit, man. Why?"

"I don't know. I didn't want to be Cary Redding. I mean, if I had told him who I was, he might have expected me to be something I'm not."

"Like a successful musician?" Aiden shook his head.

"No." Cary was squirming now.

"Like you deserve someone like him? You know... someone nice?" When Cary said nothing, Aiden continued, "That's it, isn't it? But you *do* deserve—"

"Look, Aiden," Cary interrupted, feeling suddenly very shaky, "I've gotta figure this out. It's been a crappy few weeks. I haven't exactly been at the top of my game. And I'm sure as hell not what you think I am." Cary rubbed the bridge of his nose.

Aiden frowned. "Okay. I'll let it drop. For now, at least. So how long before the cast comes off? You gonna be able to play again?"

"Yeah. I'll be fine."

"I wished you'd called me. I could've helped."

"I didn't want to impose."

"I'd like you to impose. I'm your friend, remember? Your fucking *best* friend, last time I checked."

"Thanks," Cary said. "You are. And you're right, I should have called." And for once, he meant it too.

They parted an hour later, Aiden having extracted Cary's promise they'd have lunch again in a week.

Back at his apartment after dark, Cary lay in his bed, unable to sleep. He knew Aiden was right. What good was it doing to lie to Antonio? He stared up at the ceiling and watched the lights from the cars bounce across it.

It's not like you're looking to marry the guy. So what difference does it make? He had given Antonio more than enough signals, and in two weeks, they hadn't even kissed. And eventually Antonio would figure out what Cary really was.

And then what? Why even bother seeing him again?

As he finally drifted off to sleep in the early hours of the Milan morning, Cary was filled with a sense of uneasiness—an anxiety he couldn't quite explain that lingered just out of his reach. Who was he fooling? He knew he'd see Antonio again regardless. The siren call was simply too powerful to resist.

CHAPTER  8

HOME TO ROOST

THE day after his lunch with Aiden, and in spite of the nagging voice at the back of his mind that said he was in way over his head, Cary was seized with the brilliant idea of calling Antonio. Cary knew nothing about "dating" in any conventional sense of the word. He had never "dated." Ever. And he was sure he sounded like an idiot.

"Hey, Antonio. Just thought I'd… you know… say hello. I… ah… had a great time last week. At the circus, I mean, not afterward. Shit. I didn't mean it like that. I had a great time afterward too." He paused, his cheeks hot, when he realized what he had just said. "I… ah… I'd like to see you again. When you have time. I know you're probably busy. So… right… um… call me if you have a chance."

Total fucking idiot.

He didn't really expect Antonio to call him back, at least not right away. But Antonio left him a short message the same day saying he'd call again once he was back in town.

Nearly a week passed without a call from Antonio, however, and Cary began to wonder if Antonio was a lost cause. He had probably come to his senses. Which would have been fine. *Should* have been fine, really. Only Cary realized that he no longer felt compelled to frequent his via Padova haunts, and even the nearby park seemed to hold no interest for his cock. He couldn't get Antonio out of his thoughts. And it was making him anxious. Antsy.

Cary was doing some crunches on the floor of his bedroom when his cell phone rang. He answered it, half out of breath. "*Pronto?*"

"Connor?" Antonio said over the connection.

"Antonio?"

"You sound strange."

Cary's heart began to race. "Sit-ups," he responded in English, at a loss for the Italian word. But it wasn't the sit-ups that had him breathless, and Cary knew it.

"Ah, *capisco*," Antonio replied after a pause. "*Gli 'addominali'*. It sounds like they're very hard for you."

"Give me a break, macho man. It's not as easy as you'd think when you've got a broken wrist."

"*Poverino*." Antonio's voice dripped with mock sympathy, and Cary was sure Antonio was smiling. *Poor little thing.*

"Thanks. So you're calling to make me feel like an invalid, or was there another reason?" He didn't care either way.

Right. Keep telling yourself you don't care, and maybe you'll believe it!

"Ah, *sì*. Yes, two reasons, in fact. First, I wanted to let you know I was back from my business trip to Japan. My flight just landed."

Today? The guy was calling from the airport?

"How was Japan?" Cary covered the microphone with his thumb and forced himself to slow down his breathing.

"Not very interesting seen from the inside of an office. But I was able to wrap up the contract. And the food was good."

Cary chuckled.

"The second reason I called," Antonio continued, "was to invite you this Friday."

"Another circus?"

Antonio laughed. "No, not the circus this time. A client gave me two tickets to the symphony. Would you like to come?"

"Sure," Cary said without hesitation. *Great. So much for not sounding desperate!* "I'd like that." He hoped he sounded both interested and not.

"Why don't I pick you up around six, and I can make us some dinner before?"

Cary grimaced at the prospect of another of Antonio's home-cooked meals. "How about dinner out this time? My treat."

"You sure? I'm happy to pay for dinner."

"I'm sure, Antonio. I'd like to treat you."

"All right. Thanks. I know a little place nearby you'd enjoy. Do you want to eat before or after the concert?"

"I don't mind an early dinner. That way I can just meet you at your place." Cary had other ideas that didn't involve eating food. "That'll save you the trip to pick me up."

"That sounds great. I'm looking forward to it."

"Me too."

CARY arrived at Antonio's apartment on Friday night, dressed in a pair of khakis and a wool blazer with a simple silk tie. It had been far more difficult than he imagined to find just the right thing to wear. Too expensive an outfit and Antonio might suspect that his story of being an out-of-work musician working as a waiter was a sham; too casual and he might embarrass the man. In the end, he had gone shopping in a vintage store not far from his apartment, where he had found the English wool blazer. It fit as though it had been made for him.

"*Buonasera*," he said when Antonio answered the door. The look of pleasure on Antonio's face told him his efforts had paid off.

"*Buonasera*, Connor. You clean up well."

"Contrary to popular belief, I own some clothing of my own," Cary quipped. "I can also bathe myself, although it isn't as fun as when you helped me."

The pink flush on Antonio's cheeks was way too charming.

Dinner was at a tiny restaurant Cary would have completely missed if Antonio hadn't opened the door for him and gestured him through it. They were met by a round-faced woman whose eyes lit up when she saw Antonio. "Signor Bianchi, I have missed you! It has been far too long." She then proceeded to kiss him soundly on both cheeks.

They sat at a small table in the back corner of the restaurant. Cary guessed by the set of stairs they descended and the ancient bricks lining the walls that this had once been a cellar for a store. The tables were set with candles, the walls were hung with paintings of the city, and the music was classical: baroque, understated. A hint of garlic hung temptingly in the air, and the meal was one of the best Cary had eaten in Milan, except perhaps for a dinner at home of Roberta's paella, a recipe that had been handed down to her by her Spanish grandmother. It was also dirt cheap. Antonio had obviously taken pains to make sure that Cary didn't have to spend a lot of money.

Throughout the meal, he and Antonio talked comfortably. The bottle of red wine they had nearly finished between them put Cary at ease, and he found himself focusing through slightly hooded eyes on the top button of Antonio's white cotton shirt. A hint of downy hair peered out above the button, the same dusty blond of the curls that had a habit of falling onto Antonio's forehead when he spoke animatedly.

"So," Antonio said as they ate Signora Tuzzi's cannoli (Antonio said it was Massimo's favorite, and after tasting it, Cary could understand why), "what kind of music do you like?"

"Any, really. Jazz, classical. I'm not a big country music fan, except maybe the classic stuff. I love rock too."

"What is it you like about rock?" Antonio asked.

"What do you mean?"

"What does it make you feel?"

Cary paused to think about the answer. It was an interesting question, and one he had never really considered. "I don't know... free, I guess. And a little dangerous."

Antonio chuckled. "I think you're usually dangerous. But I understand what you're saying. It's the same for me when I listen to classical music."

"The dangerous part?" Cary said as he chewed on his lower lip.

"It makes me feel something. I forget about the little things that get to me, and I just *feel*."

Cary stared down at his empty glass, the warmth of the conversation fading as he had a momentary vision of himself, the first time he had performed. He had been four or five years old. He'd felt something then: excitement, to be sharing the music which had up until that moment been only his. Love, even? How long had it been since he felt anything even approaching that?

"Are you all right?"

"I could use some more wine," Cary said with a tilt of his head.

"Of course." Antonio poured Cary the last of the bottle, and their eyes met.

Cary shivered, suddenly cold in spite of the warm restaurant and his wool jacket. What was it about those blue eyes that made him feel as though they could pierce his skin and see inside of him? It was as if Antonio *knew*....

Cary shrugged off the thought and gulped his wine.

"Good?" Signora Tuzzi asked with an expression of eager anticipation.

Thank God, Cary thought, relieved at the interruption. *"Perfetto!"* he said aloud. "The best I've ever had."

The woman left, and Antonio reached across the table and laid his hand on Cary's. It was an unexpected gesture that took Cary by surprise.

"I remember the first time my papà took me to La Scala," Antonio said. His expression was pensive. "He loved opera. We saw *La Traviata*. It was so beautiful, I remember wanting to run up on stage and join the singers. But I never could sing."

"Funny, isn't it? And I remember thinking how much fun it would be to play football. My brother was really good. I tried, but my mother always worried about me. She didn't want...." Cary's voice trailed off at the realization that he had told Antonio far more than he intended.

"We all wish we could be someone else sometimes." Antonio squeezed Cary's hand gently and met his gaze.

"Yeah. I guess that's true."

More than you know.

Cary wanted to look away, but he couldn't. He wanted to tell Antonio the truth, but the fear that Antonio would push him away was more than he could face. In the end, he said nothing.

Just one more night. The clock strikes midnight and Cinderella is dressed in rags. Tonight, he wanted to enjoy the music with someone else who loved it as much as he did. Tomorrow, he'd come clean.

THE Milan Auditorium looked different from the vantage point of their orchestra seats. Cary had never attended a concert here, but he had played several, including one three months before.

"What do you think?" Antonio asked as they took their seats.

"I love this place." Cary looked around the hall with genuine appreciation. "Modern, but the wood makes it feel warm." Antonio's thigh was warm against his own, as well. "The acoustics are amazing."

"It's my favorite hall," Antonio said.

"Really? I'd have thought you'd like La Scala better."

"I love La Scala, but it's a little like listening to music in a palace. This is more accessible."

"So what are they playing tonight?"

"The Shostakovich Fifth Symphony and the Mahler Fourth."

"Do you like twentieth century music?"

"The earlier works, yes. Romantic, with a bit of a modern edge. Mahler, Strauss, Sibelius, Dvořák. I prefer this style to Mozart or Beethoven. How about you?"

"Love the Shostakovich. I'm not as big a Mahler fan."

"What kind of music do you write?" Antonio asked.

"I haven't really written anything since school," Cary admitted.

"I'd like to introduce you to the conductor. He's a wonderful composer, as well. Maybe you've heard of him. Maestro David Somers? I met him a few years ago through a mutual friend. David's the one who gave me the tickets."

Cary did his best not to gasp. He had known David was in town rehearsing the opera with Aiden. He just hadn't figured on David conducting this *particular* concert. He too counted David Somers as a friend and not just a colleague. He even stayed with David and his partner, Alex Bishop, when he played in Chicago. The same Alex Bishop he had played with in this very hall. And it was David who had encouraged him to move to Europe after school. When Cary had first moved to Milan, he had stayed with David until he had found an apartment. He was even planning on having Thanksgiving dinner with David at his villa outside Milan in just a few weeks.

"Wow," he said, doing his utmost to sound excited. "It's pretty cool you know someone like that."

Antonio shrugged. "We can go backstage after the concert and I can introduce you."

Holy crap. A vague thought niggled at the back of his brain, but he promptly shoved it away. *Of course he doesn't know. It's just a coincidence.* "I... I...," he stammered, but before he could manage a single coherent word, the lights dimmed.

He had wanted to enjoy the concert. He *really* had. He had also wanted to enjoy Antonio's company. Instead, he spent the entire second half of the program working out a plan to avoid being "introduced" to David afterward. That was, after he spent the entire *first* half of the program trying to decide if he should just come clean and tell Antonio who he was.

And what then? You'll be lucky if he doesn't dump you in the Po River and watch you drown. And with a smile on his face.

"Something wrong?" Antonio asked after Cary spent the better part of intermission in the men's bathroom, trying to gather his thoughts.

"Pain medicine makes me sick sometimes." He didn't have to fake the pain in his gut, either, although he could hardly lay the blame on the meds.

"I can take you home, if you'd like." Antonio eyed him with concern, putting his hand on Cary's clammy forehead. "Maybe the wine and the pills were a bad combination."

Oh God. You are so screwed. Now the guy is worried about you!

"I'll be fine." He wasn't entirely convinced he would be fine after the evening played out, but he wouldn't add pulling Antonio away from the concert to his growing pile of guilt.

Before Antonio could protest, the lights dimmed once more.

THERE were few conductors Cary admired as much as David Somers. And when the orchestra began the first movement of the Shostakovich Fifth Symphony, he nearly forgot the mess he had managed to get himself into. The dark opening with the lush strings and poignant dissonances of the canon seemed to mirror the turmoil in his own heart.

By the time the concert ended, Cary was ready to cut his losses. It was one thing to lie to the nameless, faceless fucks who didn't give a shit about Connor Taylor. It was entirely another thing to lie to the oh-so-fucking-gorgeous, nicest-man-in-Milan-and-maybe-on-the-planet with the cute little brat of a kid who had done nothing more to warrant this idiocy than take care of him. Not that he wanted a relationship with the guy, he told himself, but he couldn't just keep lying to him like this.

"Antonio," he began as Antonio offered him the scarf from around his neck, "I really need to tell you something. I'm not—"

"I'm taking you back to my apartment," Antonio interrupted, steering him into a taxi. He gave the driver the address; then, over Cary's protests, he tucked the scarf under Cary's jacket.

"I can't do this, Antonio. You need to hear—"

This time, it was Antonio's big arm around his shoulders that silenced him. The faint scent of aftershave settled between them, and he knew he had no strength to fight. He was so far gone, wanting this beautiful man, lusting after him like he had never lusted before. He just couldn't tell Antonio the truth.

"Shh." Antonio moved closer until Cary couldn't help but put his head on his shoulder. Well, he *couldn't* help it, could he?

"I'm so sorry," he whispered into that strong shoulder. And he *was* too. Sorry he didn't have the guts to be honest about who and what he was.

"You don't need to apologize. I understand."

"HEY." He peered into the living room, having spent yet another night in Antonio's bed while Antonio slept on the couch. The smell of freshly brewed coffee wafted in from the kitchen, and his stomach rumbled in response. Antonio lay on the couch, hands supporting his head. He was smiling.

Cary hadn't even attempted to make a move after they had gotten back the night before. It had been all he could do not to sneak out of the apartment with his tail between his legs after Antonio had fallen asleep. In the end, he still wasn't sure why he had stayed.

"Feeling better?"

"Sort of," Cary admitted. A good night's sleep and eight hours without alcohol had helped, although they'd done little to assuage his guilty conscience. "I'll just get dressed and get going."

"I was hoping you'd spend the day with me." The smile on Antonio's face faded, replaced by a look of hopeful anticipation. "Do you have any plans?"

"No," Cary admitted without a second thought. He had been occupying his time with studying some new music he'd been considering adding to his repertoire and working on exercises for his bow arm, but without the use of his left hand, there hadn't been much else for him to do. That had just given him more time to think about Antonio, and what a shithead he had been to lie to the man in the first place.

"Good. I don't have to work today, and I was thinking we could do some shopping."

"Shopping?"

"Christmas shopping," Antonio explained. "One of the disadvantages of having a large family—I do a lot of it. There's this incredible toy store that Massi and I found."

"Sounds like fun."

They ate a light breakfast and were out of the apartment by ten. Cary decided he most definitely could get used to borrowing Antonio's silk camp shirts—they were soft, and they smelled like Antonio. And even though he had gotten better about buttoning things for himself with his cast, Antonio had insisted on buttoning the shirt for him. Even now, as they walked to the red line Metro station from the apartment, Cary imagined the feeling of those fingertips against his bare skin.

The toy store, housed on the ground floor of an old building, was already full of people when they arrived. Children were everywhere, much to Cary's chagrin, scooting about, shouting in delight with each new discovery, always underfoot. They walked around, getting the lay of the land. Antonio had some very definite ideas for a few of his nieces and nephews: dolls and wooden models of buildings and bridges, paints and oil crayons, outdoor toys for vineyard visits.

At one point, Cary became uncomfortably aware that Antonio was studying him as they explored the store. "What?" he asked at last, unable to restrain himself.

"You look like the children."

Cary shot Antonio a confused and slightly irritated look.

"You look as though this is your first time in a toy store. How do you Americans say it, 'like a child in a candy store'?"

"I've been to a toy store before," Cary snapped, feeling suddenly defensive. Well, he *had* to have been to a toy store before, right? Every red-blooded American kid made at least a few trips to Toys"R"Us with his or her parents. But when he thought about it some more, he realized he didn't *remember* ever having gone himself. Sure, he'd ordered toys online for his nephews, but…. "Or, at least, I'm pretty sure I've been," he added, knowing he sounded far less convinced than he had just a moment before.

"If you don't remember, then it's been far too long." Antonio took Cary by his good arm and dragged him off toward the back of the store.

"Where are we going?"

"You'll see." Antonio just grinned like a fool.

Cary raised his eyebrows and sighed as he allowed himself to be pulled through the store like some of the children pulled their parents.

Their destination became obvious at the doorway to a large rectangular room that took up nearly the entire back of the building. Behind the railing that ran the length of the room was an enormous model railroad complete with mountains, lakes, and waterfalls. Overhead, a make-believe sun had begun to set, casting shadows over the miniature cities and towns. The lights dimmed, and stars were now visible overhead.

Cary knew he must look like an idiot, with his mouth hanging open and his eyes wider than some of the children nearby, but he'd never seen anything even remotely like this. "Wow," he muttered in English, at a loss for words.

Antonio put his arm around Cary's shoulders and beamed. "You like it?" It was clear to Cary that Antonio already had his answer.

"It's incredible," Cary whispered. He leaned over the railing to get a better look at a bus stop where people were unloading skis and snowboards. A tiny chairlift rose on a nearby mountain slope, carrying its occupants to the top.

"I was hoping you'd like it. Massi and I spent a few hours here, just trying to see everything."

"Justin had a train set when we were little. I used to love to watch that thing just go around and around and around. But *this*...."

Antonio, too, leaned over the railing, his left arm pressed against Cary's right. Cary repressed a sigh at the feel of that solid arm. In that instant, he envied Massimo. He tried to remember a time when he had ever felt as happy as Massimo had seemed at the circus. What did it say about him, he wondered, that apart from his music, this was the closest to happy he had ever really felt?

CARY sipped his hot cocoa and watched the flames dance in the fireplace of Antonio's apartment a few hours later. The vestibule was filled with bags of toys, including those Cary had chosen for his nephews.

"Good?" asked Antonio.

Cary nodded. "Reminds me of when I was really little, at my grandmother's house." The memory warmed him, and he smiled. "She died when I was about seven, so I don't remember much about her. But she'd make me hot chocolate and she never asked me to—" He broke off, realizing he had almost said, *She never asked me to practice when I visited her.*

"Never asked you to do what?" Antonio repeated.

"Never asked me to do the dishes."

"My nonna used to knit me sweaters." Antonio settled down beside Cary, appearing pleased that the fire was now managing quite nicely without his help. "You know," he added, closing his eyes and tilting his head backward as a grin spread across his face, "I still have a few. Massi's almost big enough to fit in them now."

"He's lucky, to be able to spend time with his grandmother."

"Grandmothers," Antonio corrected. "Francesca's mother is almost as doting as mine. They spoil him."

They watched the fire and sipped their cocoa in comfortable silence, their shoulders touching. The firelight made Antonio's blond curls look almost orange.

"Do you mind if I put on some music?" Antonio asked after a few minutes had passed.

"That'd be great."

Antonio picked up the remote and clicked it several times. The sound of mellow jazz was a perfect complement to the warmth of the fire. Cary recognized the music: *The Lake*, David and Alex's jazz album.

The music simmered softly in the background as Antonio leaned back on the sofa once more, this time putting his arm around Cary and drawing him against his broad chest. The sigh that escaped Cary's lips came as a surprise. He had never been one to snuggle, but somehow this just felt *right*. He looked up and realized Antonio was watching him with an odd expression, as if he were unsure what to do with this strange creature who had somehow insinuated itself into his life.

"I like this album. I can imagine the view of Lake Michigan from a Chicago penthouse. The boats on the water," Cary said as he closed his eyes. He knew that view well—the view from David's apartment.

I can't do this anymore.

Cary sat up. He fully intended to tell Antonio the truth. Instead, though, he reached for Antonio's face, bringing it gently toward his own and brushing his lips against Antonio's. He felt Antonio tense, and Cary waited for this advance to be rejected, just like all the others. To his surprise, however, Antonio wrapped his arms around his shoulders and drew him inward.

The kiss was almost chaste, the only hint of more a slightly shuddered breath from Antonio. Cary's fingers moved of their own accord to comb Antonio's hair. And oh, but that hair was as soft as he had imagined it would be! He felt his body respond and, without thinking, pushed Antonio back onto the couch so Cary could sit on the edge, in the slight indentation of Antonio's waist. Antonio was effectively pinned against the back of the sofa.

"Connor...," Antonio began as Cary worked the silk shirt free of Antonio's pants with his good hand. Cary probed the broad chest beneath the silk fabric with his long fingers, finding a nipple and rolling it about. "I don't think this is a—"

"Shh," Cary whispered as he leaned down and kissed Antonio a second time. Antonio's chin and upper lip were rough with stubble, serving to intensify the sensual contact.

He slid his tongue inside Antonio's mouth as the other man's lips yielded. There was a hint of chocolate in that warm mouth, but it tasted so much better than any dessert. Cary wanted to plunder that mouth, to explore every inch of it. He wanted to take his time and just....

Antonio pushed him gently off and got to his feet. "I'm sorry, Connor, but I'm supposed to meet a client for dinner. I really need to get going."

"Oh." Cary did his best to hide his shock and disappointment at the brush-off.

"Cheer up, caro," Antonio told him with a lopsided grin. "I enjoyed that as much as you. There will be time for more later." He offered his hand to help Cary up. "I'm having a friend over for dinner tomorrow night," he added. "Would you like to come?"

"Sure." The invitation put Cary's mind at ease, at least a little. He figured Antonio wouldn't have bothered to invite him if he really didn't want to see him again. Still, he couldn't shake the feeling that something was wrong.

"Seven o'clock."

"Okay. Anything I should bring?"

"Nothing but yourself, caro," Antonio replied, using the traditional term of endearment again. Cary decided he liked it far better than Roberta's "beanpole," but then, Antonio could have called him "*stupido*," and he'd probably have liked that too.

CHAPTER 9

FACING THE MUSIC

"CONNOR, I'd like you to meet David Somers. David, this is Connor Taylor." The entire scene played out in slow motion, from the moment Antonio opened the door until Cary came face to face with the conductor of the Chicago Symphony Orchestra. Conductor and Cary's good friend and longtime mentor.

Oh fuck.

"Good to meet you, David," Cary said. He couldn't bear to look at him.

"A pleasure, *Connor*." David Somers had always been an intimidating figure for Cary, with his cool patrician manner. Cary felt like a scruffy dog standing in the middle of a Persian rug, having tracked the mud in from outside, tail firmly between his legs.

I can't do this.

"I can't stay." Cary turned and reached for the door.

"I don't understand." Antonio put his hand on top of Cary's. Cary avoided Antonio's gaze but focused intently on the silver door handle. "You said you were free for dinner."

"That's before I...."

Before I what? Before I realized I was totally and utterly screwed? Before I blew whatever chance I had of spending more time with you?

As chaotic as Cary's thoughts were in that instant, the realization that he wasn't just thinking of sex with Antonio anymore but about spending time with the man came as a complete shock. He was falling for Antonio.

"Before you what?" Antonio repeated.

"I really think I should leave," he croaked. "I apologize, David." *For so many things. I just hope you'll forgive me, Maestro.* He figured there was little chance Antonio would do the same.

"You needn't apologize," David said. "I was just leaving."

"Wait a minute." Cary backed away from the door and frowned at the two men. "I thought you were here for dinner."

Much to Cary's surprise, David just smiled back at him. "Change of plans. Besides, I'll see you both for Thanksgiving dinner next week. Alex flies in tomorrow. He said to send you his regards, and he asked me to tell you to bring your cello if the cast is off and you're up to playing by then. Something about an arrangement of 'Night and Day' he found."

Cary had expected to see confusion in Antonio's face. Instead, the corners of Antonio's mouth edged ever so slightly upward. And was that a wink David shot at Antonio?

David put a hand on Cary's shoulder. "Antonio told me what happened. I'm glad to hear your wrist is healing well."

"He... he... he *told* you? But how would he know you...?" The universe shifted sideways, and the only thing Cary could hear was his heart pounding against his ribs. Something in his mind clicked, and Cary finally understood. "He would only have told you—"

"If I knew who you were?" Antonio's face was unreadable.

"You know? I mean, you *knew*?"

"I'll be going now," David said, opening the door. "I'm guessing you two have a few things to discuss. Antonio, I'll call you next week about the contract. And Cary," he added with a sympathetic smile, "try to stay out of trouble. All right? I'm expecting you to play the Dvořák in March, remember?"

Cary just nodded as he watched the conductor leave and close the door behind him. "I should go too," he said after a minute's silence.

"Why? Do you have somewhere you need to be?"

"No. But after what I've done, why would you want me to stay?" His voice sounded small to his own ears, tentative.

Antonio ran a hand through his hair and sighed. "I let you stay before. Why would I change my mind now? Nothing is different."

"Nothing...? I mean, you let...?" Cary choked out. "You... you mean you *knew*? Before David?" He was sure he wasn't making any sense. His head pounded and his stomach did somersaults and backflips.

"I've known all along, Cary."

"Shit."

Antonio laughed, a warm and inviting sound that made Cary's knees wobble. "Why don't you sit down." Antonio gestured to the couch. "We can talk."

Cary did as he was told. "How…? When…?"

Christ! Get it together.

"I heard you play before we met. Several times. I thought you looked familiar when I found you that night, but you were pretty banged up. I realized who you were while I was waiting with you in the hospital." He chuckled, then added, "And when I heard you humming the New World Symphony in the bathroom that first night, I was sure I was right."

Cary opened his mouth to speak but decided against it. What could he say, anyhow?

"I go to a lot of concerts because of my work. I heard the Brahms Double Concerto you performed with Alex at the Milan Auditorium and the recital you played in July."

"Wait a minute." Cary struggled to put the pieces together. "What did David mean about a contract? I thought you did business law."

"Perhaps I should have explained it better. I help musicians and artists with their businesses. I handle all of David and Alex's European contracts. I'm what you Americans call an entertainment lawyer."

"So when we heard David conduct…?"

"I'm sorry about that. I didn't mean to upset you. I had hoped you'd just tell me the truth on your own, but when you didn't, I decided to push you a little. It was a mistake."

"If I didn't already feel so bad about lying to you all these weeks, I'd be seriously pissed."

"After the concert," Antonio added, "I knew you wanted to tell me the truth, and I felt terrible for putting you in that position. I could see how horrible you felt. I spoke with David a few nights ago. I asked him what I should do."

Cary knew his mouth was hanging open, but he didn't care.

"He was the one who suggested making up the story about dinner. He was worried about you."

Cary made a mental note to call David and apologize again. "You certainly surprised me."

"He cares a lot about you," Antonio said. "He talks about you. And when I called him from the hospital—"

"You called David Somers from the hospital?" Cary couldn't quite wrap his brain around it.

"Yes. I wasn't sure what to do, and I knew David was in Milan. He suggested I keep an eye on you just to be sure you were all right. But Cary, why didn't you just tell me who you were to begin with?"

Cary felt his gut tense at the look of hurt on Antonio's face—he knew he was the cause of it. "It's a long story." Oh, he *so* didn't want to do this!

But what difference does it make now, anyhow?

"We've got plenty of time," Antonio said. He leaned back against the pillows and waited patiently.

"I guess I owe you that, don't I?"

"No," Antonio responded. "You don't owe me anything. But I'd still like to know."

Cary absentmindedly scratched the skin on the inside of his left arm, just under the edge of the cast. How had he ever thought this—*any* of this— was okay? The broken wrist? The weeks away from practicing? The lies? He had only himself to blame for all of it.

"I'm the worst kind of self-centered asshole," he said at last. "I play my music and I do fine. But when I'm not playing… let's just say I've been in trouble a few times."

"You were coming from a bar when I found you?" There was no judgment in that resonant voice, just patient understanding.

"Yeah. And not the reputable kind *you* go to."

"I've been in my share of dives." Antonio met Cary's gaze unflinchingly. "We all have, I think."

Cary ignored this and plunged forward. It was better to get this over with quickly so he could leave Antonio in peace. He'd get it off his chest before he said his goodbyes and crawled back under his rock with whatever pathetic shred of dignity he still possessed. "I got arrested in Paris for public indecency a few years back. Promised my agent I wouldn't tarnish the Cary Redding name. I mean," he added as if it somehow justified his actions, at least in part, "he has a family to feed, and I need to pay the bills. So I created an alter ego. Someone I didn't give a shit about and who nobody else would either."

"You figured I'd ask questions," Antonio said, "that I'd make judgments about you."

"Who wouldn't?"

"*I* wouldn't. Not everyone is like that, Cary."

Oh, how he loved to hear that name—his *real* name—on Antonio's lips. *If only I hadn't botched this whole thing so entirely....*

"When you introduced yourself, I figured I'd never see you again. It just seemed easier. I mean, a guy like me. Why would you even look twice? But I had no idea...."

That I'd end up liking you, he finished silently. *That I'd want to get to know you better.*

"Well," he added, "that's about all there is to tell." He stood up to leave.

"Where are you going?"

"I've already overstayed my welcome."

"Did I say that?"

"You didn't have to say it," Cary said with resignation. "I just want you to know I'm really sorry about being such a fucked-up—"

His words were cut short by Antonio's lips on his.

Oh, good God, he thought as Antonio wrapped his arms around him. It was so overwhelming: the way Antonio smelled, the hard body against his own, the acceptance he felt in that moment.

"You...." Cary gasped as the kiss broke. "You're not pissed with me? After all I've done?"

"Yeah, I'm pissed."

Cary could see the anger now, where before he had been too inwardly focused to notice. "Then why... I mean... why did you do that? These past four weeks, you kept pushing me away."

Antonio took a deep breath. "As much as my brain tells me to run away from you as fast as I can," he said, "I just can't seem to help myself. I want you. More than that. I want to know *you*—Cary Redding. Without the bullshit. Without the lies."

"You don't *want* to know me, Antonio. What I... do."

"I figured it out."

Cary looked everywhere but at Antonio. He knew?

"No. You don't know. You can't, really. Because anything you've heard—it's a hundred times worse. I... I can't help myself. This... us... you don't want this. You *can't* want this. Someone like me. A...." The word *slut* danced on Cary's tongue, but he couldn't bring himself to say it.

That's what you are, isn't it?

"I didn't want Connor Taylor. I wanted *you*, Cary. The real Cary Redding."

"But—"

"I like you, Cary. How you live for your music. How you are around Massi. How you look at things like a child sometimes. How you seem so lost. I…." Antonio hesitated for the first time that evening. "I want to show you the way."

"I lied to you. For almost a month. I told you I was something— *someone* I wasn't."

"You also showed me what's inside of Cary. You pretended it wasn't you, but I know it was."

Cary said nothing. He was too stunned to speak.

"I *am* angry. I don't like being lied to. And if you lie to me again…."

"I won't," Cary whispered. "I promise." He meant it too.

"I never wanted Connor Taylor," Antonio repeated. "Besides, you were trying too hard."

"I wasn't try—"

"Kiss me, Cary. And, how do you say it in English? 'Cut the crap'?"

Cary should have had a smart comeback—he usually did—but how could he possibly resist the one thing he'd been obsessing over for the last few weeks? He did the only reasonable thing he could: he did exactly as he was told.

Antonio parted his lips to allow him entry, then teased him with a brief taste of his tongue until Cary had no choice but to lean against the taut body and pull that pale, beautiful face to his own with his one good arm. A moment later, Antonio lifted off Cary's shirt and eased it gently over the cast. He wasted no time but found the hard nipples of Cary's chest with his thumbs, rubbing in narrow circles until Cary growled and pressed his groin against Antonio's muscled thigh.

No one had touched him like this in years. He had imagined the first time with Antonio would be rough and fast, but nothing in that gentle, insistent touch was anything like what he had imagined. It was *so* much better.

Antonio kissed a line from the base of his neck, over his Adam's apple, and up to his right ear. "Oh fuck," Cary moaned, not sure if he had spoken English or Italian or even if he had spoken at all. Antonio pulled at the lobe of Cary's ear with his teeth and licked around the outside until Cary trembled.

"Come." Antonio backed away from the couch with an outstretched arm. "There's no need to rush this evening. I want you to be comfortable while I make love to you."

Make love? Cary wondered from a distance. *Is that what this is?* He didn't like things slow and deliberate, did he? But even as those thoughts crossed his foggy brain, he knew he had no will to resist, and he'd be a fool if he did.

A moment later he was facedown on the bed as Antonio pulled down his jeans and briefs. He felt that hot mouth on his skin, the tongue licking and tasting, the teeth biting at his thighs and his ass until he cried out. "Fuck me," he hissed. "Oh, please fuck me."

But Antonio's mouth did not cease its insistent exploration, and his mouth was soon joined by his large hands as they ghosted over Cary's skin with surprising gentleness. He wasn't sure why he had expected them to be rough, but they weren't. Powerful, yes, but smooth and oh so sensual.

"I'm not in a hurry," Antonio whispered. "And we have the whole night."

Cary wanted to protest, to tell Antonio he couldn't wait, that he needed this *now*, but Antonio was feathering kisses up his spine, and his ability to speak seemed to dissolve somewhere between his brain and his mouth. And he loved it. Loved the tender touch of those lips upon his skin and the tickle of blond curls that followed close behind. Loved the attention he hadn't even known he'd craved.

The bruises on his back had mostly faded, but Antonio found each and every one and licked the skin there as if to make him forget the pain. "You didn't make it easy on me," Antonio whispered as he came up for breath. "God. From that first night, when I saw you standing naked in this room, I wanted this. You don't know how hard it was not to take you right there, bruises and all."

Antonio's words made Cary shiver.

He wanted me all along? He felt dizzy, overwhelmed at the realization. And so, *so* turned on.

Cary tried to roll over, but Antonio stopped him. "So impatient," he chuckled as he began to massage Cary's tense shoulders.

"Oh fuck," Cary moaned. This was torture, having the man so close and being unable to touch him. And yet, as he lay there, unable to do anything but feel those fingers and that mouth upon his skin, he felt as though the stress of the evening had been driven away, his guilt forgotten.

"Better?"

Cary watched as Antonio stepped back from the bed a few minutes later and began to unbutton his shirt. "Mmm."

Antonio's shirt fluttered to the ground.

Although Cary had traced the outline of that powerful chest the night before, seeing it now for the first time, the urge to touch it again proved too strong. He got up from the bed and ghosted his fingers over the pale, downy hair. He kissed one nipple and then the other, then licked a line down the center of his chest until he was on his knees and reaching for the buckle of Antonio's belt.

Slowly, ever so slowly, he unfastened the belt and the pants, then pushed them down until Antonio stepped out of them. Now that Antonio was wearing only a pair of boxers—silk, of course—Cary really did feel like the proverbial kid at Christmas. He bit his lip and looked up at Antonio as he pulled the shimmering silk to the floor.

This night had reminded Cary of many things, and the fact that it had been years since he'd given another man a blow job was yet another. For as long as he could remember, sex had been uniquely about his own satisfaction. And while he still wanted that now, he also wanted to please Antonio.

He reached out with his good hand and cupped Antonio's ass. He felt the firm muscle beneath the supple skin. He squeezed it and scraped it with his fingernails. He watched as Antonio's cock responded and his body tensed at the touch. It was a beautiful cock, Cary thought with satisfaction. Long and thick and cut: just the way he liked it. And Antonio was as aroused as he.

Antonio reached out to rub his fingers over Cary's face. Cary licked one of Antonio's palms and heard his partner inhale sharply. Then he leaned in and flicked his tongue around the head of Antonio's cock. Antonio snaked his fingers through his hair and urged him closer still.

"I thought you said we had all night," Cary teased in a low voice.

"Damn Americans. Always pointing fingers."

Cary responded by taking Antonio deep into his mouth, using his teeth to gently scrape the underside of his erection, then released him so he could probe the slit with his tongue and circle the head until he heard Antonio's sharp intake of breath. With a quick glance upward and a grin for good measure, he swallowed Antonio to the hilt once more and held him prisoner there. He groaned with pleasure, and Antonio shivered in response to the vibrations from his mouth.

For Cary, the sensation of being in control was exhilarating and new. He pulled back and tasted a hint of precome on his tongue, then licked the crown again to coax a bit more.

Antonio growled and pushed him gently away. "You'll make me come like that," he warned, his pale cheeks flushed and his breath hitching as he spoke. "It's been too long."

Cary grinned as he allowed himself to be pushed back onto the bed. He wasn't sure why it mattered, but the thought that he was Antonio's first in a long time made him feel good. Special, even.

And then it was his own cock in Antonio's willing mouth. He arched his body upward to meet the warmth as large hands slid underneath his ass, gripping and guiding him. He watched, mesmerized, as Antonio worked his way up and down his length, pulling and sucking. He cried out when Antonio found the tight ring of muscle between his cheeks and breached his opening with a finger while cupping his balls and rolling them around with his other hand.

"Fuck, oh, fuck," Cary moaned as Antonio eased his finger inside and began to move it about in rhythm with his mouth. Cary hadn't even noticed Antonio use the lube coating those big fingers; he had been too inwardly focused to appreciate anything beyond what he could touch or feel himself.

Antonio's eyes reflected the dim light from the streetlamp outside, and something in his expression left Cary nearly breathless. He struggled to understand the emotion behind that glittering gaze. There was hunger there, certainly. And there was something else, something Cary wasn't sure of but which both intrigued and frightened him. But when he felt another finger press inward, any coherent thought he had fled with the telltale tingle at the base of his spine.

"I'm going to come," he panted. Antonio released Cary from his mouth, using his hand now to keep up the delicious pressure, and pressed a third finger inside Cary's ass. The dual stimulation of Antonio's hand on his cock and the probing of his fingers was too much for Cary. His balls drew up tight, and he came into Antonio's hand, crying out so loudly he hardly recognized his own voice. He gripped Antonio's arms, forgetting about the cast and not caring when he felt a twinge of pain in response.

As the warm haze of orgasm began to fade, Cary noticed Antonio watching him with a ghost of a smile. He drew Antonio down once more. He kissed Antonio's lips, tasting himself there. Then, after pushing him so he lay with his back on the sheets, Cary began to bite and lick at the pale nipples, sucking until he was rewarded with a gasped "*Sí!*"

"Condom?" he asked, at which Antonio gestured to the nightstand. Cary leaned over and pulled one out, then proceeded to roll it over Antonio's cock, stopping halfway through to bite a pebbled nipple and study the result with satisfaction. But when he tried to turn over to allow easy access to his ass, Antonio stopped him.

"No," Antonio said. "I want to see your face."

Cary couldn't remember the last time he *hadn't* gotten fucked from behind, and the thought made him uneasy.

Why? Afraid if he sees your face, he might see something that will frighten him away?

Antonio held out a hand, and in spite of himself, Cary took it. He straddled Antonio's hard abdomen, then slicked up his fingers and rubbed Antonio's erection, easing himself over it as Antonio's hands found purchase on his hips. And—*oh God!*—as that hard cock pressed against his ass and the first set of muscles stretched to admit it, he felt that incredible burn.

"Oh... damn... oh fuck!" he cried out as Antonio filled him completely. Delicious pain melted into familiar warmth.

Antonio's stuttering breaths of anticipation became groans of satisfaction as Cary began to move upward, then back down again. His movements were slow at first as he savored the sensation of that hard width inside of him. And even when he began to pick up his pace and felt his muscles clench around Antonio's cock, it was nothing like the frenzied fucking he had always found so satisfying. It was better. *Much* better.

"Cary. *È così bello.* It's so good...." He pushed Cary's body up and down his shaft and leaned his head back on the pillows, his eyes closed.

Cary knew Antonio was close, and he slowed his movements to give him time to catch his breath. Had it been less than an hour ago that he had wanted it fast and hard? But now, seeing the look of hunger on Antonio's face and realizing *he* was in control—that Antonio was *giving* him that control— he knew he didn't want this to end too quickly.

Antonio opened his eyes as Cary stopped moving and teased Antonio's nipples once more, then grazed his fingernails over skin and muscle. Their eyes met, and Cary understood Antonio had achieved a victory of sorts: they had been "making love," and Cary was enjoying it. It was a battle Cary was happy to have lost.

We'll do it your way, Cary thought, *at least for now.*

Antonio reached out to take Cary's reawakening cock in his hand and began to stroke him. Cary, in turn, moved with slow deliberation, never taking his eyes off Antonio's face. He was rewarded with a look of sheer bliss as he leaned back and ran a slicked finger between Antonio's cheeks. The position was awkward, but it was more than worth it.

"Cary," Antonio pleaded in a low, husky voice. "Caro... please...."

So *much better than "beanpole."*

Antonio did not move but let Cary take the lead, allowing him to move up and down on his hard cock, setting the tempo. Cary continued to tease Antonio's opening with his fingers.

"Oh, caro...," he moaned. "I can't... even I have my limits...."

Cary laughed and moved faster, feeling the burn in his thighs and knowing his own release would follow soon. He couldn't remember sex ever having been this incredible. "Oh fuck, yes!" he shouted as the thrusts became frenzied and demanding, and Antonio's grip on his own erection grew tighter. "Feels so—"

His words were cut short by the powerful wave of his orgasm and by Antonio's stuttered cries as he came too. Antonio reached around his body, gathering him close as he shook with release. The warm come on Cary's belly seemed to forge a connection between them, and for a moment, Cary wasn't sure where Antonio ended and he began.

"Caro," Antonio rumbled as he kissed him on the lips.

What the fuck just happened here? Cary wondered as he watched a naked Antonio return from the bathroom a few minutes later, washcloth in hand. The thought persisted as Antonio washed them both and then settled back into the bed and pulled the thick covers over them. And the thought still hung at the back of Cary's exhausted, sated mind as he fell asleep on Antonio's chest with the sound of his soft breaths in his ear.

CHAPTER

FITS AND STARTS

CARY whimpered in his sleep and woke with a start in Antonio's bed. Antonio reached over and drew Cary against his chest, murmuring something reassuring into his hair. It felt so natural, so comforting to be held like this.

Cary struggled to remember the dream but, as always, came up empty. He had a vague sensation that he had seen his mother's face, but that's all he was sure of. The end result was always the same: he felt like a child. Lost. Unloved. Until Antonio kissed his cheek.

Cary sighed as Antonio kissed him again and stroked his face. "Better, caro?" he asked.

"Yes."

"Good. Now sleep."

And Cary did.

LIGHT filtered in from the window, and Cary, still half-asleep, rolled over in bed to avoid it. His arm fell across something solid, and he opened his eyes.

Antonio.

"*Buongiorno,*" Antonio said, gathering Cary into his arms. "I was hoping you'd still be here."

Cary was surprised he *was* still there. He had never spent the entire night with another man. He was also more than a little embarrassed about waking Antonio up in the middle of the night.

"Why?" he quipped, doing his best to shake his discomfort. "Was there something you were hoping I'd do if I stayed?"

"I can't decide between sex or a bath before breakfast. I was hoping you might be able to help."

"You just need a little imagination, Signor Bianchi." He got out of the bed and pulled Antonio along with him toward the bathroom. "In the States, we call it 'multi-tasking'."

"Ah, I see. Is that what this is?" He leaned over and licked a line up Cary's neck, found the lobe of his ear, and bit it.

"We haven't made it to the bathroom yet," Cary pointed out.

"Mmm." Antonio grabbed a condom from the drawer by the bed and held it up with a grin.

"Good point. We might want one of those."

"Might?" Antonio asked with a raised eyebrow. "If you're going to help me, we *need* one."

"Okay. Fine. We definitely want one of those." Cary bit his lower lip and waited for Antonio to join him in the bathroom.

A few minutes later, they kissed in the large bathtub as it filled. In the sunshine from the skylight above, Cary got his first good look at Antonio's naked body. His skin was smooth over the ridges that defined the muscles of his chest and abdomen. Sunlight caught the drops of water that dotted Antonio's arms and shimmered there.

Cary took the bar of soap and slid it over Antonio's skin. For the first time, he noticed the jagged scar that ran from Antonio's waist over his hip and down his left thigh. "That looks like it was painful," he said.

"It was." Antonio did not elaborate. "But you were supposed to be cleaning me, weren't you?"

"Demanding, aren't we?" The soap slipped from Cary's fingers into the water as Antonio leaned forward on his knees between Cary's legs.

"I'm always demanding." Antonio reached into the water and retrieved the soap. "But I think *you* need a little cleaning here"—he pointed to Cary's abdomen and soaped it up—"and here." Cary bit his tongue as Antonio worked his way down to the dark curls at the base of his jutting erection.

"Mmm. Yeah. Right... ah... oh shit... there...." Cary tried to keep from shaking as Antonio cupped his ass, pulling it upward so that the object of his attentions was right above the water line.

Cary's ears were now just below the tiny bubbles at the surface of the bathwater, and he realized the muffled growls he heard were his own. With Antonio's body so tantalizingly close, he moved to reach out and touch it, catching himself at the last moment before his cast slipped into the water and ending up with his entire head underneath in an effort to keep his wrist dry.

"Maybe we should try this a bit differently." Antonio chuckled as Cary righted himself, coughing and spluttering, still managing to keep the cast above the bathwater. "Turn around and put your arms over the side."

Cary complied with a broad grin. His cock stood at attention at the thought that, at last, Antonio would take him from behind. Biting his lower lip, he adjusted his legs underneath himself so his ass barely broke the surface of the water. He was rewarded with a single finger moving across his hole.

"Leave your hands there," Antonio ordered as Cary reached to grasp his own erection. "I have no intention of explaining to your doctor why the cast needs to be replaced. I can take care of that too."

Cary closed his eyes as Antonio breached his opening with his fingers and began to stretch it. "God, Antonio, I'm dying here. Just hurry up and fuck me!"

This elicited a full belly laugh from Antonio, who pressed the head of his cock against the tight entrance. Cary, ever impatient, pushed backward to seat Antonio inside and nearly slipped under the water once more.

"You're bound and determined to break your neck." Antonio rescued Cary by grasping his waist with a powerful arm.

Cary opened his mouth to protest, but Antonio pressed smoothly inside this time, and Cary's gasp was lost in the sound of the water as it splashed about the tub. "Oh, damn... right... there," he moaned as Antonio pulled out and then angled back in, hitting his prostate.

Once Cary was leaning safely over the tub, Antonio took one hand off Cary's hips and reached around to clasp Cary's cock. He let his thumb rub the sensitive tip, pressed down into the slit to Cary's keening cries, then stroked it in tandem with his thrusts.

"Harder. Please... I want... I need...."

Antonio did not object but moved faster, sending the water flying about the tub and beyond. "So tight. So good... I'm going to come like this, caro."

The term of endearment put Cary over the edge. He spurted onto Antonio's hand and the side of the bathtub, and Antonio followed in short order, shuddering and panting his release before he collapsed against Cary's back, his hands planted firmly beside Cary's to prevent him from slipping backward.

"How did we do?" Antonio asked after he had caught his breath.

Cary turned around and held out his arm with a self-satisfied smile. "Only a few drops. Nothing to worry about."

"Good. I'm not sure I can say the same about the floor." He leaned over to kiss Cary's neck, and Cary shivered in response. "Now, where's that bar of soap?"

AN HOUR later, Cary stumbled out of the bedroom to the smell of coffee and fresh pastries. "Don't you need to go to work?" he asked Antonio as he sat down at the dining table.

"Normally, yes. But I'm taking the day off. Good thing too, because I'm going to need a nap after breakfast. I didn't get a lot of sleep last night, you know."

"Really? Would you like company?"

"Definitely. Although I can't promise much more than sleeping," Antonio added. "It's not as easy for us old men." He winked.

"How old are you?" Cary asked as he pulled a piece off of a *cornetti*, the Italian version of a croissant.

"Thirty-three. But right now, I feel a lot older." Antonio laughed as he poured them both coffee.

"I'm not all that much younger."

"Five years makes a difference, caro. But I'll give you a little leeway for that wrist."

Cary tried not to look overly pleased that Antonio knew how old he was. It wasn't as if it was a secret, but the thought that Antonio had taken the time to find out made him almost giddy. "So," he began after a moment's pause, "tell me. How the hell is a guy like you still single?" *Gorgeous man, easy personality, great fuck....*

For the first time since they had met, Antonio appeared ill at ease, looking briefly away before meeting Cary's eyes again. "It's a long story." When Cary waited patiently for more of an explanation, Antonio added, "And one I'd prefer not to talk about now. Perhaps someday...."

"Sorry. I didn't mean to pry." Cary thought of the photograph in the bedroom and what Massi had said about his namesake. He was pretty sure the man pictured with Antonio was Massimo, and he was just as sure Massimo was the "long story."

"You aren't prying." Antonio stood and began to gather their dishes. "And you don't need to apologize.

"So, caro mio," Antonio said a few minutes later with a full-out yawn, "after this nap, will you come with me to pick Massi up at school?"

"The little monster?"

"He finishes in about two hours. I thought maybe after, we might make some dinner here."

"I really should go back to my apartment at some point." He was beginning to crave Roberta's cooking. Antonio was a gracious host, but the thought of another dinner of chewy meat and salty sauce wasn't exactly appealing. He smiled and fingered the soft fabric of his shirt—Antonio's shirt. "I need to check my mail and make sure Roberta isn't ready to file a missing-persons report to the police."

"Roberta?"

"My housekeeper. The Rock of Gibraltar. She keeps my agent from hopping the next plane from Paris when I do stupid shit, *and* she's an amazing cook."

Antonio grinned. "I'm jealous." He put an arm around Cary's shoulders and kissed him on the neck as they walked back to the bedroom.

"I'm a horrible cook. My mother was too. Justin and I grew up on a steady diet of frozen dinners and canned fruit. It's amazing we survived."

"Are you two close?" Antonio shut the bedroom door behind them.

"I always wanted us to be" was Cary's slightly wistful answer. "I was so busy traveling to gigs when I was a kid, I didn't see much of him."

"I read your bio," Antonio admitted as he pulled back the covers and climbed back in bed with an outstretched hand. Cary settled into the crook of Antonio's arm. "Sounds like a difficult life for a child."

Cary tensed, but Antonio held him close. "I was lucky," Cary said. It was a mechanical response, conditioned by years of practice. "How many fourteen-year-olds get to play with the Chicago Symphony?"

"Very few, I suppose."

"But?"

"But nothing, caro. I've heard you play, remember? You're a wonderful cellist and a beautiful musician."

Cary's shoulders relaxed. *Why are you so defensive?* "Sorry," he said as he settled back against Antonio's chest.

Antonio kissed his forehead. "No need to apologize, caro mio."

"PAPÀ! Connore!" Massimo shouted from the gates of the school yard. He ran, dodging the other children on the sidewalk until he reached Antonio's outstretched arms, throwing himself headlong into them and allowing himself to be hoisted into the air and swung about. "Connore! You came!"

"Hey, Massi. How was school?" Cary asked, then looked to Antonio, who mouthed, *You're doing fine.*

"It was okay," Massimo said with an overly dramatic shrug. "But Cosina and Giovanni wouldn't let me play football with them at recess."

"They're jealous," Antonio pointed out with a wink in Cary's direction. "They know you'll beat them every time."

"I didn't know you played football," Cary said, using the European term for soccer. He glanced once more at Antonio, who nodded in encouragement. "Where did you learn how?"

"My papà taught me. I'm going to play in the pros when I'm grown up."

"I'm sure you will," Antonio agreed with a smile for Cary.

As they headed down the street, Massimo circled happily around them, babbling and singing. "Where are we going?" he asked when he finally realized they were not walking in the direction of Antonio's apartment.

"We're going to my house," Cary told Massimo.

He had expected a protest, but instead, Massimo said, "Really?" His blue eyes were wide with excitement.

"Really."

"This means you like my papà, doesn't it?"

Antonio lifted an eyebrow but said nothing, leaving a very embarrassed Cary to flounder.

"Yes, it means I like him," Cary said with a sigh.

"And that you'll stay with us?"

"Massimo, remember what we talked about?" Antonio shook his head in warning. "You're asking too many questions."

"It's okay," Cary said. "I'm sure it means I'll be seeing more of you both. But I have my own place, remember?"

Cary's words seemed to remind Massimo of where they were headed, and he took Cary's hand with a quick glance upward to make sure Cary didn't object. And what could Cary do, anyhow, but hold that squirmy, slightly sticky hand?

"SIGNOR REDDING!" A very surprised Roberta peered up at them from the doorway. "Oh! You have company."

"This is Signor Bianchi and his son, Massimo," Cary said as she waved them inside. "Antonio, Massi, this is Signora Roberta Capello."

"So nice to meet you," Antonio said as he took Roberta's hand in his, then covered it with his left. "I hear you keep Cary out of trouble."

"I try, signore, I try." Roberta clucked her tongue against her cheek. "But my little *stangone*, he is a challenge."

Antonio laughed. "Oh, I know that quite well."

Roberta shot a glance at Cary, who ignored her pointedly.

"I'm hungry. Are we staying for dinner?" Massimo asked from across the room.

"I don't know—" began Cary, only to be interrupted by Roberta.

"That would be wonderful! I will make you all a little snack, and I will go out and buy some shellfish for paella."

"What's pella?" asked Massimo.

"Pa-e-lla," Antonio corrected.

Roberta smiled and bent her knees so her face was eye-level with Massimo's. "It is a little like a rice stew, with sausage and shellfish. You know, lobster, crab, clams?"

"I *love* clams!"

"It's good, then," she said, clapping her hands together. "Come with me first, little man, and I will get you some bread and cheese. Later, if you'd like, you can help me with the clams, okay?"

Massimo jumped up and down. "She's going to let me help! Is that all right, Papà?"

Antonio looked at Cary, who shrugged in resignation. "It's fine, Massi."

Massimo followed happily after Roberta, disappearing into the kitchen a moment later. "Sorry," Antonio said. "I didn't mean to invite us over for dinner."

"I don't mind. You've fed me more than a few times—it's the least I can do. Besides, it'll make Roberta happy."

"I take it you don't have many dinner guests, then?"

That would be an understatement.

"No. Not many."

As in, none at all. Ever.

"I'm flattered."

"Papà!" Massimo ran out of the kitchen, panting breathlessly. "Signora Roberta says I can help her make the rice too!"

"Are you going to work hard?" Antonio winked at Cary.

Massimo nodded with a somber expression and bounded back to the kitchen, his feet barely touching the floor.

"You think it's all right?" Antonio asked after Massimo had gone. "I don't want to put Roberta out."

"She loves kids. Her son lives near Rome, so she only sees her grandchildren a few times a year. And let's face it, he's cuter than me and a hell of a lot more interesting."

Antonio walked over to Cary and kissed him. "That all depends on who you ask."

"Then let me ask. Why do you find me interesting?"

"Other than the obvious? Because I think most people would find your career choice an interesting one."

"Other than the obvious. I find it hard to believe someone who handles the business end of things for artists and musicians finds my career very fascinating."

"Then you'd be wrong," Antonio said, taking a seat on the couch and waiting until Cary joined him there. "Why do you think I do what I do?"

"Because it pays well?"

"Only in part, caro."

"Then why?"

"Because I have no talent at all. I can't sing. I can't paint. I have no artistic ability whatsoever. But I adore all of these things. What better way, then, to enjoy it all?"

"Why do you love it so much?" Cary heard himself wonder aloud.

The question seemed to take Antonio by surprise. "I'm not sure. But I often wonder what it would be like to express myself the way an artist does. Or a musician." He reached out and put his arm around Cary's shoulder. "You told me once rock and roll makes you feel 'dangerous'."

"That was true," Cary said in a defensive tone. In spite of Antonio's acceptance of all his lies, Cary still felt guilty.

"I know. It's why I bring it up now. But what you didn't have the chance to tell me was what your *own* music makes you feel."

Cary hesitated.

Antonio, perhaps sensing that hesitation, took Cary's hand. "You know the expression 'the journey is the destination'? You don't need to know the answer, caro."

DINNER was delicious, and after some cajoling, Roberta reluctantly agreed to join them. Dessert was a delicate lemon flan, and while Roberta worked on the dishes, Cary set Massimo up in his studio with a DVD of *SpongeBob SquarePants*, which Aiden had given him for his twenty-seventh birthday as a gag gift. Massimo seemed pleased and not at all disturbed that the characters spoke English.

When they were alone in the living room once more, Cary poured them both shots of tequila from a bottle of Patrón Silver he had bought at Duty Free on his last trip to the States.

"Aiden and I watched the DVD while we polished off a bottle of twenty-year-old cognac," Cary said with a snort. "David Somers sent the cognac as a birthday gift. *SpongeBob* is definitely funnier when you're drunk."

Massi's laughter rang through the apartment, and Antonio said, "Apparently not if you're five years old." He took a sip of his drink and looked up at Cary with apparent surprise. "This is very good."

"I love tequila, but don't tell David. Between the cognac and the tea he likes to send me, sometimes I feel like I'm a bartender at an old and very expensive hotel. Not that this stuff is cheap, but…."

"My lips are sealed."

Three rounds later, Roberta left for the evening, having exacted Antonio's promise to bring Massimo back to help her bake a cake for New Year's. Cary, any hesitation dulled by the onslaught of alcohol, finally got up the nerve to ask the question that had been nagging at him since the circus. "Who was Massimo? The person Massi was named after, I mean."

Almost as quickly as he had spoken the words, Cary regretted asking them. Antonio's expression, which had up until then been open and relaxed, was now visibly tense. Pain glittered briefly in his eyes—the same pain Cary had seen when he had asked Antonio why he was still single. But before he could tell Antonio it was okay, that he didn't need to know, Antonio said, "It's… complicated." He appeared momentarily at a loss for words. "He was my lover. We were together for eight years. He died a year before Massi was born."

"I'm sorry."

Oh, that's perfect! You're "sorry?" The one thing you hated to hear when your mother died, and that's all you can manage to say?

There was an awkward moment of silence before a very sleepy Massi stumbled into the living room a minute later. Cary was silently thankful for the interruption. He also made a mental note not to bring up the subject again.

Let Antonio bring it up when he's ready. You have enough skeletons in your own closet you wouldn't want to talk about.

"We should be going." Antonio reached down to pick Massimo up. Cary handed him the boy's jacket and helped Massimo—who would not let go of his father to put it on himself—thread his arms through the sleeves. Then he did the same for Antonio. "I had a wonderful time," Antonio told him. "Please thank Roberta again, for both of us."

Cary watched Antonio walk down the hallway to the elevator with the tousle of blond curls against his shoulder. Antonio turned back briefly to smile at him and disappeared into the elevator.

CHAPTER *11*

BACK-ALLEY BOY

"CARY. I just got back from Korea. I hope I can see you this weekend. Call me when you have a chance, caro."

Cary stared at the cell phone. Five days since they'd had dinner at Cary's apartment, and Cary had pretty much given up on hearing back from Antonio. Four sleepless nights. And now this.

Not that Cary had called Antonio, either. They'd talked about Thanksgiving the next week at David's, but had Antonio mentioned the business trip? Cary seemed to remember him mentioning Korea. He'd drunk far too much tequila the night Roberta had cooked them all dinner, and it all was pretty hazy in his mind. Everything except his stupid question about Antonio's lover. Cary had just assumed he'd screwed things up again.

Face it. You're not cut out for this. It's just a matter of time before he figures out it isn't only Connor Taylor who's a lie.

He didn't need this relationship crap. He tapped his cell, deleted the message, and sat back down on the couch. The coffee table was covered with music. *His* music. The music he would have been playing—the music he *should* have been playing if it hadn't been for his complete and utter stupidity. The guilt over how he had neglected his cello these past few weeks roiled in his gut. He had only himself to blame. For all of this.

"After all I've done for you," his mother had said when he finally came out to her, *"you tell me this? Do you* want *to hurt me?"*

Fucking piece of shit! He hurled the phone against the fireplace. The back flew off and the battery landed near his feet. Just his luck; it wasn't even broken.

"Signor Redding!" Roberta stood in the doorway of the kitchen, hands on her hips, her expression one of shock. "Are you all right?"

Great. She looked scared to death. "Sorry," he said as he pretended to study the music.

She eyed him with concern, then quietly picked up the phone, back, and battery and set them out on the table above the score. "Funny thing, how these phones can just slip out of your hand sometimes, isn't it?"

"I'm going out." He stood up and averted his gaze. He didn't want to see the look of disappointment on anyone else's face. The ghosts were bad enough. "I'll be back late. Please put my dinner in the fridge."

"But—" she began.

"You worry too much, Roberta. I'll see you tomorrow. All right?"

"All right."

He walked out of the room, but the ghosts followed. They always did.

"WHISKEY," he told the bartender in the dim club an hour later. "Neat."

The bar—the same bar he had come from the night he had been mugged, weeks ago—was smoky and crowded. The music from the small dance floor blared; the dancers' bodies pressed against each other. The smell of sweat and cologne hung in the air, mixing with the powerful aroma of the alcohol in Cary's glass. He replaced his half-empty drink on the shiny surface of the bar and waited as the warmth spread to his shoulders.

How had he ever thought this thing with Antonio—whatever it was— could work? And it wasn't just Antonio. It was his kid. Cary wasn't looking for a relationship, and he sure as hell wasn't looking for an instant family. It was *this* place and places like it that made him feel alive. The sea of bodies, the primal, organic smell of sweat and musk, the tension that thrummed throughout his body, the hunger and the animal energy of the encounters to be found in this place.

"I haven't seen you around in a while," said a short, broad-chested man to his right.

"I've been… distracted." Cary waved the cast on his left arm in explanation. He picked up his drink and emptied the remainder with one long swallow. He motioned to the bartender for a refill and felt a warm hand on his thigh.

"Too bad," the man replied. "We've missed you." He put his hand over Cary's knee and edged upward between his legs. Cary grew hard against the heavy fabric of his jeans.

It's been too long.

They chatted about everything and nothing, and the bartender brought Cary's drink. He loved this, trying to focus on the conversation while his body's needs rose to a fever pitch. The denial and the knowledge that there would be satisfaction to be had in the end, were almost more exciting than the eventual fuck.

His companion toyed with the first button of his jeans, released it, and slid his hand underneath. Flesh found hard flesh, and he felt himself zone out as his companion stroked his cock.

Way too fucking long....

Cary could come like this, but he wouldn't. It was all part of the game he played with himself. He imagined the bathroom beyond the bar, which only aroused him more. He bit his tongue, then took another long swallow of the liquid, savoring the burn against his throat nearly as much as the hand on his hard cock.

The hand suddenly withdrew, and he started. When he looked to see what the problem was, he nearly choked. "Shit." He was met with a familiar face, but the expression there was hard, and the blue eyes glittered with anger and something else—lust?

"Antonio, what are you—?"

His words were cut short by Antonio's hand on his cock, squeezing and probing. Cary gasped, the sudden substitution of partners leaving him breathless and struggling for control. He managed to suck down the rest of his drink before the same hand was on his right arm, dragging him away from the bar.

"Come." There was no room for argument. Not that Cary wanted to argue. Cary thought the entire situation was hotter than hell.

Antonio kicked open the bathroom door and shoved him inside. A man stood at the mirror, comb in hand.

"Get out," Antonio ordered. The man's eyes widened, but he left without comment. Antonio locked the door and rounded on Cary.

"Is *this* what you want?" His jaw was rough with stubble, and he wore a T-shirt and jeans, as if he hadn't been planning to go out. He shoved a few coins into the vending machine to retrieve a condom, then pushed Cary into the largest of the stalls and shut the door behind them. The same stall Cary had been in weeks before, the night they had met.

Oh, the irony of it all....

"I… I…," Cary stammered. He knew he should be angry. What right did Antonio have to come here and judge him? But he was so turned on, he could barely think straight. He offered no resistance as Antonio unzipped his jeans and pulled them down, followed by his boxer-briefs, exposing his white ass.

"You want to be fucked?"

Cary nodded. Hell, he wasn't proud. And right about now, he was as raw as anyone could possibly feel. "Please," he panted as he leaned on the toilet with his good arm, ass pointed skyward in open invitation.

He heard Antonio's breath in his ear and felt his teeth bite the lobe. He moaned as Antonio yanked his head back by his hair—not too hard, but hard enough that Cary had to grab his own cock to keep from shooting his release so soon. He felt Antonio's tongue flick around his neck, his teeth nipping at the skin from time to time, leaving small red marks. Claiming him.

A finger probed his hole, then pushed roughly in. "Oh shit!" He liked it this way, without lube. The burn was heaven, and he whimpered not because of the pain, but because he wanted more. "Oh hell. Please… please…."

He couldn't see the look on Antonio's face, but he knew Antonio was just as turned on. He could hear it in the muffled gasps and deep growls, and he felt it in the way a second finger joined the first, stretching him. There was no hesitation, no delay. There were no protestations of taking time to "make love." He heard the foil packet being ripped open, and his mouth watered. And when he heard the zipper of Antonio's pants and felt that beautiful cock against his hole, he gritted his teeth and shoved backward.

"Fuck me."

Antonio did just that. Hard and fast, just the way Cary craved it, skin against skin, the rhythm familiar, Antonio's large hands grasping his hips so hard, he knew there would be marks the next morning. "Yes, oh God, yes! Oh fucking hell!"

"Mine," the deep voice rumbled in his ear. "Only mine."

The words were Cary's undoing, and he came so hard he had to struggle to stay on his feet. Only a strong forearm, snaked around his waist, held him upright. He felt Antonio's body tense and shudder and his stuttered exhalation against his neck. Cary shivered.

Was that what he wanted? To belong to this man?

"Only mine," Antonio repeated.

They leaned against the hard brick wall outside the club a short time later, side by side, bodies touching, but not holding hands. Antonio hadn't offered, and Cary had made no move to initiate the contact.

Cary had worn his leather jacket; this time, it was not the temperature that made him shiver. His cheeks were flushed, and his body still throbbed, wanting more, even now.

"You're angry with me." It wasn't a question. He didn't need to ask—he saw it in Antonio's face, although there was something more there, as well.

He's hurt. Cary's chest ached with the realization. *I've hurt him. Again.*

"You think so?" Antonio's voice was tinged with pain.

"This—tonight—this is *me*. This is all I am."

The bitter laugh that escaped Antonio's lips echoed into the night. "Of course. You don't deserve any better, do you?"

Cary stared down at a crack in the sidewalk between his feet.

"Tell me it wasn't different. Tonight. Tell me it wasn't better than what you've had before. Tell me you don't want me again, and I'll leave."

"I can't say that." God, how could he say that? Even *he* wasn't *that* consummate a liar.

"Then tell me what you want. Because I'm not going to chase you down again. I have no intention of—" The look on Antonio's face was one of disgust and barely controlled rage as he struggled to find the right word. "—*sharing* you with anyone else. I'm a patient man, but not *that* patient. If this is the only thing you want, we say goodbye here and now."

"No. This isn't what I want. Not just this."

I want you. He wanted to *belong* to Antonio. It scared him half to death to realize it. And there was something else he realized, as well. He was jealous. Jealous of the ghost of the lover in the photograph next to Antonio's bed.

Antonio's inhaled breath caught in his throat, and he reached his hand out to Cary. Cary took the large hand and found himself pulled tight against Antonio's chest. Antonio smelled of sex and a scent uniquely his own.

"I was angry." It wasn't an easy thing for Cary to admit. "When you didn't call me. I… I forgot you were going out of town and I…."

I was hurt.

"You thought I didn't want to see you again."

Cary just nodded. He felt like a complete idiot. Like the awkward teenager taking a bow at the edge of the stage. Except this time, the audience had figured it all out. They *knew* he was unworthy. There was no place for him to hide. The thief was there, for Antonio to see.

And Cary knew it didn't matter. Because when Antonio held him tighter and kissed his hair, Cary understood that he didn't need to hide anymore. He didn't understand why, but he understood that Antonio wanted *him*. Cary Taylor Redding. The liar. The cheat. The thief. Fucked up, insecure, and undeserving.

"I'm so sorry, caro. Truly I am. I'll call you when I'm traveling the next time, I promise. But promise me you'll trust me and not jump to conclusions."

Cary nodded again.

"Good. Then come home with me. And I'll show you how I feel about you."

You are totally screwed, Redding. Totally screwed and falling hard. And for once, he was entirely okay with that.

CHAPTER

FEAR OF FLYING

Milan, Italy—February

"CAN we start from number twelve one more time?" David Somers asked, looking over the piano stand at Cary. "I want to be sure I give you enough time with the next section. If you're up to it, of course."

"No problem," Cary said with a broad grin. "My wrist feels great. Eight weeks of torture—I mean physical therapy—and I'm as good as new."

David played the measures leading up to the finale of the first movement of the Dvořák Cello Concerto in B Minor. Cary took a deep breath and followed, managing without difficulty the challenging chromatic double-stop scales that ended in thumb position at the farthest reaches of the fingerboard. He had spent the better part of the last month working back up to this, and the satisfaction of regaining the use of his left hand was tremendous.

"Excellent!" David said as he played the final phrases of the movement.

Cary leaned back in his chair and sighed with relief. It felt so *good*, playing again. Better than before, really. It felt almost joyous. For so many weeks, this studio had been a constant reminder of what he had nearly lost. But now....

"*Bellissimo*," came the deep voice from the hallway. Antonio leaned on the door jamb and smiled his approval. "So, I take it he's ready for Chicago next month?"

"Most definitely," David said. He put his reading glasses away, gathered the score, and slid it into the leather portfolio on the piano. "I'm looking forward to it. Alex and I will take good care of him for you."

"I'm counting on it," Antonio said with a grin. "I'm expecting you to keep him out of trouble."

Cary shook his head and laughed as he put his cello back in its case.

"I didn't expect you until later," Cary said after David left a few minutes later. He laced his arms through Antonio's and claimed his lips.

"I finished up early, and I thought I'd stop over here before heading home. I figured since you were gone last weekend, I'd start this weekend a bit sooner." He tightened his hold on Cary, who relaxed into the embrace. Most of Cary's trips out of town had been short one- or two-day stints, but this last trip had lasted the better part of a week.

For nearly four months since they'd first met, they spent every weekend together at Antonio's apartment, except when Cary's performing schedule took him out of Milan or Antonio traveled on business. On weekends when she worked, Roberta had taken to making them dinner at Antonio's. Even Cary had to admit that Antonio's place was starting to feel more like home than his own.

"I missed you." Antonio buried his head in Cary's hair and inhaled his scent.

"Me too," Cary said with a soft yawn.

"Long day?"

"Yeah. But a good one. Playing with David is always a blast, even if it's just with him on piano."

"I can hear it in your playing," Antonio said, leading him over to the couch and pulling him down so Cary's head lay on his chest.

"Really?"

"There's something different when you play with him. I've heard you practice the piece enough, I can hear the difference."

"The man's a genius. I've performed this piece dozens of times, and still he finds something new to show me."

"You seem happy, caro." Antonio ran his fingers through Cary's hair. "It makes me happy too."

Am I happy?

AN HOUR later, they were seated on the balcony of Antonio's apartment, enjoying the unseasonably warm weather and drinking coffee.

"Gentlemen." Roberta peered outside. "I'll be going now. Signor Bianchi—"

"Antonio," Antonio corrected.

"Antonio," she said with a blush on her cheeks, "I've left instructions on how to reheat the dinner. Dessert is in the refrigerator."

Cary looked from Roberta to Antonio. "Instructions?"

"A little something special Roberta agreed to make. *Grazie mille,* Roberta."

"*Prego.*" She shot Antonio a sly wink and closed the glass doors behind her.

"What was that all about?" Cary eyed Antonio with suspicion and cocked his head to one side. "Special dinner? Instructions? Am I missing something here?"

"Nothing at all, caro."

Antonio stood up and offered Cary his hand, then led him inside to the dining room, where the table was set for four. The smell of seafood and saffron wafted in from the kitchen, and there was a vase filled with flowers in the center of the table.

"Wait a minute," Cary said as he met Antonio's gaze. "We weren't expecting company. What's going on?"

But before Antonio could respond, the doorbell rang. Cary went to open it to find David standing there.

"Did you forget something back at my apartment?" Cary asked, confused.

"No," David said as he walked past Cary into the apartment, followed by his partner, Alex Bishop. "But I think perhaps *you* forgot something."

"Happy birthday, Cary," Antonio said. "*Tanti auguri.*"

"I... I forgot," Cary stammered.

"I know, caro." Antonio kissed him tenderly on the lips.

"For you." Alex handed Cary several bags filled with gifts and hugged him. David shook Cary's hand and clasped his shoulder warmly. "Aiden and Sam send their regards. There's a bottle of tequila somewhere in here. Aiden said you'd appreciate it."

"Thanks, guys," Cary said, overwhelmed.

The Reddings hadn't done much to mark birthdays. Cary had been on the road so much of the time that birthday parties weren't particularly easy to plan. Other than his birthday two years before, which had included the

SpongeBob and cognac celebration with Aiden, Cary couldn't remember the last time he'd noticed he was officially a year older.

"DAVID says you'll be staying with us in March," Alex said as they sat down to a dinner of Roberta's paella and a couple of bottles of a heady Chianti Riserva that David had chosen with obvious care.

"That's the plan," Cary said as he dug into his food with relish, spearing a shrimp with his fork.

He couldn't help but notice the way David and Alex always seemed so comfortable together and the way they touched each other—light touches that communicated the intimacy of their relationship and their commitment. Cary had known David Somers even before David had met Alex Bishop and long before they'd moved in together, but it was the first time Cary realized how much happier—more relaxed—David was at Alex's side. He wondered if someone might see the same thing, looking at him and Antonio.

"Sounds like you have a little free time on your schedule after Chicago." Alex shot a conspiratorial glance at Antonio. "I've got an idea of something we could do together."

"Don't tell me you want me to play at that jazz club with you again."

Alex laughed. "That'd be fun. But it seems David also has a little time on his schedule, and so do I." He winked at David and took a sip of wine.

"Give it up, guys. One surprise an evening is more than enough. What do you know that I don't?"

"Antonio has managed to negotiate all three of us a recording contract," David said, smiling over the top of his glass.

"Are you serious? The Brahms Double Concerto?"

"You got it," Alex said triumphantly. "And the musicians union just signed on to the deal yesterday. All this baby needs is your John Hancock, Cary Redding."

Cary grinned and pulled Antonio in for a sloppy kiss. "You're a fucking genius! So that's what you've been up to with the evening meetings." It had been nearly three years since the last time Cary had recorded anything. Not only would it give him the extra financial security he had been hoping for, but he adored the Brahms, and he couldn't have chosen a better violinist to play it with. Or a better conductor.

"Happy birthday, caro." Antonio lifted his glass, and the other two men followed suit.

LATER, they lay in bed together after what Cary deemed his "best birthday ever," Cary nestled in Antonio's arms, his head against his chest. Since they had started seeing each other regularly, he had not once longed for the seedy clubs and back-alley encounters, although he still preferred it hard and fast and from behind. But the uneasiness he had felt in "making love," as Antonio put it in his sexy-as-fuck bass-baritone, had dissolved into an insistent, thrumming need for Antonio's touch.

More than that, really. Need. Pure and simple. The need to be the object of someone else's attentions, and not because of his music.

"What are you thinking about, caro?"

"Nothing," Cary lied, happy that the semidarkness hid the blush on his cheeks. *You really are a fucking Disney princess!*

"Hmm."

"All right, all right," Cary protested. "I was sort of thinking I like this."

"This?"

"Shit, Tonino. You really like watching me squirm, don't you?"

"*Sì*."

"Fine," Cary said, sitting up and glaring at Antonio. "I like being here, with you."

"I like hearing that." He pulled Cary back down and kissed him on the lips. "I know it's not an easy thing for you to admit."

"I guess not." It was more than that, Cary knew. The entire thing—their relationship, the growing commitment he felt toward Antonio—frightened him to no end. And he wasn't sure *why.*

Instinctively, Cary glanced over to the bedside table. The photograph of Massimo and Antonio was gone, replaced by a newer photo—one of Cary and Antonio, laughing and raising their wine glasses for the camera. Aiden had snapped it at David's Thanksgiving celebration just a few months before, and Cary had been happy to see it appear by the bed shortly after that. The photograph of Massimo was now part of the large collection of photographs of Antonio's family out in the living room. Cary still hadn't asked Antonio about Massimo, although he longed to know more.

"I know it's a little soon," Antonio said after a prolonged silence, during which he held Cary close, "but I'd like you to think about the two of us getting an apartment together. Something big enough for your studio, with an extra room for Massimo."

"Why?" The minute the question was out of his mouth, Cary regretted asking it. He wanted to know the answer, but he feared it as well.

"I want to wake up to you every morning," Antonio said in an undertone as he drew Cary against his chest once more. "I want to be the person you come home to when you've been traveling."

"Why?" His voice was small and muffled against Antonio's chest. He imagined himself as a little boy in front of the crowd of people, deathly afraid they'd learn his secret: that he was unworthy.

"*Ti amo*, caro," Antonio whispered. "I love you."

For the first time he could remember, Cary fought back tears.

Antonio sat up and gazed down at Cary, then bent over and kissed him on the lips. Cary sighed audibly as Antonio trailed his lips over his cheeks and nose. Cary shivered at the delicate contact and closed his eyes as he just let himself *feel* for a moment. Antonio moved to straddle him, ghosting his mouth over Cary's neck and pausing to lick at the indentation at Cary's throat.

"God... Tonino... that feels so—"

Cary's words were interrupted by Antonio's mouth on his nipple, his tongue circling until it hardened. Using one hand to support himself over Cary, Antonio combed his fingers through Cary's hair, nails scraping his scalp. Cary drew a deep breath that caught in his throat. In the silence, it felt so loud, so vulnerable to Cary's ears.

What had become of the man who craved hard, nameless fucks? Even the voice of insecurity—the thief who had struggled to reassert himself only moments before—fell silent. This was everything. This man who had just told him he loved him, who wanted *him*, Cary Redding. *Antonio* was everything.

"Tonino, I—"

"Shh, caro. Let me show you how much I love you. How much I want you."

Cary felt wet heat as Antonio glided his mouth further downward. He heard Antonio inhale the scent of him. Soft hair tickled his belly as Antonio probed and licked, his firm hands supporting Cary's body to draw it closer.

"Roll over," Antonio said in the deep, sexy voice that made Cary weak with need.

A moment later Cary felt Antonio's hands massage the tightness in his shoulders, his strong thumbs pressing under Cary's shoulder blades to release the tension there. Antonio continued the sensual massage as he kneaded the muscles of Cary's ass, nipping and licking the skin so that Cary moaned into the pillow.

"*T'amo.*" The words were whispered into his waist and followed by another feathered kiss.

Cary's hunger, his need to have Antonio inside of him, burned hot, but for once, he did not protest Antonio's slow and deliberate ministrations. He reveled in them. And when Antonio gently spread the globes of his ass and he felt a warm, wet tongue press against his hole, he keened and rose to meet it. Patterns of colorful light flickered and burst across his vision as Antonio worked his way inside, and Cary's already hard cock throbbed.

"So good... ahhh... so good." Cary's brain didn't want to work properly, but he couldn't stay silent.

"Touch yourself," Antonio said as he came up for breath. "I want to hear you say my name when you come. I want to feel it when you do."

He probed further inward as Cary knelt and took his erection in his hand, stroking and pulling on it as Antonio's mouth and tongue continued to play with his hole. Antonio moaned, and Cary gasped as he felt a finger replace the tongue, reaching for the place inside that sent shockwaves throughout Cary's body.

"More," Cary begged. "Please... more...."

A second finger joined the first, and then a third. "That's it," Antonio said, his free hand scraping the skin behind Cary's cock.

"Please... oh, please...."

"What do you want, caro mio?"

"I want you inside of me when I come...."

Cary felt Antonio's fingers withdraw, replaced by Antonio's cock pressing inside, filling him. It wasn't the first time since they had been tested that they had made love bareback, but it had never felt so sensual before, the feeling of Antonio's bare skin. Cary heard Antonio's satisfied hiss as he pressed back to seat Antonio completely within.

Antonio's movements were slow and deliberate, his hand coaxing Cary's own erection, adding to the intensity of the experience. Cary didn't even fantasize about the bars anymore—he dreamed of *this*. He wanted Antonio's smell in his nostrils. He wanted the feel of Antonio's hard body against his own, the soft pads of his fingers on his nipples, his hair against his back. He wanted everything that was Antonio.

"I'm going to come," Cary said.

"Do it. Say my name and do it."

"Tonino! Oh fuck! Tonino!" Cary struggled for control, then gave up. Why try to control it? Why fight it? "Tonino. Tonino," he repeated as he felt Antonio's body tense and heard his lover's cries as he came, as well.

Oh God, Tonino! "I love you too."

CHAPTER *13*

LIFE AS WE KNOW IT

Chicago, Illinois—March

"MAN, I love this place!" Cary opened the glass doors of the penthouse onto the large patio overlooking Lake Michigan. A blast of cold air blew off the water, and he shivered, his T-shirt and pajama bottoms giving him no protection from the harsh wind.

"Do you have a death wish, Redding?" Alex growled from behind him. "It's barely above freezing."

Cary followed Alex back inside a moment later, laughing. "Not my fault your old man only wants to hire me in the winter."

"You're the one who's always saying how much you hate Milan in winter, what with Fashion Week and Carnivale. I'd think you'd be happy to get out of that place. Besides, it's spring."

"You wouldn't know it out there, now would you?" Cary snorted and shook his head. "Tell your partner I want to perform in summer, next time."

"Disparaging the host?" David walked past them, coffee in hand, eyebrow raised in feigned indignation.

"The maestro is having a bit of a midlife crisis," Alex joked.

David sniffed loudly enough for Alex and Cary to hear, and kept walking toward his studio. The sounds of a piano could be heard throughout the apartment a few minutes later.

"Great job at the dress rehearsal last night, by the way." Alex motioned Cary to take a seat at the breakfast table, where Sarah, the housekeeper, had set out a large continental breakfast of bread, croissants, cheese, and meats.

"Thanks." Cary poured them both large cups of coffee with hot milk. "David makes it easy. So what's the schedule to rehearse the Brahms?"

"We'll go over it, just the three of us, today and tomorrow. David won't want to play anything but the Dvořák or the Beethoven the day of the performance. Besides, you'll want to rest up. After the concert, we'll have another week to get it polished up. We've got three full days of studio time to record."

"Great. That's more than I'd expected." Cary popped a piece of cheese in his mouth. "Sushi for dinner tonight? Not that we don't have it in Milan, but...."

"You got it. First dinner out in Chicago—it's tradition, right?"

"It should be."

Alex took a long drink of his coffee and leaned back in his chair. "So, have you spoken to Antonio?"

"Called him last night before the dress rehearsal. Massi was spending the night with him. Took me ten minutes to explain to him how my cell phone works over here. Gotta love the brat."

"Sounds like you do."

Cary sighed. "Tonino wants us to find an apartment together. You know, something big, with a rehearsal studio for me and a bedroom for the kid."

"Sounds serious."

"Yeah." Cary picked absentmindedly at a croissant. "And it scares the shit out of me."

"*And*?" Alex leaned over the table and grinned.

"And I think I'm going to tell him yes."

"You *think*?"

"It's not exactly something I'd ever really given much thought to," Cary shot back defensively. "I hadn't planned this... *any* of this."

"No kidding. So what gives?"

"I'm in love with the guy. *That's* what gives. And what isn't there to love? He's smart, funny, sexy as hell, and he treats me better than I deserve."

"You don't give yourself enough credit."

"Sorry. That was a bit defensive, wasn't it?"

"It's okay. And I agree—he's a great guy."

"But?" In Cary's experience, there was always a "but."

"But it's not easy... relationships... living with someone," Alex answered in a gentle voice.

Cary looked down at his coffee and sighed. "I have no clue what I'm doing, Alex. I've never even dated before. And now it's like instant family, with Massi. I haven't even met Tonino's mother and sisters yet, and I—"

"They'll love you, Cary. That's the easy part. The other part, the relationship part, that's more work. Tell Tonino what you're feeling. It's been a while for him."

"Did you know Massimo?" Cary still hadn't had the courage to broach the subject with Antonio again, although it nagged at him. He wanted to know what happened, to understand. Francesca had said only that it was Antonio's story to tell, and Cary hadn't pushed the issue.

"No. I met Antonio through David about four or five years ago. The only thing I know was that Massimo was killed in a car crash and Antonio nearly died, as well."

So that was it. It explained the scar and Antonio's reaction when Cary had asked him about it. "He said they were together for eight years, and that he died a year before Massi was born. That would have made him what—nineteen?—when they first got together. But that's all he's been willing to tell me."

"Give him time."

"I know. I will." What other choice was there, really?

Besides, isn't it a little juvenile to be jealous of a dead man?

THE next few days were spent in David's studio, rehearsing the Brahms. As promised, David did not ask them to practice on Saturday, the day of Cary's performance with the symphony. Instead, he treated them all to high tea at Russian Tea Time, a light meal consisting of sandwiches and scones along with the house tea.

"You'll eat plenty at the reception tonight," Alex said when Cary looked with skeptical resignation at the modest meal. "Doris Pinchley-Bates has the best spreads. She's been gushing about you since last year, so I'm guessing it'll be even more over-the-top than her usual shindig."

Cary spent the first half of the program listening to the Beethoven from the wings. At last, on stage an hour later, he closed his eyes and listened to the long orchestral introduction to the Dvořák, noting with pleasure the richness David was able to coax from the string section and the clear, powerful tones of the horns as they took over the melody from their stringed counterparts.

He adored this music, from its dark and demanding opening theme to the more subdued secondary theme in the brass and the woodwinds. The warmth of the sound from the orchestra behind him sent chills down his spine as he opened his eyes once again and looked up for David's cue. The conductor met his eyes with a trace of a smile on his lips, then lifted his baton.

The opening measures of the solo flew by with their arpeggio passages, giving way to the secondary theme with its lilting melodic line. Back and forth, soloist and orchestra wove the complex tapestry the composer had envisioned. In this piece, the cello and the orchestra were both integral to the music. Perhaps this was why Cary adored it so much, and the sense that he and David created the music together made this performance so much more satisfying than any other until now. For a short while, Cary just lost himself in the music as his fingers found their way with ease through the treacherous double-stops and arpeggios that made this such a virtuosic composition.

His eyes filled briefly with tears as the last notes resonated from the cello and the final movement came to a close. For a moment, he was utterly lost to understand the depth of his own emotion. How many times had he played the same notes over the past twelve years, since he had mastered the piece? And yet this time, it was entirely different. He came back to himself with the thunderous applause from the audience, and struggled to regain his composure.

"I've never heard you play as well," David said as they both walked to the edge of the stage to take their bows. It was true; he never had. And he was pretty sure he understood why.

Back in his dressing room afterward, Cary sank into the couch and closed his eyes for a few minutes. It had become a bit of a habit for him to meditate after a performance—it was something Aiden had suggested to him years ago and which he had initially laughed off. Today, more than any other, he needed the time to decompress.

The door opened a crack and Alex Bishop peered inside. "You decent?"

"Never," Cary answered with a snort. "Come on in."

"I hope you don't mind." Alex walked into the room. "I brought someone with me."

Cary was about to say something clever when he caught a glimpse of blond hair in the doorway. "Antonio?"

"I was in the neighborhood," Antonio said, "and someone told me the music here was good."

Grinning broadly, Alex closed the door behind him on the way out.

"You came all this way just to hear me?"

"Why not?" Antonio said, taking Cary into his arms and giving him a tender kiss.

Cary melted into the warm embrace, partly out of sheer exhaustion, but even more out of relief. "I missed you," he whispered. Why was he afraid to say it louder? He loved this man.

Antonio kissed his hair and exhaled, his breath hitching with emotion. "I missed you too, caro mio. Two weeks is too long."

"How long can you stay?" Cary knew he shouldn't feel so needy, but the performance had left him a bit off-kilter, and he needed reassurance that Antonio wasn't leaving the next day.

"I've asked my colleague to handle things at the office. I'm going to stay until you've finished the recording. If you'll have me, of course."

"I'll have to think about that." Cary edged over to the door and locked it behind him. "But first I need to get out of this sweaty tux and take a shower."

"I could help. I'm told I'm good at bathing other people."

Cary pulled Antonio's jacket off, unknotted his tie, and began to undo the buttons on his crisp white shirt. "That's just what I was counting on."

ANTONIO lay back on the couch half an hour later while Cary, still shirtless, hummed and combed his damp hair. There was a knock on the door, and Cary opened it to find the stage manager standing there.

"I'm sorry to disturb you, Mr. Redding," she said, "but there's a gentleman outside who says he needs to speak with you. He says his name is Redding."

"Justin?" Cary wondered aloud. He hadn't been expecting his brother. Cary smiled at the thought that Justin had been able to take a day off work to make the drive up. "You can send him on in," he told the woman.

He walked back into the changing area and quickly pulled his shirt off the hanger and put his arms through the sleeves. "Sorry, Justin," he said as he turned and headed back into the sitting area, "I didn't realize…." But it was not Justin.

Antonio had gotten to his feet and was closing the door behind a man whom Cary did not recognize. The newcomer was about Cary's height, and looked to be around fifty years old, judging by the graying hair at his temples and the lines around his eyes and mouth. He had gray-green eyes, his face was pale, and he looked nervous. For a split second, Cary could almost imagine he was seeing a much older version of his brother, with the same strong jaw and high cheekbones.

"I'm sorry," Cary said. "When the stage manager said your name was Redding, I just assumed you were my brother."

"I didn't mean to take you by surprise," the newcomer replied. "I had meant to do this with a bit less drama, but I wasn't able to reach you by phone, and I really needed to see you." He offered his hand and Cary shook it, noting the tremor that ran through the other man's arm. "My name is John Redding."

John Redding? The room suddenly felt hot and cramped. He dropped John's hand and took several steps backward, nearly backing into Antonio. *But that's....*

Antonio stepped forward to reach out and shake the man's hand. "Antonio Bianchi. Good to meet you. Are you Cary's relative?"

"I... yes," John Redding said, now looking nearly as uncomfortable as Cary. "I... I'm Cary's father."

For nearly a minute, Cary stared dumbly at John. "No," he said at last, his mind unable to make sense of this pronouncement. "My father died when I was a baby."

"I...," John began in a halting voice, "I had hoped to handle this better. Give you time before I showed up at your doorstep and dropped the bombshell."

Cary felt his jaw tighten. "Give me one good reason why I shouldn't call security and have you hauled out of here," he demanded, glaring at his visitor.

"Because you need to hear me out. Because even if you believe what I'm telling you is a pile of garbage, you want to know for sure. Am I right?"

"Cary," Antonio said in Italian, "I'd be happy to escort him out of here if you'd like."

"No." Cary finished buttoning his shirt and tucked his shirttails in. "It's all right." Then he added, in English, "You've got two minutes to convince me this isn't all bullshit. And don't think I won't have you thrown out if you're messing with me."

"Would you like me to wait outside?" Antonio asked under his breath.

"No." Cary took Antonio's hand and squeezed it. "Stay. Please." *I need you.* Then, addressing John, he repeated, "Two minutes."

"Fair enough." John sat down heavily on the couch.

Cary took one of the chairs facing John, and Antonio stood behind the chair, his hand resting on Cary's shoulder in a silent gesture of reassurance. "Go on," Cary said, taking strength from Antonio's solid presence and drawing a deep breath in an attempt to calm his racing heart. "Tell me why I should believe any of this."

"Your mother was Janet Fontana, and your older brother is Justin," John Redding began. He looked at Antonio but appeared to find no reassurance there, because he quickly looked back at Cary and continued, "You grew up in a suburb of St. Louis, in a three-bedroom ranch on Athena Drive."

"Anyone who has access to the Internet would know those things." Cary knew he sounded harsh, but he didn't care. He was angry. And although he'd hardly have admitted it, he was also curious.

John looked down at his hands, as if trying to decide what more he could say. "I met your mother at Washington University. I was an English major. She was a music major. Choral studies and composition."

Choral studies? Composition? I didn't even know she had been a music major. It made sense, though. Funny, how he had always accepted the fact that his mother knew so much about music. Still, he said nothing but waited to hear more, unconvinced.

"We dated for about a year before she got pregnant," John continued. "She dropped out of school when we got married. Your brother was born six months later. About four years after, you came along.

"It was rough. I had a hard time finding a job in my field, so I started working construction to make ends meet. Janet was depressed... she had trouble sleeping, and she lost a lot of weight. Right after you were born, she was diagnosed with lupus."

Cary swallowed hard to hear this. His mother had never told anyone except him and Justin about the lupus.

"Ironic, isn't it, that she died of cancer, in the end?" John added with a bitter shake of his head.

Cary stood up abruptly and pulled his tie off a nearby table. "So you expect me to believe...," he began as he struggled to knot the tie with shaking hands. "You expect me to believe that you've known how to find us all these years, but—what?—you just... *didn't?*"

"I left her, Cary. Filed for divorce. She was hurt. Angry. She didn't want me around you boys. Said I was a bad influence. I can't really blame her, either. I had nothing. I lost my job, and I couldn't find any other work."

He sighed. "At least there was some money in our retirement account to cover the house payments after the savings ran out."

Cary looked at the pathetic knot he had tied. *Fucking tie!* He unknotted it and, by sheer force of will alone, managed to retie it so that it wasn't so lopsided. "What do you want?" he asked without turning around. His voice was even and controlled, but he shoved his hands into his pockets so John wouldn't notice how they still shook. He caught Antonio's eyes reflected in the mirror and saw both concern and sympathy there.

"What do you mean?" John asked.

"You want money?"

"No. I want to get to know you. Be a part of your life again. Justin's too, if he's willing."

"You're joking, right?" Cary felt bile burn at the back of his throat. *Twenty-eight years, and now he wants a relationship?*

"No," John repeated. "I just—"

There was a knock on the door, and Alex peered inside with a knowing grin. "Hey, guys. I know it's been a while since you've seen each other, but…. Oh, damn. I'm sorry. I didn't mean to interrupt."

"You're not interrupting anything," Cary said. "My visitor was just leaving. Tonino and I will meet you in a minute. Tell David I'm sorry for taking so long."

"Sure. No problem." Alex closed the door, leaving the three men alone once more.

"Listen, Cary—"

"No," Cary snapped. "*You* listen. I'm not interested in getting to know you. I've been doing fine for—what?—all of my *life* without you." He tossed his clothes and toiletries into a small rucksack and pulled on his suit jacket.

"Please. At least think about it before you tell me to go to hell. I can wait as long as you need. A week. A month. Whatever." He reached into his jacket and pulled out a piece of paper, which he offered to Cary. "This is my cell number. I'm staying with friends outside of the city, but I'll be moving to New York in a few weeks."

Cary snatched the paper out of his father's hand and shoved it unceremoniously into his pants pocket.

"I think you must leave now, Mr. Redding," Antonio said, his voice firm.

"Please just think about it, Cary. Please."

Antonio opened the door and motioned John through it, then closed it with a deep sigh and turned back to Cary. "Caro," he said. "I'm sorry."

"For what?" He tried to sound as though nothing was wrong, as if he didn't care. He knew Antonio wouldn't buy it for a second, but he also knew Antonio wouldn't press the issue, either. "We have a party to go to, right?"

Antonio took Cary in his arms and held him tight. "I love you."

Cary's muttered "Thanks" was barely audible over Antonio's sigh. He would *not* cry. He *didn't* cry, he reminded himself.

It was nearly three in the morning when they fell into bed. Antonio, jet-lagged, had fallen asleep during the limousine ride back from the donors' party. All evening, Cary had been outgoing, making small talk with the guests, laughing and flirting with the symphony's donors (male and female), who clearly relished the attention. The life of the party, Doris had called him.

Underneath the extroverted persona, however, Cary teetered on the brink of an emotional precipice. He knew Antonio had seen the fear in his eyes and the way his hands trembled. Now, as he lay with his head against Antonio's chest, he also knew Antonio was forcing himself to stay awake a little longer, even though Antonio wouldn't press him about what had happened in the green room. He would wait until Cary was ready.

"Why did she lie to us?" Cary whispered into the darkness. "I know she must have been angry with him. But still… to lie to us…."

"Would it really matter now?" Antonio asked. "To know why she lied?"

"No. I guess it wouldn't change anything, would it?"

Antonio kissed his head, and when Cary didn't say anything, he said, "My father died when I was an adult. At his funeral, there was a woman I did not recognize." He took a deep breath and exhaled slowly. "I asked my mother who she was. She told me the woman was my father's mistress. Just like that. As if it was usual. Like it didn't matter."

"She came to the funeral? Knowing you were all there? And your mother *let* her stay?"

Antonio's smile was sad. "Yes. I think the woman really loved him. My mother loved him too. Maybe they understood each other. I don't know."

"Shit."

"That day, I realized my father wasn't the man I thought he was. And I was very angry with my mother, that she knew what he had done, and didn't tell him to leave."

"Did you speak with the woman?"

"No," Antonio admitted. "But I yelled at my mother. I said some terrible things. Things I regret, even now, years later. But she forgave me, of course. She's my mother. On that day, I acted like a child."

"Why? It seems pretty reasonable, being angry at your parents about something like that."

"Yes. It was. For a *child*. A child expects his parents to be perfect. But a man understands his parents have problems, that they make mistakes, and they can be selfish. A child cannot easily forgive that. But a man—an adult—he can *understand* it. And then he can forgive."

Silence hung between them, punctuated only by the sound of Antonio's heart in Cary's ear. After a minute or two, Cary said, "I used to dream about my father. What he was like. What my life would have been like if…." He let out a long, shuddering breath.

"I know." Antonio kissed him again, lingering with his lips pressed to Cary's hair.

"I don't know what to do."

"You don't have to decide right now, caro. But whatever you do, I'll be here if you need me. I promise."

CHAPTER *14*

UNDER THE MICROSCOPE

Milan, Italy—May

"MASSI," Antonio said with a chuckle as Massimo launched into the tenth repeat of "Frère Jacques" from the backseat of the car, "your French is very good, but I think Cary would like a little quiet tonight."

Please God! Cary leaned his head back on the seat rest and closed his eyes.

The hour-long drive from Milan to Antonio's mother's house near Stradella already felt as though it had lasted several days. He loved Massimo—he really did—but, dammit, he was just about at his wits' end with the constant babbling and singing.

"But I'm happy," Massimo announced, as if this made all the difference. "Cary is going to meet Nonna! And Gisella, and Isabella, and Constanza, and Marg—"

"I think maybe Cary is a little nervous about meeting them," Antonio interrupted as he ignored the scowl on Cary's face.

Not nervous. Terrified and feeling like I'm about to puke.

Cary looked out the window of the car at the gentle hills and vineyards of this part of the Po Valley, trying to remind himself how beautiful it was here. Late spring, and the trees and fields were a lush green, and the fragrance of the season wafted in through the half-open windows. Cary watched the sun as it began to set a deep orange on the horizon, and did his best to clear his mind.

"Why?" Massimo's question brought Cary back into the moment.

He sighed; "why" was Massimo's new favorite word. Most days, Cary was happy to humor Massimo, enjoying answering the constant questions. But tonight, it was like Massi's buzzing airplane noises in his ears all over again.

Breathe. Just breathe. It's going to be fine. If they hate you, you can go back to your lonely, pathetic life, and all will be well with the world. Only he knew he was *so* past the point of no return—his agreeing to meet the entire Bianchi brood was proof positive.

"Remember how you felt the first day of school? How you were worried the other children wouldn't like you?" Antonio asked in his usual patient voice. Cary could see the mop of blond curls in the back seat bob up and down. "It's the same for adults, sometimes."

"Why?"

Because we're idiots, kid. Because we do stupid shit like falling in love even though we know it means we have to put ourselves through hell and meet the in-laws.

Blessedly, Massimo forgot he asked the question when Antonio pulled the car through the familiar landmark gate.

"We're here! We're here!" he chanted happily. This was followed by a through-the-window tour of places where Massimo had fallen and skinned his knee, broken his arm, scraped his chin, and—the clear favorite—where his cousin Violetta had vomited.

After the long recitation, Cary was almost relieved when the car stopped in front of the large house and Massimo hopped out to trot down a stone walkway and leave Cary alone with Antonio. Cary's relief was short-lived as he contemplated getting out of the car.

"How are you doing, *caro*?" Antonio's face was half-sympathetic and half-amused to see Cary so anxious.

"Just great. You sure you want to do this? Because I'd be perfectly happy to go right back to Milan now and—"

Antonio's warm lips pressed against his own, and he sighed. "They'll love you, *caro*. I promise." He trailed two fingers across Cary's cheek, his eyes warm and forgiving. "They will love you because I do."

"You sure you want to tell them?" Cary asked. "Seems like enough, just introducing me. Can't we save the announce—"

"Cary. I know you're afraid. But it'll be fine. Really." He leaned in to kiss Cary again. "I want to tell them we'll be living together. It makes me happy."

Cary managed a wan smile. It made him happy too. And really, was that such a bad thing?

AFTER driving down the dirt road through the lush vineyard, Cary expected the house to be quite grand, much like David Somers's villa. Instead, it was quite modest: stone, with vines of flowers and ivy that snaked their way up, digging into the mortar that held the irregular stonework together. Ancient shutters, painted a soft green, hung at either side of the windows. They were not purely decorative, and Cary had no doubt that during the hot summer months or the dead of winter, they would be closed.

The flower beds at either side of the building were in full bloom with an eclectic mix of daisies, poppies, bachelor buttons, snapdragons, and a few dozen others Cary did not recognize. The effect was charming and unpretentious, and the backdrop of the vineyards was stunning. It was far more a home than the grand estate he had envisioned. Simple and down to earth, much like the man who walked at his side down the pathway to the front door.

Cary had also expected a convergence of adults and children at the front door to greet them, so he was pleasantly surprised when the only person waiting there was a petite woman with white-blond hair and blue eyes.

"Tonino, caro!" Antonio's mother exclaimed happily as he bent down to kiss her cheek.

"Mamma," he said as he turned to Cary, "I'd like you to meet Cary Redding. Cary, this is my mother, Oriana Bianchi."

"It's a pleasure to meet you," Cary said stiffly, offering the woman his hand. She ignored it, instead throwing her arms around him and hugging him with such enthusiasm that he was momentarily speechless.

"Oh, carino," she cooed in lilting Italian, "it's so good to finally meet you." When she released him, she frowned at her son, although the adoring look in her eyes belied her stern expression. "You have been hiding him too long, Tonino." She hugged Cary again, then added, "Welcome, Cary. We're so happy to have you join us."

"Thank you," Cary mumbled, unused to such an effusive greeting and not quite sure what to say.

"Come." Oriana took Cary by the hand and led him through the house to the large kitchen. "I want you to meet my children."

They sat down at the long table behind the house an hour later, a thoroughly overwhelmed Cary relieved to have a glass of red wine in his hand and a plate full of food in front of him. The back patio overlooked the vines that lined the sloping hills. The flagstones were slightly uneven, and the spaces between were moss-covered and soft to the feet. The smell of garlic and butter mingled with the scent of flowers growing beneath the canopy of vines and around the supporting posts. Antonio's mother, sisters, and brothers-in-law sat around two large tables, and a multitude of children, ranging from two to thirteen years old, buzzed about. Several large outdoor heaters kept the area warm in spite of the evening chill.

Antonio's large hand found Cary's thigh, and Cary relaxed with the touch. Across the table, Antonio's oldest sister, Gisella, smiled at him with real warmth. Of course Antonio had been right. He always was, wasn't he? There was nothing but acceptance to be found in this beautiful setting.

Dinner was a lively affair, and the children disappeared after a short while, leaving the adults to their conversation. Most of the questions, of course, were aimed at Cary and Antonio. Cary told a rapt audience about how Antonio had rescued him on the Milan street seven months before (leaving out a few of the pertinent details, of course). For his part, Antonio told them about Cary's playing, which led to a surprising discussion about classical music, with Antonio's mother suggesting that what Beethoven and Brahms needed most were more young artists like Cary and Alex Bishop to inject life into the genre.

The food was plentiful. Cary noted with pleasure that Oriana was, unlike her son, an excellent cook. By the time they had cleared the table and set out the dessert, the children had returned, a few of them sporting dirty knees and smudged faces. No one seemed to mind.

A few reminders to wash hands later, Oriana set down a large dish of panna cotta and began to portion it out, adding a bit extra to Cary's plate with a smile in Antonio's direction. "He needs to eat more," she said.

After the plates were emptied—several literally licked clean by the younger children—Antonio stood up and raised his glass of sparkling water. He motioned Massimo over, and Massimo climbed without hesitation onto Cary's lap, yawning as he settled in comfortably.

Cary clenched his hand around his wine glass as Antonio thanked his family for welcoming Cary into the fold. Antonio put his free hand on Cary's shoulder, glancing briefly at him, then around at those gathered. "The next time we meet will be in Milan," he said with eyes wide with happiness. "Massimo, Cary, and I would like to have you come to our new apartment."

Massimo, who had been slowly falling asleep on Cary's shoulder, now looked up at his father and bounded off of Cary's lap, dancing around with renewed energy. "You *are* staying, Cary! I knew you would. I *knew* it! Is Roberta coming too?"

"She's coming too," Antonio confirmed with a quick smile for Cary.

As they said their goodbyes an hour later, Oriana took Cary aside while Antonio carried the now sleeping Massimo into the car and belted him in. "Carino," she said as she clasped his hands in hers, "it's been too long since I've seen my Tonino so happy. And I think it's been even longer for you."

He looked at her in surprise, noting the understanding in her eyes.

"You will be good for him." Then, without waiting for him to respond, she kissed him on the cheek and embraced him as she had her own son, hours earlier. "He will take care of you," she added. "But you must also take care of yourself, Cary. For him."

AFTER dinner the next evening, Cary took a wrinkled bit of paper from his wallet and studied it while Antonio looked on in silence. Cary took a deep breath, then pulled his cell phone from his pants pocket. His hand shook and his shoulders tensed, his fingers clutching the phone as if it might slip from his grip.

Please.

Funny, how he had no idea what he was asking for. Something. A sign, perhaps, that he wasn't making a huge mistake. He had so much now—his own family with Antonio and Massi—was he being greedy to wish for more? But there was no thunderclap, no moment of great clarity as he heard the call connect, just the mundane drone of traffic from the street and the low rumble of the washing machine as it spun wet clothes about.

"Hello?" came the voice on the other end of the line.

"Uh....," Cary began with a slight tremor in his voice. "J-John?" As he had the night before, he felt Antonio's solid hand on his shoulder. He knew he couldn't have done this alone. He wouldn't have had the strength.

"Cary? Is that you?"

CHAPTER  15

PROMISES MADE

Milan, Italy—June

MASSIMO bounded past Antonio and Cary into the empty apartment, feet tapping against the wood floors as he explored one room after another.

"Massi," Antonio called from the doorway, "shoes!"

Two small shoes landed in the hallway outside of one of the bedrooms, and Cary laughed. "Pretty efficient, that kid."

"Better that than have the downstairs neighbors complaining before we've even moved in." Antonio leaned over and took Cary in his arms. "Welcome home, Cary."

"Welcome home, Tonino."

Home. It felt strange to call it that. They had been to the apartment before, of course, but this was the first time since the paperwork had gone through. It was *their* apartment now. The deed revealed nothing but a business partnership. But they owned it. Together. Cary took Antonio's hand and, smiling, led him into the living room.

"Is this my room?" Massimo stuck his head out from one of the bedrooms.

"If you want it to be," Antonio replied. "You can choose that one or the one next to it." He squeezed Cary's hand and pulled him close again. They had discussed giving Massimo his choice of the two smaller bedrooms. Cary would take the other one for his practice studio.

"I like this one." Massimo disappeared once more into the room, singing and talking to himself.

"I called Francesca," Cary said in a low voice. "She'll come over and paint his room before we move in."

"It was a great idea. Wait until he sees it. He loves surprises."

Cary grinned and kissed Antonio. "Happy?"

"Are you serious?" Antonio said with a sigh. "Very happy."

"Me too."

Cary led Antonio over to the balcony and opened the glass doors. The air was warm and slightly humid as they walked over to the railing and looked out on the city. The sun was beginning to set on the horizon, and the street lamps had begun to light up around the neighborhood. The sounds of modern jazz filtered on the breeze, an open-air concert—one of many throughout the summer as part of Milan's Notturni in Villa. In a few weeks' time, Cary himself would be playing several unaccompanied cello pieces in a downtown park.

Cary loved this time of year in Milan with its festivals and markets. He and Antonio had stayed out all night the Friday before for "La Notte Bianca," a nightlong celebration when many Milan bars, restaurants, shops, and movie theaters stayed open until six in the morning. In the past, Cary had used the festivities as just another excuse to spend the night out cruising the bars. With Antonio at his side, they had eaten at a new restaurant, shopped for artwork for their new apartment, and even gone swimming at 3 a.m. in a pool a few blocks away from their apartment.

"I have a surprise for you too, caro," Antonio said as he closed the doors behind them.

"I'm not great with surprises."

"I think you'll like this one. At least I hope you will." Antonio swallowed hard and reached into his pants pocket. With a hopeful expression, he pulled something out, keeping it hidden and taking Cary's right hand in his left.

Cary felt the faint tremor in Antonio's fingers and realized Antonio was nervous. Really nervous. Cary decided it was kind of cute.

"I know things are... different here. In Italy," Antonio began. He glanced over Cary's shoulder into the apartment, and Cary guessed he was looking to see if Massimo was still occupied. "I... I only wish that it could be different. But I... I want you to know how much I love you, caro. I want to show you. I want to give you something that will remind you of me."

Antonio slipped a ring on Cary's finger: a simple white gold band. Their eyes met, and Cary could see the question burning there. Antonio put his hand back in his pocket and pulled out a matching ring.

"Will you stay with me, Cary? Be my partner? Forever?"

Cary's hand shook as he took the ring and slipped it over Antonio's finger.

"Yes."

The word was whispered on the breeze and barely audible above the sound of the traffic from the street below.

Cary blinked back tears as Antonio took him in his arms. *He wants me? Forever?* He was beginning to appreciate his inner Disney princess.

"I love you, Cary." Antonio's voice cracked as he spoke the words.

"I love you, Tonino." *More than I can ever say.*

"Papà! Cary Papà!" Massimo ran out onto the balcony, laughing. "I can see the park from my room!"

Cary turned away in an effort to master his emotions. A small hand tugged at his, and he looked down at Massimo.

"Are you all right, Cary Papà?"

"I'm fine, Massi," Cary answered with a broad smile. He caught Antonio's eye over Massimo's head and saw that he wasn't the only one whose eyes were watery. "Just happy."

"Grown-ups are weird. You say you're happy when you look sad." Massimo crossed his arms over his chest and frowned.

"Your father just gave me this," Cary said, squatting down so his face was even with Massimo's and showing him the ring.

Massimo's eyes grew wide. "Is that like the one Mamma wears? The one Marissa gave her?"

"Yep. The same kind of ring."

Massimo threw his arms around Cary, nearly knocking him off his feet. "I told you we'd make you stay, Cary Papà! Didn't I?"

"Yes. You did. I didn't believe you back then."

Massimo walked over to Antonio, took his father's hand, and turned it over to inspect Antonio's ring. "Grown-ups think they're smart," Massimo said, doing his best imitation of Antonio. "But really, kids are smarter."

"I think you're right, Massi," Cary said with a wink in Antonio's direction. "We just need to listen to you more."

"WHAT are you thinking about?" Antonio asked as they lay in bed that night in Antonio's apartment.

"Lots of things. You. Me. Massi. Sometimes it's a little overwhelming." Cary played with the ring, turning it around on his finger. "I just never expected… I never really thought, you know, that this would be me. I never thought I deserved it, I guess."

Antonio's lips brushed Cary's cheek, and Cary sighed.

CHAPTER *16*

PRELUDE

New York, New York—September

ANTONIO rolled over and began to follow the line of Cary's neck with his tongue, his hand probing beneath Cary's pajama bottoms.

"Even jet-lagged, you're a morning person," Cary said as he rolled onto his side and caught Antonio's lips.

"Are you complaining?"

"Nah," Cary said between gasps. "Besides, I need to get up anyhow."

"I think you're already there," Antonio teased as he cupped the globes of Cary's ass and pulled him tight against him.

Cary wrapped his arms around Antonio's chest and murmured happily, "This is much, *much* better than any wakeup call I've ever gotten."

Two hours later, having devoured a bagel with lox and cream cheese in a small deli next to the hotel, Cary left Antonio with a brief peck on the cheek and headed for the subway. It was a short walk over to 42nd Street to pick up the Q train, which would take him directly to Sheepshead Bay, at the southern tip of Brooklyn.

For the past few months, Cary had been corresponding with his father by e-mail, short and impersonal messages that revealed nothing of the turmoil in Cary's heart. Still, the communication had given him the courage to take the next step: meeting his father at his new apartment.

Cary had called his brother not long after that first call to his father. "Jus," he said after they had discussed plans for Cary, Antonio, and Massimo to spend Thanksgiving in St. Louis, "there's something I need to tell you. Something you need to know." He then proceeded to tell Justin about the Chicago concert several months before, and of John's visit.

"I kind of figured he was still alive," Justin told him, an admission that had Cary nearly forgetting how to breathe.

"You... *what*?" Cary spluttered.

"I remember him. How he and Mom used to fight. And then, one day, he was just... gone. I asked Mom, years later, why I didn't remember his funeral. She said something like I was too young, so I didn't go. But then Aunt Charlene would always make a face when I mentioned his name. And Mom never really defended him. Later, I started to wonder...."

"Why didn't you say anything?" Cary bit back his anger. "I mean, he was *my* dad too."

"I didn't know if I was right. I really didn't. The last thing I wanted to do was have you worry about it or get your hopes up. I knew I could be wrong. And what then? And if it was true, that he was alive... what kind of a jerk did it make him, staying away so long?" Justin's sigh was audible, even through the receiver.

Cary wanted to protest. He was so damn *angry*. But he knew he wasn't really angry with his brother. He was angry with his mother for lying to them, and angry with John for not having tried to contact them, even after his mother's death.

"It's okay," he said at last. "You only did what you thought was best. You didn't really know either."

"I'm sorry, Cary."

"I know." Cary inhaled slowly, trying to clear his fuzzy head. All of this was so overwhelming. "So do you want to talk to him?"

"Me?" Justin's voice was bitter. "No fucking way."

"But—"

"But nothing. Bastard left us. He left Mom too. He can't wait twenty-eight years and then just expect me to come running. My father's dead. Rest in peace. End of story."

In the end, Cary made his uneasy peace with Justin's decision not to contact John. He had felt the same way, after all. If Justin was going to come around like Cary had, it would have to be in his own way and in his own time.

NOW that Cary was sitting on the nearly empty train, his heart raced. It had been Antonio's idea to tag along on this gig, and Antonio had offered to come with him for this first meeting. Cary had turned him down. "I'll probably regret it later, but I think I need to do this myself," he had told his lover. And as he walked the two flights of stairs up to the apartment, he regretted his decision. It would have been nice to have Antonio by his side.

Breathe. What do you have to lose?

His hand shook as he knocked on the door.

"Cary," said John Redding as he motioned him inside, "it's great to see you. Please, come on in."

"Thanks" was Cary's mumbled reply. Funny, he thought, how much more nervous he was for this meeting than he had been to rehearse with the New York Philharmonic the day before.

The one-bedroom apartment was tiny but bright. Cary looked around, more to avoid meeting his father's eyes than out of curiosity. The place reminded him of his college apartment: sparsely furnished but neat and clean. The couch, he guessed from the way it sagged in the middle, could double as a bed. An old dresser stood beside the tall windows at the far end of the room. The kitchen was small but serviceable. The bedroom door was open, the bed neatly made.

"Something to drink?" John asked as he walked over to the fridge. Cary caught the faint scent of spearmint from the gum John was chewing. "Water? Juice? Beer?"

"Beer." It was barely lunchtime, but Cary didn't care. It would help calm his frayed nerves.

John pulled a bottle out and popped off the cap. "Need a glass?"

"Nah." Cary took the bottle from him quickly, hoping the other man didn't notice the way his hand continued to shake.

John pulled a glass down from a cabinet, tossed a few ice cubes in, and filled it with tap water. "Please, Cary, have a seat."

"Nice place," Cary said after a long pull from his beer.

"Thanks. I moved in about a month after I saw you in Chicago. Been wanting to move back to the city for a few years now, and a friend of mine told me about this place. It's a little farther from Midtown than I'd like, but the rent's reasonable." John sipped his water, then asked, "Did Antonio come with you on this trip?"

"Yeah. He tries to travel with me when he can. We've got tickets to the theater this week, and a friend of mine got me tickets to an opera he's singing in at the Met." Cary took another drink of his beer and felt the tension in his shoulders ease ever so slightly.

"Nice, to have friends like that. What's your friend's name?"

"Aiden Lind. We met through David Somers."

"Aiden Lind?" John appeared both pleased and surprised. "I heard him sing at Chicago Lyric. *Don Giovanni,* was it?"

"It's his signature role." Cary smiled, and this time, the smile reflected the comfort of the familiar territory of the conversation. "Bread and butter, although he prefers Italian *verismo* to Mozart."

"I could see—hear him—singing Verdi," John agreed.

"I didn't know you knew so much about music." As always, the words were out of Cary's mouth before he realized how they might sound, as though he had expected his father to be uneducated, uncultured.

John just chuckled. "I've always enjoyed classical music, although I knew nothing about it. It was one of the things that first attracted me to your mother. She was ushering at an orchestra concert at school when I first saw her." He looked away for a moment, as if recalling the scene in his mind's eye, then said, "You might say I became much more versed in music as a way to woo her."

In spite of himself, Cary smiled. He tried to imagine his mother as a young, carefree college student, with little success.

"She saw right through me. Eventually, though, I learned from her. I can still guess the composer when I hear a piece on the radio."

The next few moments passed in silence. Cary fought the urge to hum, as he often did when he was nervous. John studied his glass intently, then drank once more. Finally, he said in a tentative voice, "I... I'd have understood if you had never called me, after Chicago."

"I almost didn't." Cary's face warmed with the admission, but at the same time, he felt his anger flare.

"Can I ask what changed your mind?" John too must have felt his son's mixed emotions, because he added, "If you don't mind telling me, of course."

Cary took a deep breath. The truth was he was grateful for his own second chance, after his near-disastrous start with Antonio nearly a year before. What he said instead was also the truth, although not nearly as revealing. "I realized I was angry. I've cooled off since Chicago."

"I... I appreciate that, Cary. Sounds like your brother wasn't as reasonable."

Cary forced himself to take a deep breath. *Wasn't as reasonable? Is it so unreasonable to be pissed as hell when your long-lost father shows up out of the blue?* But all he said was, "Justin needs to do what's right for him and his family."

"Of course." Cary's father's words were conciliatory, but Cary saw the pain in John's eyes.

That's not your battle to fight, he reminded himself. *Justin needs time too.*

When he left the apartment an hour later, having arranged for John to meet him and Antonio for dinner the next evening, Cary felt as though he had survived a self-created trial by fire. After all the worry and soul-searching, he had found John to be charming and intelligent. He could only wonder what had gone so terribly wrong to cause his parents' marriage to fall apart so spectacularly.

"SO, SIGNOR REDDING—" Antonio began in English.

"Please call me John."

"Only if you'll call me Antonio."

"Of course, Antonio."

"So, John," he began again, "what do you do for a living?"

"I'm a freelance writer. I write copy for press releases and annual reports, and when I'm lucky, I sell my articles to online journals and print magazines. It pays the bills. Things have been a little more difficult in this economy, but I'm not averse to taking a job bartending from time to time."

It was nearly ten o'clock, but all eight of the tables at the small Brooklyn Heights restaurant were occupied. The Storehouse was run by the brother of one of Antonio's clients, Sean Josephson, and had quickly become one of Cary's favorite places to come when he was in New York. In spite of its name, The Storehouse was a tiny restaurant, decorated in an eclectic mix of modern art from the 1960s and '70s and atomic-era furniture and lighting.

It was Sean himself who brought their desserts to the table, and he embraced Cary and Antonio warmly. "Sean, this is my father, John Redding," Cary said formally as Sean and John shook hands. "John, this is Sean Josephson, the man who fed us so well tonight."

"After tonight's amazing dinner," John said with a charming grin, "I'm afraid I'll be a regular fixture for dinner. My son's fault, entirely."

Sean bowed and put a hand to his head to keep his chef's hat from tumbling off his short dark hair. "As long as he keeps giving me tickets to his concerts, I'm happy to feed all the Reddings. My sous chef keeps threatening to walk off the job if he doesn't get to hear you play someday, Cary. You and Antonio going to make it here for brunch on Sunday?"

"Are you kidding? Our flight home doesn't leave until late afternoon, so we'll probably leave for JFK from here." Cary leaned over to his father and added, "Sean makes the best brunch in the city."

"Perfect. It was great to meet you, John. I look forward to seeing you."

"I have to admit," John said a few moments later, as they ate their desserts, "it's a bit strange to be introduced as someone's father. I'm liking it. Especially the added bonus of free symphony tickets."

Cary managed an uncomfortable smile.

"Cary's career is certainly more interesting than mine," Antonio said between bites of a delicate pear mousse.

"I don't know," Cary replied. "You certainly work with interesting people. I've never met a performance artist who 'paints' with food before."

"What type of law do you practice, Antonio?" asked John.

"I'm an entertainment lawyer. My clients are mostly classical and jazz musicians, along with the occasional fashion designer and artist. And one client who paints in different pasta sauces."

"Sounds fascinating. And has Cary been taking advantage of your expertise?"

"My colleague, Valentia, handles Cary's contracts. Cary and I decided it was best to keep business and pleasure apart. Although many of my clients are also friends, it's different when you live with someone."

"I can imagine," John said with a quick smile in Cary's direction. "And Cary, I see you've been busy lately." When Cary blinked at him with surprise, John added, "I took a look at the schedule on your website. Quite impressive."

"I do all right." Cary took a quick sip of his coffee and felt Antonio's hand on his thigh. His entire body was, once again, full of tension. He loved the way Antonio could sense that about him, and he put his hand on Antonio's in a silent "thank you" of sorts.

"I know your mother would have been proud," John said with genuine appreciation. "Did you know she was a classically trained pianist?"

Cary swallowed hard. "No. I mean, I knew she could play. She accompanied me at home when I was little."

"Janet was always the practical one. She was talented enough to make a career of it, but she knew a job as a choir director was a less risky proposition. She conducted the choir at Christ Methodist Church until about the time you began to perform publicly."

"You followed us… I mean, her?"

"As best I could. I know it probably doesn't mean anything now, but I came to a few of your concerts over the years. Only to the bigger venues—I didn't want to cause trouble for you."

"Really? I didn't think you'd have been interested." How many times had he looked out into the audience and imagined his father was still alive and sitting out there, listening? And now to hear he *had* been there. Cary wasn't sure how he felt.

"Whenever I could. Mostly when you were performing around the Chicago area." John's smile was warm and a bit wistful. "I am curious, though," he continued. "Why did you decide to move to Europe?"

It wasn't an easy question. There were many reasons Cary had decided to leave the US. Mostly he had just been lost after his mother's death. In spite of their differences, he had never really known a home other than the one she had made for him. He had wanted to start fresh somewhere far away from St. Louis, and Europe seemed about as far as he could run. But as usual, he found himself revealing only part of the truth to his father.

"I don't know. The majority of my gigs are in Europe and Asia. After I graduated from New England Conservatory, I spent a month in Milan working on some new music with David Somers, and he showed me around. It didn't hurt that his villa outside of town is incredible, either. I hadn't met Aiden yet, so I really didn't know anyone in Europe other than my agent. Milan just seemed like the best place to land."

IT WAS nearly midnight when Cary and Antonio walked John to the Clark Street subway station and said their goodbyes. "Mind if we walk a little?" Cary asked.

"I'd love to walk. Where did you have in mind?"

"The promenade. It's a few blocks down from here, and there's an incredible view of downtown and the Brooklyn Bridge."

Cary took Antonio's hand and led him out of the station and down Clark Street, toward the East River. The air was cold, but there was almost no wind as they reached the pedestrian walkway.

"It's beautiful," Antonio said as he leaned on the railing and looked out across the water to see the Manhattan skyline, still illuminated even at such a late hour.

"This is my favorite spot in the city." Cary loved how it felt peaceful here, and yet under his feet he could feel the low rumble of traffic from the Brooklyn-Queens Expressway.

"I can see why." Antonio leaned in to kiss him, and they just held each other for a few minutes without speaking. "How are you doing?" Antonio asked at last. "Are you glad you made time to see your father?"

"Yeah. I'm glad I did. I think I'd like to see him again."

"Would you like to invite him to visit us?"

"In Milan?" The suggestion took Cary by surprise.

"Why not? I know money's tight for him, but we can send him a plane ticket. You could choose a time when you're not working and show him around. Get to know him better."

"You wouldn't mind?"

"Why should I?"

"I don't know. I guess it seems like it's asking a lot, having him there."

Antonio chuckled and kissed Cary on the forehead. "I suggested it, caro. I wouldn't have if I didn't think it was a good idea. We'll look at the calendar and see what kind of time you have. We can ask him to come for a few weeks, and if you want, you can ask him to stay longer."

"I'd like that," Cary said. "Thanks."

"My pleasure." Antonio pulled Cary close once again. "It makes me happy to see you happy."

"I love you, Tonino." Cary pushed away the familiar niggle of doubt from his mind.

"I love you too. *Sempre.* Always."

Just accept your inner Disney princess, thought Cary as he melted into Antonio's arms. *She's a lucky girl.*

CHAPTER 17

NOW I KNOW WHY TIGERS
EAT THEIR YOUNG

Milan, January

"CARY PAPÀ!" Massimo tugged on Cary's T-shirt as Cary bent over the counter, mixing up a batch of pancakes. Cary had brought back a few boxes of mix when he'd visited the States a few months before, but this was the first chance he'd had to make Antonio and Massi breakfast, since he'd been performing nearly every weekend since.

"Hey, Stinker." Massi peered over at the bowl, and Cary tilted it so the boy could see.

"That looks weird. Are you sure it's not bread?"

"I'm sure," Cary said with a grin. "Wait until you taste it. And with the maple syrup I brought back—"

"Carlo called," Massi interrupted. "He's going to meet me in the park to play some football."

"Now?" Cary stopped mixing the batter and looked down at Massi. "But we're supposed to have breakfast with your father when he gets up."

"He's lazy. He shouldn't be sleeping in so late." Massi glared at Cary in open challenge.

"He got back late from his trip. He'll be up in a little whi—"

"Carlo said if I don't get there in ten minutes, he'll choose someone else to play goalie." Massi stomped his foot as he spoke the words.

Cary smiled at him. "Then he'll get someone else to play goalie. You can meet him after breakfast. Besides, since when do you play goalie?" Cary added. "I thought you wanted to play right midfield in the pros, like David Beckham."

"I need to learn other positions too."

"You can learn them another time, then." Cary reached up and pulled a frying pan down from the cabinet. "This morning, we're having breakfast together."

Massi scowled and put his hands on his hips in a gesture that reminded Cary of Francesca when she scolded Massimo for not cleaning his room. "That stuff is disgusting," Massi said. He pursed his lips as though waiting for Cary to argue with him. "I don't want to eat your stinky American breakfast, anyhow."

Still holding the frying pan, Cary turned and stared at Massi. In the nearly six months he and Antonio had been living together in their new apartment, Massi had never once talked back to him. He tried to remember what it was like to be seven years old, without much success. Cary felt his gut clench and willed himself not to react to the taunt.

Cool head. He's the kid here, not you.

"You can go play after breakfast, Massi."

"But Francesca and Marissa are coming over this afternoon."

"They're not coming over until dinnertime. There'll be plenty of time for you to play later."

"But I—"

"That's the final word, Massi." Cary sure hoped it was, too. "We're having breakfast together. And if you keep pushing me on this, you won't get to go play football at all."

This last statement seemed to push Massi over the edge. "You can't do that!" he shouted, his voice echoing throughout the kitchen. "You can't tell me what to do! You're not my father!"

Cary felt as though he'd just been kicked in the chest. Until that moment, he thought he was doing okay with the kid. He'd responded the way he'd seen Antonio respond when Massi pushed the boundaries. But the truth in Massi's words was something he couldn't deny. He *wasn't* Massi's father. He never would be, either.

Before Cary could collect himself enough to figure out what to say, Massi stormed out of the kitchen, running headlong into Antonio, who was rubbing his eyes and frowning. Cary walked over to the doorway, unsure of what he should do but glad that Antonio was intervening.

"What's going on here, Massimo?" Antonio asked. His voice was calm, but his expression made it clear that he was irritated.

"Cary won't let me go play football with Carlo." Massi was still openly defiant, although Cary thought he was less so than before. "He says I can't go until after breakfast."

"Then you won't be going until after breakfast." Cary nearly sighed with relief to hear Antonio speak the words; he'd worried that he'd overstepped.

"But that's not fair!" Massi's voice cracked as he shouted, and Cary knew he was crying.

"That's enough, Massi. If Cary says you can't go until after breakfast, that's just how it will be."

"But he's *not* my father!"

Cary saw Antonio draw a deep breath. "Massi," Antonio warned, "if Cary says something, you have to listen to him. He's as much your parent as I am. Now go to your room until breakfast, and if you don't, you're not going anywhere at all this morning. And no TV for the rest of the day. I won't have you speaking to Cary like that. Understand?"

Massi turned around and shot Cary a steely look, then ran to his room and slammed the door behind him.

"Shit," Cary said. "I'm really sorry, Tonino, I didn't mean—"

"There's nothing to be sorry about."

"But he's right," Cary protested. "I'm not his father."

Antonio shook his head, then walked into the kitchen, took the pan that Cary was still holding, and set it down on the counter. "You're his parent and you're part of this family, caro." He took Cary's hand and brought it to his lips, then added, "You're also the adult, and if you tell him to do something, then he must listen to what you say."

"I don't know. I mean, maybe I was wrong to tell him he couldn't go."

"Even if you were wrong, I wouldn't go against what you said. I might talk to you about it later on, but I wouldn't undermine your authority, especially in front of him. I trust you to make the best decision you can. But I don't think it was wrong of you to tell him to stay for breakfast, caro. "

Cary closed his eyes as Antonio hugged him. "Thanks." He didn't doubt Antonio's words, but he still doubted himself. More than that, Massi's words had stung, even though he knew the kid hadn't meant them. Not really.

"So what's for breakfast?" Antonio asked a few minutes later, meeting Cary's gaze in a gesture of silent reassurance.

"Pancakes and maple syrup."

Antonio grinned broadly. "And afterward?"

"Massi needs to go to the park," Cary reminded Antonio.

Antonio sighed theatrically. "All right. But maybe later, when Roberta gets here, you and I can figure out something else to do with the syrup."

THAT evening, Francesca and Marissa joined Cary, Antonio, and Massi for dinner. Massi, who had played in the park most of the afternoon, had said very little to Cary since breakfast and was still sulking. After they finished eating the main course, Massi stood up and announced, "I'm done."

Antonio frowned. "Are you asking to be excused, then? You know once you leave, you can't come back for dessert."

Massi looked over at Cary and glared at him. Then he turned back to Antonio and said, "I know that. I want to be excused."

"All right. But no TV, remember?"

"I remember." Massi huffed loudly enough to be heard, then walked to his room and closed the door noisily behind him.

Antonio put his hand reassuringly on Cary's shoulder, and Cary sighed.

"Tonino told me about this morning," Francesca said. "I'm sorry he was so badly behaved."

"It's fine, really." Cary tried to sound convincing.

"No, it's not," Francesca said. "But it's probably a good thing. It means he's beginning to see you as a parent."

"I'd be happy to skip the growing pains and stick to the easier part of parenting." Cary took a sip of his wine and leaned back in his seat. "The fun stuff like tossing a baseball around, reading bedtime stories. That sort of thing."

"At least you got a few months' grace period," Marissa added with a laugh. "He still does that to me sometimes, you know. Tells me I'm not his 'real' mother."

"Really?" Cary knew he shouldn't be surprised to hear this, but he was anyhow. "But you've been his mother since he was born."

"He's understanding more about our family," Marissa said. "When we told him how he was conceived, I think it made him think about it. He knows I want him to see me as his mother. And when he's angry...."

"He doesn't intend to be mean," Francesca finished. "But kids that age want to be in control. They want to be grown up, so they push you sometimes."

"He'll get over it soon enough," Marissa added. "You just need to be patient with him. It sounds like you handled it well, though.'"

"Thanks," Cary mumbled, feeling awkward. In spite of the reassurances, he still felt woefully inept. He decided it was best to change the subject. "So, Francesca, how's the gallery doing?"

"Business is pretty good," she answered, although something in her expression made Cary wonder.

"You don't sound all that excited about it," Antonio pointed out.

"No, I guess I'm not. I asked Bruno, the owner, for more responsibilities. I hoped he'd put me in charge of bookings—that he'd trust me enough for that now. The few shows I've arranged on my own have been much more successful than the others."

"Bruno is a control freak," Marissa interjected.

"You should look for something better," Cary told Francesca.

"I've been thinking about it." Francesca smiled at him. "Marissa thinks I should too."

"Then we all agree," Antonio put in.

Cary raised his glass and smiled. "A toast," he said. "To Francesca and her job search."

The others raised their glasses as well. "To Francesca!"

"YOU want me to put the stinker to bed?" Cary asked Antonio, who was up to his elbows scrubbing a pot from dinner. They'd sent Roberta home—she wasn't supposed to have been working on a Saturday, anyhow—and Cary knew that Antonio always felt a little guilty about having her work overtime.

"You all right with that?" Antonio eyed Cary warily.

"I'm fine with it. I'm not so sure Massi will be."

"He will. He loves you."

"Yeah." Cary sighed. "If you hear loud crashing noises, though...."

"I'll come rescue you, princess."

"Oh, you are *so* going to regret calling me that!" Cary chastised, swatting Antonio's ass with the towel.

Antonio pulled his wet hands out of the sink and grabbed Cary around the waist. Cary took the towel and wrapped it around Antonio's neck, then pulled him close and kissed him. God, he loved the way Antonio could make him feel better, stronger, just by making him laugh.

"Wish me luck," Cary said as the kiss broke.

"*Buona fortuna.*" Antonio smiled at him. "But you won't need it."

"HEY, Stinker. Time for bed."

Massi was sitting on the bed, reading a book. "Okay," he said.

"Want me to get your pajamas?"

"I can do it myself."

"Okay." Cary watched as Massi pulled on the pair of flannel pj's Cary had brought back for him from the US. They were printed with drawings of vintage airplanes and Massi loved them, but the fact that Massi chose to wear them tonight still surprised Cary. "Teeth, Stinker."

Massi padded off to the bathroom. Cary pulled down the bedcovers and waited until Massi came back.

"Hop in."

Massi complied. After a moment, though, he looked up at Cary and asked, "Where's my blanket?"

Cary knew Massi was looking for the ragged baby blanket he still slept with. He'd sworn both Cary and Antonio to secrecy. He didn't want his friends to know about it, although Cary guessed most of Massi's friends also had their own little "secrets."

"Under your pillow. It was on the floor."

Massi reached under the pillow and pulled the blanket out. He held it to his nose and inhaled the smell of it. "Thanks."

"You're welcome." Cary lifted the covers and pulled them over Massi's shoulders, then bent down to kiss his forehead. "Good night, Stinker."

Massi rolled onto his side, facing away from Cary. Figuring that was about as well as he'd do, Cary walked toward the bedroom door.

"Cary Papà?"

Cary stopped and turned back to Massi. "Yeah?"

"I love you."

Cary's vision blurred at the words. He walked back to the bed and reached out for Massimo, who jumped into his arms, causing him to fall back onto the bed. He held Massi as the boy clung to him tightly.

"I love you too, Stinker," he whispered against his tears. It scared him to death how much he loved the kid, how much he wanted to be a father to Massi, and how much he wanted Massi to see him that way. But he knew he wouldn't want it any other way. "I love you too."

CHAPTER  18

PHANTOMS AND APPARITIONS

Milan, March

MASSIMO raced across the living room, causing one of the glass bowls on the buffet table to ring with the vibration. "Massi," called Antonio, shaking his head as he finished washing the dishes, "soft feet. Remember? Signora Corelli might still be sleeping."

The early morning sun streamed in through the window near the sink. It had been one of the things they had loved about this place the moment they had seen it: the natural light that seemed to permeate every corner of the apartment. Now, nearly a year after they had first moved in, this was home: from the small practice studio that also served as guest bedroom to the room next to their own, which Francesca had painted like a sky with puffy clouds and which was filled with model airplanes hung from the ceiling.

Cary chuckled as he dried a glass and set it up on a shelf. "He told me he wants to go to the airport with us to meet his 'grandfather'."

"Are you sure it's all right with you?"

"Of course. To be honest, I think the babbling might be a welcome distraction this time."

"Nervous?"

"You think? 'Scared shitless'." The last two words were spoken in English.

"I know you don't believe me," Antonio said, wrapping two wet hands around Cary's waist, "but it'll be fine. He's probably just as nervous as you are."

"I keep telling myself it was the right thing, to invite him. But I worry you and Massi—"

"Let me do the worrying, caro. You take some time to get to know your father. Massi and I will be fine too. Besides, how often is it that we get to have you home for four weeks at one time?"

Cary slung the dishtowel over his shoulder and claimed Antonio's lips with a sigh. "Roberta said she'll be by around three. Massi's going to help her with dinner, and she'll make the bed up in the studio. You sure you're okay with me practicing in the living room while he's staying with us?"

"You're worrying again. And you know I love to hear you play." He nuzzled Cary's cheek. "We'll be here no matter what happens, caro. I promise."

"IS THAT him? Is that him?" Massi sat atop Antonio's shoulders at the exit from customs at the airport.

"Over there," Antonio said, taking Cary's hand in his and walking over to greet Cary's father. "Good to see you, John."

"Thanks for meeting me." John Redding appeared tired and pale, but he smiled up at Massi. "And this must be Massimo."

"Hello!" Massimo said. "I am Massimo. Welcome to Milan." He spoke the words in English, just as Antonio had taught him.

"Nice to meet you. You're a big boy, Massimo."

Antonio translated this into Italian, and Massimo sat straighter on his father's shoulders, beaming. "Can I have a piece of gum?" Massimo asked, noting the gum John was chewing. Cary translated this time and a moment later, the boy was happily chewing away.

"We'll go get the car and meet you both out front," Antonio told Cary, squeezing Cary's hand before leaving.

For an awkward moment or two, Cary and his father stood there in silence. "How was the trip?" Cary finally managed, offering John his hand.

"Long, but uneventful." John took Cary's hand and shook it.

"You look tired. Do you want to sit while we wait?"

"No, thanks. I'm fine. Really."

"Good." Cary shifted uncomfortably on his feet, unsure of what more to say.

"Thanks for inviting me."

"No problem."

"He really seems like a sweet boy," John said, glancing over to where Antonio and Massimo had left.

"He's a great kid. Smart, like his father." Cary shoved his hands in his pockets. "I always told myself I hated kids, but I'm kind of liking this 'parenting' thing."

"I'm glad you're giving me a chance at parenting, after all these years."

Cary fought the urge to clench his jaw, instead looking down. He thought of himself at Massimo's age, dreaming about what it would be like to have a father, and the old anger flared again. This time, however, he said nothing.

"Cary!" a high, squeaky voice shouted from the exit. "We're waiting for you!"

"That's our cue," Cary said, relieved to have something to focus on other than the awkward silence. He took the larger of his father's two bags over John's protests, and they headed out of the terminal after Massimo.

"I TOLD Giovanni that I have two papàs and two mammas," Massimo was saying a few hours later over a festive dinner of veal and risotto, "and he didn't believe me."

Antonio translated, and John laughed. "I'm not really your dad, though, Massi," Cary pointed out. Cary felt the same relief he had months before, when he had invited his father to come visit. He had worried John might not be accepting of his son's same-sex partnership, but John had never questioned it.

"He's really great with Massi," Antonio told Cary's father as Roberta ladled soup into their bowls.

"*Vino*, Signor Redding?" Roberta asked John.

"No, thank you, Roberta," John replied in Italian. Then, switching back to English, he explained, "I'm still feeling a bit tired from the flight. Pellegrino is fine."

"Of course, signore." She refilled Antonio's glass and moved on to Cary's.

"Your Italian's pretty good, John," said Antonio with a tilt of his head.

"Ever since we planned this trip, I've been trying to learn a bit. I can probably order at a restaurant, but I'm not ready for real conversation, at least not yet. I'm pretty sure Cary got his ear for languages from his mother—it sort of goes hand in hand with the musical ability."

"I'm curious, Cary," Antonio said, "why your mother chose cello for you?"

"I never asked her," Cary admitted, "although I seem to remember her saying she took me to a music store when I was about three years old so I could look at the instruments. I have this vague memory of being there and thinking it would be fun to learn to play an instrument nearly as big as I was."

"Janet's mother played the cello," John added. "It's also my understanding that there are fewer children learning cello than violin or some of the brass instruments like trumpet. Less competition. Cary's mother was a very practical woman."

Roberta came back into the dining room and began to collect the soup bowls. "The soup was wonderful, Roberta," John added in heavily accented but passable Italian. She blushed happily as he handed her his bowl, then bustled off to the kitchen again.

The conversation lagged as they waited for Roberta to serve the main course. Antonio, perhaps sensing the difficult situation in which Cary found himself, once more took charge of the conversation. "I hear this is your first visit to Milan. Is there something in particular you're hoping to see while you're here?"

"I'd love to head over to the Piazza del Duomo and maybe take a look inside the cathedral. Cary suggested we also visit Castello Sforzesco."

"I figured we could do lunch in between," Cary added. "Since John's in town for at least a few weeks, we don't need to jam everything in at once. We'll probably visit the Museo Poldi Pezzoli on Tuesday and Pavia on Wednesday or Thursday, depending on the weather. John also wants to see the Po valley. I told him we could take a day trip to some of the vineyards."

"I'm taking Massi back to his mother's tonight," Antonio told them, "so I could join you for an early dinner tomorrow after I finish up at the office. There's a nice restaurant on via Manzoni I'd love to take you both to."

"That would be wonderful," John said. "If it's okay with you, Cary."

"Sure." Cary was silently relieved he wouldn't have to spend the entire day trying to make small talk with his father. He guessed Antonio had understood this and resolved to thank Antonio later—he had a pretty good idea of how he might do that, as well.

IT WAS nearly midnight before they said their good-nights, having set John up in the studio with some help from Roberta. On the way back to their bedroom, Antonio stopped and peered into Massimo's room with Cary behind him. "He likes your father," Antonio observed as he put his arm around Cary's shoulder.

"The kid likes everyone," Cary said with a chuckle. Then, with some hesitation, he added in an undertone, "I have to admit I kind of like him too."

Antonio smiled as he closed the door. "I was hoping you'd say that. But I know how hard this is for you."

Inside their own bedroom, Cary pulled Antonio against him and briefly claimed his lips. "I couldn't have done this without you."

"Yes, you could have. But I appreciate the thought."

"Thanks for letting him stay here."

"You still talk about this place as though it isn't yours," Antonio pointed out. "You're my family, and Massi's too. This is our home."

Cary's sigh was audible. "You don't know how much it means to me that you feel that way. It's just that—"

"Shhh, caro," Antonio interrupted. "Let me make my own decisions about who I want to spend my life with." He pulled Cary over to the bed and sat him down, then began to massage his shoulders.

"Sometimes I worry you'll realize what a jerk I am." Cary was so terrified to speak the words that he spoke them in a whisper. "And you never complain when I'm gone."

"She was hard on you, wasn't she? Your mother."

Antonio's comment surprised Cary. They had never really spoken about his mother before. "Why do you say that?"

"Just a guess." Antonio planted a tender kiss on Cary's cheek.

"Am I really that transparent?" Cary knew exactly what Antonio meant, although it pained him to realize it. He felt raw, vulnerable. He hadn't realized his father's visit would reawaken his long-repressed emotions.

"The pain is still here," Antonio said as he laid his hand against Cary's chest.

For a moment, Cary said nothing, trying to rein in his now fragile emotions. "She only wanted what was best for me."

That's true. But there's more to it than that, and you know it.

Antonio said nothing, perhaps sensing Cary's hesitation and allowing him time to gather his thoughts.

"Yeah," Cary admitted finally. "She was hard on me."

"She loved you, caro. I'm sure of it."

"Sometimes I wonder." The words tumbled out of his mouth and, with them, the pain of so many years spent trying to please his mother. He had thought he was past this, that he had rid himself of the memories. But now….

Shit, Redding. Get it together. He could feel the tears well up in his eyes, and he fought them. He didn't cry, he reminded himself. He took a few deep breaths and tried to think of something else, tools that had served him well in the past. But tonight, try as he might, he could not stop the tears. His eyes burned, and he felt the hot wetness on his cheeks. He turned away from Antonio, not wanting him to see.

"She loved you," Antonio repeated, gently turning Cary's head so their eyes met. He swept a large thumb across Cary's damp cheek to brush the tears away. "She may not have been able to show you, but I'm sure she loved you."

The tears fell in earnest now, and Antonio drew him closer, cradling his head. Cary cursed himself for having the fourth glass of wine, doing his best to explain away his reaction. In the end, though, it didn't really matter what had triggered it. Whatever the catalyst, he was powerless to stop his tears. "I'm sorry," he whispered into Antonio's powerful chest. "I didn't want—"

Antonio hushed him, then kissed his head. "Don't apologize for what's in your heart."

Cary nodded, even as his body began to shake and he heard himself moan with grief. And there, in the deepening darkness, he sobbed until Antonio's shirt was damp and he couldn't cry any more.

For the first time in his life, he felt really and truly loved.

CHAPTER *19*

THE ANGEL ON YOUR SHOULDER

"GET back! Farther back! You got it, Cary!" John shouted as Cary chased the baseball across the nearly empty park. The sun was beginning to set over the treetops, and there was a hint of chill in the air as he kept running past the fountain, the smell of freshly cut grass and the first spring flowers on the breeze.

"I did it! I did it!" Massimo shouted happily. "I hit the ball!"

"Run, Massi, run!" John called to Massimo, who looked confused.

"*Corri*, Massi, *corri!*" Cary translated, still running after the baseball, which rolled down a small hill.

"Oh! *Sì!*" Massimo charged off in the direction of first base, a tree near the walking path.

"Go! Go!" John gestured for Massimo to keep running.

"That's it, Massi!" Cary crested the hill, ball in hand, waiting until home plate was within reach. "Here, John!" He threw the ball to his father, who caught it in the leather glove Cary had loaned him.

John Redding trotted off in the direction of the park bench but gave Massimo enough time to tag home plate. Laughing and panting, he collapsed onto the bench and hugged Massimo. "You did it, Massi! Great job!"

"He says you were great, kid," Cary said as he joined his father on the bench and wiped beads of sweat from his brow.

"Maybe I'll be a baseball player," Massimo said, his face lit with pleasure. "They make more money than football players, don't they?"

"Could be." Cary shook his head. "Already thinking about his nest egg at seven." He shot his father a grin.

"He'll be a lawyer like his father," John said as he tried to catch his breath. "Either that or an investment banker."

"You okay?" Cary handed a bottle of water to John, who took it without complaint and began to drink.

"Fine. Just out of shape." He massaged his chest below the collarbone and chuckled. "Don't think I'll be running any marathons in the near future."

"Me either. Sit-ups aren't exactly great for my stamina. Tight abs, no endurance." He pulled two bottles from his backpack and held one out for Massimo. "Drink, Massi. We wouldn't want Roberta to get angry with me."

Massimo giggled and took the bottle. "When I first met Roberta," Massimo said, "I thought she was your mother."

"Sometimes I think *she* thinks she's my mother." Cary ruffled Massimo's hair.

"Can I go over to the fountain, Cary? I promise I won't get wet."

"Okay." Cary held out his hand, pinkie finger sticking out. Massimo caught it with his own, and they shook. Then Massimo ran off down the hill.

"Pinky shake?" John smiled. "I didn't know kids still did that."

"Don't tell anyone," Cary said with a conspiratorial wink, "but I have absolutely *no* clue if they do. But he's still young enough that he doesn't think it makes me uncool."

"Ever thought about having your own children?"

"Me?" Cary hadn't expected the question, and it took him by surprise. "Nah. Not even for a second." But now… was it still true? He wasn't sure. Helping Antonio raise Massimo had been much more rewarding than he had expected. He liked the way Massimo accepted him unconditionally, without any adult bullshit. And he liked the feeling he got when he put a Band-Aid on Massimo's knee and even wiped the snot from his nose.

"Can't say I blame you." John sighed and ran a hand through his hair. "Sounds like it was tough for you and Justin."

Cary felt the old anger return. "We had it a lot better than some kids." Well, it was true, wasn't it? "And Justin's a great dad." He stood up to make sure Massimo was still at the fountain.

Massimo waved at them and ran back up the hill. "I'm hungry," he announced.

Cary pulled out his cell phone to check the time. "Just about time for dinner, Stinker." He popped the phone back into his pocket and let Massimo climb onto his shoulders from the bench. "You ready, John?"

"I hope someday you'll call me 'Dad'," John said as he bent down to gather up the ball, bat, and glove.

Cary didn't answer but held on to Massimo's ankles as Massimo began to sing "Take Me Out to the Ball Game" in a passable American accent, and they headed out of the park toward home. All in all, Cary thought with a ghost of a smile, it had been a very good day.

THE next morning, Cary practiced in the living room while Antonio sat on the couch, reading through a contract. Cary skated his bow across the strings of the cello. The plaintive sounds of Bach's Cello Suite No. 1 reverberated throughout the apartment. The stark beauty of the unaccompanied piece reminded Cary of the trees in the piazza outside the apartment, bare but for the hints of buds at the tips of their branches.

Antonio sighed and leaned back, closing his eyes as though he were giving himself over to the music.

With the final arpeggio chords announcing the end of the movement, Cary breathed deeply and opened his eyes as the last of the notes died on the air. "Sorry," he said with a sheepish expression. "I didn't mean to disturb you."

"You didn't. It was too beautiful to waste on a boring contract." He stood up and kissed Cary's head.

"I'm playing it in an old monastery in Villefranche-de-Rouergue next month. The acoustics there are incredible. I'm hoping to get a good recording of the concert. Georges was able to arrange it to coincide with my concert in Toulouse."

"I may have to tag along."

"Would you?" It wasn't often that Antonio traveled with him, but Cary loved it when he did.

"I'll check with Valentia to see if she can cover for me, but it should be fine." He walked over to the bedroom. "I've got a lunch meeting I need to get to. Where's your father?"

"Sleeping in. Said he wasn't feeling well. I guess the dinner last night was a little too rich for his stomach." Cary cleaned the rosin dust from the strings and fingerboard, then wiped the wood beneath the strings and set his cello in its case. He inhaled deeply; he loved the familiar pine scent of the rosin. Then he laughed and added, "I personally think it was the three bottles of wine we polished off. John can certainly hold his alcohol, can't he? And what would we do without you to pick the good stuff?"

"Right." Antonio wore a faraway expression as he rubbed the stubble on his jaw.

"Everything okay?" Cary laced his fingers through Antonio's and kissed him.

"Fine. Sorry," Antonio said, clearly distracted. "I'd better get in the shower, or I'm going to be late. Are you eating here tonight?"

"Definitely. I told Roberta to cook something easy on the stomach. And maybe we'll stick with water this time."

"Sounds good. I'll be home by seven." He ruffled Cary's hair and headed into the bedroom.

"FEELING better?"

John rubbed his eyes and coughed. "Just needed a little extra sleep, I guess. We've been going pretty fast and furious with the sightseeing since I got here last week. I'm not as young as I used to be."

"How's your stomach? Can I get you something for it?"

"Stomach?" John looked surprised. "Nah, my stomach's pretty much cast iron. But I'd love a cup of coffee, if you're offering."

"Sure," Cary answered, thinking his father's skin looked a bit pasty and deciding what John needed was food, in addition to the coffee.

"Antonio left?"

"About an hour ago. Lunch meeting."

"He works a lot, doesn't he?" John sat down at the table while Cary put the grounds in the espresso machine and heated some milk.

"I don't know. I guess I never noticed. I'm gone a lot more than he is."

"Well, that's to be expected, isn't it? What with an international solo career. Of course you'd travel."

Cary set out a few dishes and began to pull some cheese out of the refrigerator.

"I'm sure it must be hard on him."

"I… I guess maybe." Cary had never really thought about it, at least not since they had first gotten together. Sure, Antonio always seemed happy to have him around, and he seemed happy when he returned from a gig out of town, but still…. "Did he say something to you about it?" Cary asked with a sick feeling in the pit of his stomach.

"No." John took a piece of bread and spread some cheese on it. "But sometimes you sense these kinds of things."

I haven't sensed it, Cary thought with some alarm. *Maybe I should have.* He wondered if John was right. It would make sense, wouldn't it? Antonio had mentioned traveling with him to France. And that distracted look he had seen on Antonio's face—was he disappointed Cary was leaving again?

The familiar guilt returned with a vengeance. *But he never* would *complain about my traveling.* Antonio never complained.

"So what are we doing today?" John asked, interrupting Cary's thoughts.

"I promised to pick Massi up from school. I thought we'd take him for gelato. He's been pestering me for it ever since his teacher told him it was spring." Cary chuckled and sat down across the table. "I haven't had much luck convincing him it's still a little cold for ice cream."

"I have to admit the kid's cute. What's his mother like?"

"Smart, like her son. Talented too. She's an artist."

"Really? So she and Antonio are divorced?"

"No. It's a little complicated. Francesca's a little older than Tonino. They grew up together in the wine country. She was single and she really wanted a child."

"So Antonio got it up for a woman? Guess he's more man than I gave him credit for. Interesting."

For a moment, Cary was too stunned to speak.

"Oh, Cary," John said with a laugh. "I was joking. Really, don't look so offended."

"Sorry." Cary did his best not to reveal his true feelings. "I guess I'm just a little sensitive about the topic of sexual orientation."

"I'm sure you must have slept with at least one woman," John said as he brought the hot coffee to his lips.

Cary felt suddenly cold. "I don't think this is something I really want to talk about."

John looked at first surprised, then a little embarrassed. "Sorry. I didn't mean to imply…." His voice trailed off, and Cary wondered silently what other implication there might be other than that he and Antonio were somehow less "men" than their heterosexual counterparts.

"Look," Cary said at last, seeking to dispel the uncomfortable atmosphere, "I guess you could say I'm a little thin-skinned about this. Mom wasn't exactly thrilled when I came out to her." He realized his hand was now clenched around his cup, and he forced himself to relax. He didn't want an argument about this topic with his father, not when they were just getting to know each other again.

Besides, it's not like he gave you any grief when you warned him about you and Tonino. He knew what you were, and he was at least okay enough about it that he still made the trip.

"Maybe if your mother had lived longer, she'd have changed her mind about gays. I'm sorry, though, really. I didn't mean to offend you. Antonio is a wonderful man."

Cary nearly sighed in relief. "I'm glad you think so" was all he said.

See? You overreacted. Next time, just give him a chance. And yet he couldn't completely silence the small voice in his mind that told him it wasn't such a simple thing to dismiss.

"DUCK!" Cary warned as he carried Massi on his shoulders through the front door. "You don't want to hit your head." With a grin, John reached up and guided Massimo's head under the doorframe.

"We're home, Roberta," Massimo called happily as Cary set him down on a counter in the kitchen. "Grandpa John bought me an ice cream on the piazza after school!"

"Lucky boy." The housekeeper winked at Cary and his father as she joined them a moment later. "Would you like to come to the store and help me pick out some dessert for tonight?"

"Can we have chocolate?" Massimo asked.

"Are you kidding? What else would we have?" Cary asked. "You know how your papà loves it."

"What does your papà love?" Antonio said as he walked into the kitchen. He nodded to John, kissed Cary, then grabbed Massimo and hoisted him up over a broad shoulder.

"Chocolate," Massimo said between giggles. "Roberta and I are going to get some dessert at the store."

Antonio reached into his pocket and pulled out some bills. "Is this enough?" he asked Roberta.

"I'll need a few more this time," she replied as she retrieved a pile of shopping bags from out of a cabinet by the kitchen door. "I need to buy a bit more cognac and limoncello while I'm out. We're also out of beer again."

"No problem." Antonio handed her another fifty euros.

"*Grazie, signori*," Roberta said. "We'll be back in an hour. I've left some cheese out on the counter. Help yourselves."

"I'm going to take a shower," Antonio said after Roberta had left. "I'll join you both later."

"Sure," Cary said as he walked over to the fridge. "Water?" he asked his father.

"Sure. Thanks."

As he poured their water, Cary was struck by the fact that Antonio rarely showered when he got home from work. *Strange. He almost seemed like he was avoiding us.* Cary brushed the thought from his mind.

"Enjoying your visit so far?" Cary asked as he and John settled down on the couch in the living room a few minutes later.

"Immensely. And you?"

"I'm having a good time." He smiled at his father and put his feet up on the ottoman.

"But...?"

"But," Cary answered with a sigh, "I've taken too much time off from practicing. I'm going to need to get back to it."

"I heard you practicing this morning after breakfast," John pointed out.

"Yeah. But an hour or two isn't enough. I need more like six hours these days, what with the new composition David Somers wrote for me and the concert gigs coming up next month."

John said nothing.

"We can still do some sightseeing," Cary added. "I'll need to schedule a bit more practice time into our plans."

"Oh." John leaned back against the cushions and sipped his water.

"Sorry." Cary felt surprisingly guilty, although he was loath to understand why—his father knew his music was a job. He shrugged it off as his own natural tendency toward guilt, then continued, "So what would you like to see tomorrow?"

"I'll have to look at the guidebook to find something that'll fit into your schedule." John looked toward the window but said nothing more.

Shit. Cary fidgeted and did his best to get more comfortable on the couch, but with little success. "It's not a problem," he said at last. "I can skip tomorrow, if you've got something more time-consuming in mind. It'll wait a day."

His father's expression brightened. "That'd be great. I appreciate it," he said and launched into a discussion of a villa outside of the city he had been hoping to see.

"SOMETHING bothering you?" Antonio said as Cary rearranged his pillows for the fifth time since they had turned in.

"Nothing. Just restless, I guess."

"How's the new piece coming?"

"David's piece?"

"Is there another one?"

"No." Cary repositioned himself again. "It's coming along fine, I guess."

"You haven't had much time to practice since your father came."

"It's okay," he lied. "I've still got five months before the premiere."

"How about I take your father out on Saturday? That'd give you some time to yourself, without any of us around."

"But that's not fair to you. He's *my* father. I should be the one making sure—"

"And I'm your partner," Antonio interrupted. "And I'm offering."

"Sorry," Cary said. "That'd be great. If you don't mind, I mean."

"I don't mind." Antonio chuckled and rolled over to face Cary. "But if you're thankful," he continued with an evil grin, "I can think of a way you can show it."

"Really? I can't imagine how I might do that." He nuzzled Antonio's neck and began to lick around his ear, drawing a contented sigh from his partner.

CHAPTER 20

RETURN OF THE THIEF

"BREAKFAST?" Cary asked as Antonio poked his head into the kitchen.

"Where's your father?"

"Still sleeping. We got in a bit later than I'd planned last night."

Cary's head ached. He'd gotten out of the habit of drinking so much since he and Antonio had gotten together. Once he had given up the bar scene, he found he just didn't need it. He'd taken a few headache pills, but they hadn't kicked in yet.

"I noticed," Antonio said with a quick kiss to Cary's cheek.

Cary tensed and looked down at the stove, pushing around the egg he'd been frying. It had started out as over easy but was now looking more like scrambled.

"I'll take some eggs, since you're offering. Scrambled is fine." He handed Cary the carton from the fridge, and Cary began cracking the eggs into the pan. "Something bothering you?"

"Nah," Cary lied, kicking himself for being so obvious.

It's just your own fucked-up guilt. He wasn't complaining about the late night....

Antonio laced his arms through Cary's, kissing him on the neck. "Careful," Cary warned. "I wouldn't want to burn you."

"I'm already burned." Antonio's voice was husky. "But you're avoiding my question."

Cary pushed the eggs around again in the pan, although he wasn't really paying attention to what he was doing. He was trying to figure out how he could avoid this conversation entirely.

"Please, caro. Tell me."

Another moment of silence; then: "You never complain."

"What?"

"I come home after midnight, I travel a lot, and you don't say anything."

"Why should I?" Antonio asked, frowning. "You aren't a child."

Cary wasn't sure how to answer. The man had a point, didn't he? Of course he didn't have to ask permission to stay out late. And he had never made any bones about the demands of his career. "No. I guess you're right. It's just that sometimes... I don't know... you're *too* patient with me. Too... nice." Cary had wanted to hear more. Maybe something like *I don't like it when you're gone,* or *I wish you wouldn't stay out so late.*

Antonio's rumbled laugh filled the room, and Cary looked back down at the eggs once more. Antonio pushed Cary's hair from his face. Cary didn't think what he'd said was funny, and he guessed Antonio was trying to gauge his reaction.

"I'm sorry," Antonio said. "I didn't mean to offend you."

Cary turned the burner off and glared at Antonio. "I'm sure you didn't." Then, seeing Antonio's regret, he said, "Sorry. I guess I'm a little bit on edge."

"I can tell." He kissed Cary and added, "So, as you Americans put it, 'what gives?' I want to understand."

"It's really nothing, Tonino. It's stupid. *I'm* being stupid."

"You're never stupid, caro," came the warm response. "But I do want to understand."

"It's just that... sometimes I... oh shit... you're too patient with me. You know, when I do stupid things or say something.... You should be angry with me, but you never are."

Antonio appeared genuinely perplexed. "You want me to be angry with you?"

Cary turned and walked across the kitchen, shaking his head. Then, looking back at Antonio, he said, "Yeah. I guess I do. Sometimes. I know... it doesn't make any sense, does it?"

Antonio appeared to consider this statement as he leaned back against the counter and searched Cary's face. "I'm not sure."

"Crap. How can I explain it?" Cary took a deep breath. "I mean, you're always so coolheaded about things. You almost never get angry with me, and you should. You get angry with Massi more than you do with me. It's like...."

"Like I don't care?"

Cary said nothing.

"That's it, isn't it? You think if I don't get angry when you're away, if I don't worry about you when you don't come home until late, that I don't love you?"

This was such *a bad idea*, Cary thought, wishing the ground would open up and swallow him. He felt like a complete idiot. What was he doing, anyhow, feeling insecure? He didn't doubt Antonio loved him, did he?

Antonio gathered Cary in his arms. "I love you, Cary. Maybe I need to say it more."

"No. It's not that. But John and I were talking, and I realized it's a lot to ask of you. You know, my traveling. And now, having John here…."

"You're worried that I'm unhappy."

Cary sighed and nodded.

"Do I look unhappy?"

"Yes… I mean no, but—"

"But nothing. I *am* happy."

Cary fought the urge to melt into Antonio's arms as he loved to do. Why was it so damn easy to lose himself in those arms, anyhow? "But I'm always asking you to do things for me," Cary protested.

"Maybe it seems that way. But it doesn't feel like it to me." Cary said nothing, so Antonio continued, "The other day, I listened to you play the Bach. It made me happy. Music does that for me. And your music… I can't tell you how good it makes me feel to hear it. It's like I can hear your happiness in your playing."

"But that's not the same thing. I don't hold your hand or listen to you complain—"

"It might not seem like it to you, but it *is* the same. There are lots of moments like that. When I watch you teach Massi how to play baseball. When you make breakfast for me, like you're doing now. When you make love to me. They all add up."

Cary started to say something, but Antonio shushed him with a finger to the lips. "There will come a time when I'll need to complain to you and when I'll need you to hold my hand. And I'm certain that when I *do* ask you to help me, you'll be there, Cary. I'm sure of it. That's normal when you love someone. I saw it with my parents when I was little. It's not always an even give and take."

"I suck at this relationship stuff."

Antonio chuckled and kissed Cary. "No, you don't. You've just never seen it for yourself. But trust me, it makes me feel loved to know you *can* lean on me. If you didn't come to me when you needed help, *then* I would worry."

"Thanks."

"For what?"

"For loving me."

"That's easy, Cary."

Cary gave in, pressing his body against Antonio's, feeling the slight pressure of Antonio's arms, warming him. And for just a moment, he didn't wonder if he deserved it.

CHAPTER 21

IF WISHES WERE FISHES

"CARY!" Massimo shouted as he bolted from the schoolyard to hug Cary.

"Hey, Stinker." Cary laughed and crouched down to allow Massimo to climb atop his shoulders. "You know you're almost too big for me to carry, don't you?"

"Well, I *am* seven years old now. I'm *supposed* to be big."

Cary waved to the teacher as they headed down the block and back toward the apartment. It had quickly become habit for Cary to pick Massimo up from school, something Francesca appreciated even when Massimo was staying with her. For Cary, who spent most of the day practicing at home, the twenty-minute walk to and from the school was a welcome diversion. And, of course, he had come to enjoy his time with Massimo.

"Where's your papà, Cary?"

"With *your* papà today."

"Again?"

Cary chuckled. "I had a rehearsal with Maestro Somers this morning, so your papà and my papà took a drive out to the country together."

"I like your papà," Massimo said without hesitation.

"I like him too."

"Is he going to stay with us too?" Massimo pressed. "Like you did?"

"I don't think so."

"That must make you sad. It would make me sad if my papà lived far away."

Leave it to a kid to say what the grown-ups won't. The thought of his father leaving *did* make him sad. *And how strange is that?* he thought. *After all the anger….* "A little, I guess," he said after a moment.

"Then you should ask him to stay."

Such a childish thing, really, to think life could ever be so simple. And yet, Cary wondered if maybe it wasn't so unreasonable, after all. *Why not?* His father had hinted around that he'd like to stay in Milan a few weeks more before returning to the States, and Cary still had two weeks before his next gig.

"I don't know, Stinker."

Massimo bent down from his perch on Cary's shoulders and hugged him so tightly, it nearly choked Cary. "I love you, Cary," Massimo said.

"I love you too, big stinker," Cary answered to giggles. He smiled to himself with the realization of how totally and utterly he had fallen for both father and son. And was it really so childish to hope that he too could have a loving relationship with his own father?

CARY arrived back home later than he'd intended. He and Massi had stopped for gelato and fed the pigeons on the piazza near Francesca and Marissa's apartment. He had that silly, warm feeling he'd come to crave, a feeling that, more often than not, led him to his instrument and his music. Antonio and John wouldn't be back from their trip to Antonio's family's vineyard for a few hours, so he picked up his cello and played.

He'd practiced nearly eight hours already that day, so this time he just let the music take him where it wanted. He didn't stop to go over the fingering of the passage he'd been working. He didn't worry that he'd marked a section as starting with an upbow, or that he'd wanted to take more time on a rallentando where the piece modulated from major to minor. He just played, his eyes closed, feeling the vibration of the wood in his bones, with the smell of the rosin in his nostrils.

When he stopped playing, he realized he'd been at it nearly an hour. He'd lost track of the time. Antonio and John would be back any moment— they'd made plans for dinner at the tiny Italian restaurant where Antonio had taken him when he was still "Connor," and he figured he'd shower and get dressed so they wouldn't have to wait for him when they got back.

He stood in the shower, letting the warm water run over his hair. *You're happy*, Aiden had said when they'd spoken the weekend before. Not that Cary agreed at the time—he didn't want to admit that he was at least as big a romantic sap as his best friend—but he knew Aiden was right. He *was* happy, and he knew part of that happiness was because of John.

He twisted the ring on his right finger and smiled. Massi was right too. He'd talk to Antonio about having John stay longer.

When he emerged from the bedroom a few minutes later, he heard Antonio and John speaking in the kitchen. He moved closer and stopped in the hallway. He didn't mean to eavesdrop—he really only intended to let them finish their conversation—but what he heard made him pause.

"You misunderstand me," John was saying. "My relationship with Janet—Cary's mother—was not an easy one."

"You've said this before." As always, Antonio's voice was calm, although Cary knew him well enough to hear the hint of tension there.

"I don't mean to imply that *she* was the only one to blame for the end of our marriage. I'm hardly without my flaws." John paused, and Cary guessed John expected Antonio to agree. Antonio, however, did not respond.

"I was angry," John continued, sounding a bit defensive. "I stayed at work late. I worked hard for our family, but it was a difficult time, after Cary was born. When I filed for divorce, she said I'd threatened her. They believed her too. She got a restraining order to keep me away."

"Have you told Cary this?"

"Why? What would it accomplish now? It was all lies, anyhow."

"All this are lies?"

Cary frowned. It wasn't like Antonio to make mistakes when he spoke in English, not unless he was distracted. *Or upset.*

"What are you insinuating?" John asked.

"I have watched you these past weeks. I have noticed you do not tell your son the truth." This time, there was no mistaking the coldness in Antonio's voice.

"Cary is not a child, and I am not his father," Antonio continued. "I will not tell him what he must do with his life. He has already suffered too much this way with his mother. He must learn himself, and he must choose for himself. But you will not ask to stay longer."

"What?"

Cary knew it was wrong not to interrupt them, not to let them know he was listening. But he couldn't help himself. He stood rooted to the spot with a sick feeling in the pit of his stomach.

"I've heard you speak of staying here longer. I am telling you I will not permit this. Even if Cary will be angry with me."

"You're jealous." John let out a triumphant laugh. "You're afraid I'll take him away from you."

Antonio said nothing.

"That's it, isn't it?" John's voice was full of contempt.

There was a pause; then Cary heard Antonio release an audible breath. "I am not jealous. But I do fear I will lose him—"

"To me," John interrupted.

"No," Antonio whispered. "To himself."

What is he so afraid of? Cary brushed the thought aside. He had no intention of confronting either of them, although he figured he'd talk to Antonio later. For now, he'd pretend he hadn't heard anything. He needed time to think, to understand. He took a deep breath, steeling himself inwardly, putting on a mask nearly as complete as those that hung on the wall of his practice room. He was good at this. He always had been.

"Hey!" he said as he walked into the kitchen, hoping his smile wasn't overly bright. "Did you have a good time today?"

"We did," John said. His expression seemed a bit forced, and Cary found himself looking at Antonio.

"My mother made us lunch," Antonio put in as he leaned over and kissed Cary on the cheek. "She sends her regards."

"Wonderful woman," John added. Cary couldn't help but notice that John didn't look at Antonio. "Antonio's a lucky man to have grown up in such a beautiful place and with a mother like that."

Cary's thoughts strayed to his own mother, and he forced himself not to react. "Oriana is wonderful," he agreed. "And the wine—"

"I should go shower," Antonio interrupted. "I'll be ready to leave in about fifteen minutes."

"Sure," Cary answered.

"I'd better get going, then," John said. "Fifteen minutes."

A moment later, Cary was alone in the kitchen, leaning against the counter. He let out a slow breath and closed his eyes. It was going to be a long evening.

CHAPTER 22

CONFESSIONAL

"CAN we talk?" Cary asked Antonio as they sat out on the balcony eating breakfast. He'd been meaning to talk to Antonio for several days, but they'd rarely been without Cary's father or Massimo, and a string of late nights had left them with little time alone other than to sleep. That, and he was afraid to talk. Afraid to admit he'd overheard his father and Antonio talking in the kitchen. Afraid Antonio would be angry with him. Afraid of what Antonio had meant when he'd said he feared losing Cary to himself.

"Of course." Antonio refilled their coffee cups, then topped them off with hot milk. "Is John still asleep?"

"I think so." Cary chuckled, trying to act as though nothing was different between them. "He's definitely not an early riser. I must have inherited that from my mom."

"Are you enjoying his visit?"

"Yeah. Funny, isn't it? I'm starting to think I'll actually miss him when he leaves on Sunday."

Antonio's answer surprised Cary. "Of course you would," he said evenly. "He's your father."

Cary looked down at his plate and smiled. "Yeah."

"So what did you want to talk to me about? It sounded important."

Shifting in his seat, Cary began, "I… I'm thinking about asking John to stay a little longer. Only if it's all right with you, I mean," he added hastily.

Please. Tell me what happened between you two.

"I see."

"It's been really good, getting to know him. And I thought a little longer might be nice." Cary ran a hand through his damp hair and looked out over the small piazza below the building.

"Did he suggest this?"

"Yeah. I mean, he didn't want to force it on me or anything, but...." He stopped when he saw the hard expression on Antonio's face. "But if you're uncomfortable with that," Cary continued quickly, "I understand."

Please. Tell me.

Antonio rubbed the bridge of his nose, then pursed his lips. "I had hoped this might go differently," he said with a gentle sigh.

Cary tried to look surprised. "What do you mean?"

"I'd prefer he not stay."

For a moment, Cary said nothing. *Deep breath.* "Why not?"

"I don't think it's a good idea."

"I don't understand. Why wouldn't it—"

The glass door to the living room opened, and John stepped out onto the balcony. "Sorry," he said with a yawn, "I didn't realize it was so late. Mind if I join you for breakfast?"

"Not at all," Antonio said as he sprang to his feet. "I was about to leave for work. Please, take my chair."

"Are you sure?" asked John.

"Absolutely." Antonio turned to Cary and said, "I hope you enjoy your day. Francesca's taking Massi to his grandmother's, so there's no need to pick him up at school."

Cary opened his mouth to speak, but Antonio had already walked into the apartment and shut the door behind him.

"Did I interrupt something?" John asked, looking a bit shamefaced. "I didn't mean—"

"It's nothing." Cary stared at the glass doors in shock. "It wasn't important."

CARY finished practicing around one o'clock, then straightened the apartment up, popping some of Massimo's clothes into the wash. It was Roberta's day off, and he knew she'd appreciate the head start. Cary found he actually liked to help clean the apartment when he had the time, a fact that surprised him.

"Sorry," John said as he strode into the apartment a few minutes later. "I got a little lost."

"No problem." Cary, dressed in sweats, now lay on the floor with his hands behind his neck. "I thought I'd do a few crunches while I had the chance. If you want to go out, I can shower and—"

"I'm good," John interrupted as he pulled off his jacket and sat down heavily on the couch.

"Something to drink?"

"Something cold. Beer, if you've got it."

"Sure." Cary got up off the floor and went to the kitchen, wiping his forehead with a towel as he walked. He tossed the towel onto a chair, then opened the refrigerator and poked about, looking for the bottles he had seen Roberta put inside the day before. There were none.

A vague thought crossed Cary's mind. Something he felt he was missing. And then it was gone, and he just rubbed his eyes and stuck his head into the living room. "No beer. Pellegrino?"

John hesitated. "Nah. I'll make myself some coffee while you take your shower."

Half an hour later, Cary emerged from the shower, toweling off his hair. John was closing one of the cabinets in the living room, his coffee sitting on the table. "There's enough for you, if you want. On the stove."

"Thanks." Cary noted with some surprise the unique scent of cognac on the air as he walked into the kitchen. David's cognac. He frowned, then, deciding he had imagined it, poured himself some coffee and joined his father on the couch.

"Find what you were looking for at the store?"

"I got a few knickknacks to bring home. Promised my neighbor I'd find a snow globe for his collection," he explained. "The clerks at the first few stores I went to looked at me like I was crazy, but I finally found it near the train station."

As Cary sat down, a photograph on the side table caught his eye: a photo of him and Antonio in Switzerland with Massimo perched atop his father's shoulders. Smiling. All of them.

He sighed. Audibly, apparently, because John asked, "You all right?"

"Did something happen between you and Tonino?" Cary hadn't meant to voice the question, but he needed to know. If he couldn't learn the truth from Antonio, maybe John would tell him.

"Like what?"

"I don't know… it's just that I mentioned I wanted you to stay, and he seemed…." Cary struggled for a word to convey his concern but not put the blame on Antonio. "Uncomfortable with it." *Not really uncomfortable. Adamant, really.*

"I'm sorry," John said. "I'm getting in the way of your relationship, aren't I?" He finished his coffee and set it back on the table.

"No, that's not it," Cary protested. "It's just that—"

"It's okay, son. Really." John's smile appeared forced "We have this time together. And you'll be back to New York to play in the fall. I understand he wants you for himself."

The words took Cary aback. Did Antonio want him for himself? No, it made no sense.

That's not Antonio. He's not like that. Is he?

He was about to protest when the phone rang. "Excuse me," he told John. "Georges said he'd call to discuss a Japanese tour for next year. I need to take this. We can talk some more tonight, over dinner." But he knew they wouldn't, not unless he brought it up. He didn't want to; it was easier just to avoid the subject. It was also a mistake, and he knew it.

ANTONIO looked up from his book and smiled as Cary walked into the bedroom. It was nearly six, and Roberta had left minutes before, having finished her marketing and set the table for dinner. "Back so soon?" he asked.

"Are you implying I've stayed out beyond my curfew again?" Cary snapped. "Because I wasn't aware I had one."

For the past three hours, he had been shopping with his father. With each passing hour, he had grown more and more irritated with Antonio. He was just about to explode.

"I didn't mean to imply anything by it," Antonio countered with a bewildered expression. "Where's John?"

"Out." The answer was clipped and barely civil. "He said he wanted to do a little shopping. You know, for gifts to bring home."

"Oh."

"Happy?"

"About what?" Antonio asked.

"That he's leaving Sunday." Cary folded his arms across his chest and stood with his back against the door.

"No. Not particularly."

"Really? Because the way you've been acting, I find that hard to believe."

"I'm sorry if I gave you that impression," Antonio said with apparent regret. "It's complicated. I didn't mean—"

"What kind of impression did you expect me to get? You've told me you don't want him to stay. What do you want me to think, Tonino?"

"It's not a simple thing. It's—"

"Complicated," Cary finished. "Yeah, I know. You've told me. A bunch of times. But you see, if there's something to understand, then it would be helpful if you'd fucking *explain* it to me. Don't treat me like some kid and give me some bullshit."

"I didn't mean to... I don't think you're a child, caro—"

"Then stop treating me like one. And don't call me that." The words tumbled from his lips, unbidden. Until that moment, Cary hadn't realized how truly angry he was.

"All right." Antonio's tone was even and controlled, but Cary could see the tension in his body.

Cary strode across the room, stopped just shy of the bathroom, and rounded on Antonio. "Dammit, Tonino. I'm so pissed at you right now, I can't even...." He took a deep breath, then blew air from between his tight lips. "I understand you might not tell Massi why he can't do something, but this"—he fought the inclination to yell—"I... I don't get it. You tell me you want my father to leave, and then you conveniently avoid telling me *why*."

"It's—"

"This has something to do with *him*, doesn't it?" Cary interrupted. If he heard the word "complicated" one more time, he was sure he was going to scream.

He understood now. It was that word, "complicated," that had jarred his understanding. He'd only heard Antonio use that word when he brought up the subject of Massi's namesake.

"This has to do with Massimo. Your lover."

"What?" Antonio's startled expression told Cary he was spot on.

"That's it, isn't it? This has to do with *him*." Even though he was angry, the stricken look on Antonio's face made his stomach clench with guilt. He wanted to tell Antonio he was sorry, that he didn't mean to hurt him. But he knew just as surely that he needed to confront the other man's ghost. *They* needed to do it. Together.

Oh God. I love him so much.

The old fear was back again with a vengeance. Why would Antonio stay around for *this*? And if he knew Cary had eavesdropped on Antonio's conversation with John…. But even as the thought crossed his mind, Cary's anger flared once more.

"You *owe* me an explanation, Tonino. I know you don't want to talk about it, but it's making me crazy, this bullshit. You can't have it both ways. You can't drop these mega hints about John, then refuse to talk to me about why you want him to leave." He sat down on the bed. "Please. Tell me. I don't want to lose you."

I can't *lose you. It would kill me.*

For the first time since they'd met, Cary saw pain in Antonio's eyes—not hidden beneath the usually controlled exterior but raw and pulsating there.

"You're right." Antonio's voice was brittle with emotion. "I owe it to you. But I can't tell you what to do."

It had always been Antonio who had supported him; he had been the stronger one. But this time, it was Cary who moved to embrace Antonio, checking his anger long enough to regain control. "I love you."

More than you know.

Antonio extricated himself from the embrace. His expression was tender, his eyes filled with tears. "It's not my place to tell you what you should do. But I won't have him here. I…."

"I'm listening." Even as he spoke the words, Cary could already guess at what Antonio would say.

He's not the only one who's been avoiding things. This isn't just about Massimo. It's about John, and you know it.

Antonio's bittersweet smile mirrored the profound pain in his eyes. "I was so young when I met Massimo. He was a professor at the university. He was nearly fifteen years older." He sighed and pushed a stray lock of hair from his forehead.

"I knew I had to be with him. He was handsome, intelligent, and he had a wonderful sense of humor." Antonio laughed softly. "He told me I was too young for him, and ignored me. Or, I should say, he *tried* to ignore me. I can be very persistent."

Cary squeezed Antonio's hand. "I know."

"It took six months, but he finally went out with me. A few months later, we moved in together. People at school talked, but he had never been my teacher, so it died down pretty quickly. I graduated a few years later. Those first few years were some of the best of my life.

"He taught archeology, and I traveled with him when I wasn't in school. We spent summers in Greece. A few years later, I started my law studies. At first I worried it would be difficult for him—I was so busy. But we were happy, even then."

Cary swallowed hard. He wasn't sure what part of this he didn't want to hear. That Antonio had been happy with someone else? That he obviously still grieved the loss?

No. That's not it, and you know it. This is about John and about what you yourself already suspect.

"Massimo's sister became ill. She was young—not even your age—and he adored her. She was in and out of the hospital for more than a year. I watched what it did to him... and when she died... it nearly killed him too. I didn't know what to do...." He stood up abruptly and walked to the window. "I should have noticed," he said. "God, I should have seen it sooner. Maybe if I had...."

Cary got up from the couch and wrapped his arms around Antonio's waist. He had never seen Antonio cry before. Strange, how it felt good to comfort him rather than to be the one receiving the comfort.

"It's all right," he said, unsure of what to say and just as sure he needed to say *something*.

"No. It's not all right." Antonio wiped his eyes and turned around to look directly at Cary. "Because I *knew*. All along. I saw the signs. The bottles of alcohol that disappeared. The way he would get drunk every time we went out to dinner. The way he acted at parties. How he would get angry with me about the smallest things."

Now Cary was sure what this was leading up to, and he felt ill at the realization.

"For two years, I told myself it was nothing. That he was depressed. That it would pass. I did nothing."

"But it wasn't your fault—"

"No. The drinking wasn't my fault. I realize that now. But you have to understand, Cary. I *saw* all these things, and I did *nothing*. I didn't say anything. I didn't try to stop him." Antonio brushed the spot where the scar began on the side of his body. "He died because I let him drive. I believed him when he said he was fine." He turned away once more, but this time Cary pulled him back and wiped away his tears with his fingers.

"I spent more than a month in the hospital and six months in rehab," he continued, his voice now a detached monotone. "The driver and passengers in the other car survived. I think if they hadn't...."

Antonio shook his head, then added in an undertone, "I asked you once what it was about music that you loved so much."

Cary nodded.

"When I was in the hospital, music kept me going. I know it sounds strange, but I think it saved my life. It was the only thing that seemed to make sense to me. To give me comfort."

Something in Antonio's words resonated with Cary, and he began to cry. How many times had he thought the same thing?

"I still don't see how you can blame yourself," Cary said after a moment.

He had expected to be interrupted again, but Antonio only shook his head. "I *knew* he needed help, but when he told me I was wrong—that he was fine—I should have done something. Instead, I closed my eyes. And I hated myself."

"You think John is an alcoholic." The minute Cary spoke the words, he knew they were true.

"What do *you* believe, Cary?"

"I... I...," he stammered. "I'm not sure what to believe."

"Have you asked him why he left your mother?"

"No." It was true, Cary reasoned. He hadn't asked, even if he'd heard the answer.

"He told me the same thing he told you when you first met him. About how difficult life was for them around the time you were born. But he also told me your mother said he was an alcoholic. And he denied it."

So that *was the part of the conversation I missed.*

Cary remembered the beer that had disappeared so quickly, the smell of cognac in John's coffee, the chewing gum, the nights John would disappear to "take a walk" and come back smelling of stale cigarettes and booze, then explain it away by saying the café had been smoky.

"Even if it's true, what am I supposed to do about it?" He knew he sounded like a child, but he couldn't help himself. "I'm worried about him."

"I know. And you should tell him that. Talk to him."

"And then what?"

"I can't tell you what to do. I *won't* tell you what to do." Cary relaxed a little as Antonio held him tighter. "I know you want me to."

Cary laughed. "You know me too well."

Antonio's eyes glittered in the fading light from outside. "And I know you love me."

"Yeah. You're right."

Oh God. When did things get so difficult?

"Thanks," Cary said after he kissed the rest of Antonio's tears away.

"For what?"

Cary smiled up at Antonio. "For letting me decide. And for loving me."

CHAPTER 23

CHOOSING SIDES

"YOUR mother lied. I don't deny I drank, but I'm not an alcoholic and I never *have* been. Have you ever seen me drunk?"

"No," Cary said, "but—"

"Where is this coming from, Cary? Have I done something to upset you?"

"No. I'm just wor—"

"Then why would you even ask me about this?" John's eyes were fixed on his, and Cary felt suddenly very small—like a petulant child deserving to be chastised.

"I… I'm sorry," he stammered. "I just want to understand what happened between you and Mom."

The noise in the restaurant seemed at once louder, more strident to Cary's ears. He wished Antonio were here with him. As angry and confused as he was, Antonio's quiet strength would have made this entire conversation so much easier.

No. Tonino was right. This is something I have to do on my own.

John Redding sighed and replaced his glass of wine on the table. "I've already told you what happened, son. Obviously Antonio has been taking my words out of context."

"I think he's concerned, that's all. So am I."

"Has it occurred to you that maybe he has a reason to interpret what I've said in a particular way?"

"What?" Cary frowned and bit his lower lip. "I don't understand."

"All I'm saying is maybe he has a reason to make it sound as though I have a problem."

"Why? Why would he do that?" It wasn't like Antonio, he told himself.

"I think he knows I want you to come home with me when I leave on Sunday. To the States."

"With you?" Cary forgot to breathe. Antonio had said nothing about this when they had spoken the night before. "But my home is here...."

"Just hear me out," John said as he refilled their wine glasses. "I'm not suggesting you leave for good, but we both know I can't stay here. There's no work for me in Europe."

"But you could work remotely," Cary protested. "Lots of people do that these days."

"We both know Antonio doesn't want me to stay." Until that moment, Cary had thought he was impervious to the power of words, or at least thick-skinned enough that the pain was tolerable. But these words—John's words—hurt more than anything he had ever experienced before. Even worse, it was the truth. All along, Cary realized he had sensed this coming, and now....

Please don't make me choose between you.

It was the first time he had realized that what was lurking around the next darkened corner was true pain. It didn't matter if he stayed or if he left; either way, he would lose.

"I think Antonio's just—"

"He's jealous. He's afraid of losing you. He said it himself."

Is that true? Is he afraid? But there's no real choice here, is there? I can't lose him, no matter what. I just can't....

"This is my home, John. I can't leave. I love him. I love Massi. They're my family too."

"You know I'd never judge you," John said. "I only want what's best for you. But what happens when things get rough? You can't get married to him. And Massimo isn't yours; he never will be. What happens when you grow apart? He leaves with Massimo and you're all alone. What happens then—"

"No." Cary stood up abruptly, knocking over his wine glass. The red liquid ran over the tablecloth and splashed onto his shirt. He didn't care. "I want to know you better, John. I want a relationship with you. I really do. But I can't—I *won't*—leave Tonino."

He pulled a few large bills out of his pocket and set them down on the restaurant table. He wasn't hungry anymore, and he couldn't sit here, not after all that had been said. He needed to think. He needed Antonio so badly it hurt.

"I'll see you back at the apartment later, John," he said, striding away from the table even as he spoke the words. "I'm sorry. Really, I am."

CARY leaned over the balcony railing. He didn't realize that he was gripping the metal so tightly until he saw his knuckles were white. He stood there, shivering in the cool evening air, for nearly an hour after vomiting up what little food he had eaten at lunch. Antonio hadn't been home. Had he said he had a dinner appointment? Cary couldn't remember now, his thoughts were so scattered after the conversation with John.

Antonio? Jealous of his father?

It's not true, and you know it. You know him. Is Tonino afraid to lose me?

There was something that rang true in John's words. And Massimo. Was John right? If Antonio left him—and God knew he wasn't the best catch, with his traveling and his past history—would that be it?

Stop it! You don't need a fucking marriage certificate to make a relationship permanent. They had committed to each other, hadn't they? *Tonino isn't leaving.*

The glass doors behind him opened. "Hey, you," Cary said as he turned around.

"You okay?" asked Antonio.

Cary nodded.

"Want to talk about it?"

Cary let out a long breath. "He asked me to come back with him. To New York."

"Oh."

For a moment Cary stared at Antonio, stunned at his response.

"That's *it*?" he said at last. "Just 'oh'? Maybe you should just say 'ciao' and be done with it."

"No," Antonio said, obviously struggling. "Not that. Never. But I don't want to—"

"Tell me what you want, Tonino." Cary's voice broke. "Don't just stand there and tell me you don't want to interfere. Tell me, dammit. Tell me what you want. I need to know."

I need to know you want me to stay.

Antonio's eyes filled with tears. "Please," he whispered. "Don't leave. I don't know what I'd do if you left."

Cary swallowed hard, then took Antonio in his arms and embraced him tightly. "I'm not leaving." He was surprised at how his voice didn't waver when he said it.

"Oh, caro…," Antonio whispered against his ear. "You don't know how much I hoped you'd say that."

"Then tell me."

"It means everything that you'll stay. Everything."

"I could never leave you, Tonino. I realized that tonight. You and Massi… you're my life and my home. You're what inspires me."

"You already decided, didn't you?" Antonio asked, pulling back and searching Cary's face.

"Yeah, I guess I had. I just didn't realize it." Was this him talking? Bang-Me-in-the-Bathroom Redding? The man who had sworn over and over that he didn't want a relationship? The man who hated kids? When had he changed? Why hadn't he noticed?

"Somehow," Cary continued, his mind a whirl of thoughts, "hearing you say you wanted me to stay… I guess I needed to hear you say that to know for sure. I know it's stupid, but I worry… you know… that I'm selfish, and maybe you'll figure it out and—"

Antonio's kiss was crushing, and every thought in Cary's mind fled with the onslaught of emotion the kiss evoked.

"Will you come with me? To visit him in New York?" he asked a moment later, still in Antonio's embrace. "I've got a concert in August at Lincoln Center. I still want to see John again."

"Of course." Antonio looked at him with something approaching admiration. "I'd love to. And maybe we can bring Massi this time. He keeps asking about coming to hear you play. He's never been to New York, and he's out of school then."

"Really?" Cary nearly bounced up and down, but he stopped himself when he realized he was acting just like Massimo might. "Because I could get tickets to a Yankees game, and we could take him to the Bronx Zoo, and—"

Another kiss.

"Stop that," Cary chastised with a sloppy grin. *As if I want him to stop!*

"Not happening." Antonio kissed him again. "Ever."

"I love you, you romantic Italian fool."

"Isn't it about time to get ready for dinner?"

"Dessert before dinner," Cary announced as he dragged Antonio inside and toward their bedroom. "We've got about two hours before Roberta and Massi get back from Francesca's."

Antonio grinned outright as Cary took him by the hand and led him inside to their bedroom. Cary closed the door behind them, seated Antonio on the bed, and stood in the middle of the room, facing him.

"Tell me what you want."

"What?" Antonio asked with obvious surprise.

"Tell me what you want me to do." Cary looked at Antonio in silent challenge.

"I don't need—"

"Tell me what you want me to do to you." Cary wasn't angry; he knew this was difficult for Antonio. "I don't want to guess. I want to hear it. Tell me, Tonino. How do you want me to make love to you?"

Antonio did not immediately respond, but Cary could see understanding in his eyes. "Take your shirt off," he said, his voice a sensual undertone.

Cary complied in silence. "What now?" he asked.

Antonio took a deep breath and appeared to consider the question. He leaned back against the pillows. "Come closer to the bed," he said at last. "And take your clothes off. Slowly. I want to look at you."

"Shit, Tonino, I—"

"You told me to ask for what I want."

Cary said nothing but pulled his shirt over his head. He waited until he saw the look of approval in Antonio's eyes, then trailed his hand down his belly to the button on his jeans. He was already hard in anticipation. He was also a little embarrassed. Bang-Me-in-the-Bathroom Redding was self-conscious about his body. It was a surprise.

"I'm waiting. I told you to take all your clothes off."

Holy shit. Cary unzipped his jeans and pushed them down, along with his briefs, then stepped out of them and stood at the foot of the bed. Waiting. For a moment, Antonio said nothing, just bit his lip. Cary tried to relax, but every muscle in his body was screaming to be fucked and his cock stood at attention.

When Antonio didn't speak, Cary said, "What do you—"

"Touch yourself, caro. Pretend it's me touching you."

Cary swallowed hard. He felt his heart pound against his ribs and took a deep breath to steady himself.

"And don't come until I tell you to," Antonio added as the ghost of a smile danced on his lips.

"Okay." Cary's voice sounded rough to his own ears as he took his cock in his hands and began to stroke it.

Antonio unbuttoned his own shirt. It fell open to reveal his chest, and he reached up to his neck and began to stroke the skin there with his fingers in a slow, sensual pattern. Cary blew air from between his lips and swallowed again. "God, Tonino, you're going to make me come like—"

"You can't come until I tell you to," Antonio reminded him. He was smiling outright now.

"I think you're enjoying this way too much."

"You're the one who said I should tell you what I want. And right now, I want to hear you, caro. But I don't want you to talk."

It wasn't as though Cary had to try very hard to make a sound. He'd practically been panting up until that moment. So when Antonio undid the fly of his pants and reached beneath the fabric, Cary didn't even try to stifle his moan.

Antonio was obviously pleased, because he began to stroke himself, matching Cary's movements. "Come closer," he said. "Onto the bed. But stay at the end of it, and keep touching yourself."

Cary complied, kneeling at the end of the bed. He ached, wanting to come but knowing he wouldn't, not without Antonio's permission. It was hotter, he realized, than the bar had ever been, denying himself like this.

Antonio shimmied out of his pants, so he was now as naked as Cary. Without looking away, Antonio reached into the drawer at the bedside and pulled out the bottle of lube they kept there. He shoved a pillow under his hips, emptied a good amount of the lube on his hand, tossed the bottle onto the other pillow, and covered himself with the slippery liquid. His left hand strayed back beneath himself, and Cary gasped audibly in response.

"So fucking sexy...," Cary hissed.

"I want you to fuck me." Cary realized he must have frozen in place at these words, because Antonio just laughed and reminded him, "You're supposed to be touching yourself."

"You... you...," Cary stammered. "You want...?"

"I want you to fuck me." Antonio's expression was full of heat. Cary had no doubt his lover wanted this. Even more of a surprise: Cary wanted it too.

"Oh hell, yes." In the year and a half they'd been together, Cary had never topped. It wasn't as if Antonio never offered, but Cary had always been more comfortable with their traditional roles when making love. Until now.

"Then get over here and show me you want it."

Cary didn't hesitate. As Antonio continued to stroke himself, Cary traced his fingers over Antonio's chest and downward, behind Antonio's cock, and pressed a finger inside Antonio's hole.

"*Ti voglio scopare.*" Cary's voice was a low rumble. *I want to fuck you.* He'd heard the words before, but he'd never spoken them himself. He worked a second finger inside as Antonio kept pulling and fisting himself, then added his own hand to Antonio's. He could see the struggle on Antonio's face—he wanted to come, but he, too, would wait. "So fucking hot...." English, this time, as Cary's Italian failed him.

"That's it," Antonio encouraged Cary. "More. Harder." Cary fucked Antonio with three fingers now.

"You're so tight." Cary's voice sounded like a growl to his own ears.

"It's been a while." Antonio's laugh became a moan. "Fuck me now, caro. I want you inside."

Cary pushed Antonio's legs up and pressed his cock to Antonio's entrance, pausing there just a moment so he could see Antonio's face.

"Do it. Fuck me."

Cary pushed inside and felt the tight muscles clench around him. He looked at Antonio again.

"Do it," Antonio repeated.

This time, Cary didn't stop but pressed himself inward until he was seated deep inside. He had to stop and catch his breath—Antonio hadn't given him permission to come yet, he reminded himself. It was almost more than he could bear. He was so turned on. He guessed that Antonio was nearly as close as he, because he, too, was still, his expression one of focus and concentration.

"Move," Antonio commanded after a moment.

"You feel so good around me, so warm," Cary murmured as he slowly pulled out, then pushed back in. "But I don't think I can last long. I—"

"Then come, when you're ready. And tell me when you're coming so I can come too."

Cary didn't need any more encouragement. He moved faster now, letting himself go at last. He leaned forward so that their cheeks touched. He felt the hint of stubble on Antonio's cheek and heard Antonio's panted breaths close to his ear. "Caro," Antonio moaned. "Oh, caro."

"I'm coming," Cary said as he held fast to Antonio's legs and felt his thighs burn with effort. "It feels so fucking good. God, Tonino!" He felt the spasm run from his body to Antonio's as both of them clung to each other, shuddering, shaking, panting. He released his grip just long enough to free Antonio's legs, then fell on top of him, the sweat and come hot between them. Their breaths, at first ragged, relaxed and slowed, but they held each other still. Cary didn't want to let go, and he guessed Antonio felt the same. At some point, Cary drifted off, feeling safe and warm against his lover's body.

"WHAT made you decide?" Antonio asked as he held Cary in his arms an hour later.

They had showered and ended up back in bed, pressed up against each other. The feel of Antonio's naked body against his made Cary's heart warm. He'd never felt so safe. So *sure*. Even the ache in his heart—the pain of impending loss when John returned home—was bearable now.

"To stay here?"

"Yes."

"It's all the kid's fault," Cary said with a chuckle.

"How's that?"

"I kept on thinking, 'How can I leave when I promised Massi I'd stay?'"

"For someone who hates kids," Antonio pointed out, "you seem to care for him a great deal."

"I couldn't do it to him." Cary found it hard to choke out the words. "I know I'm not his father, but I couldn't do it. Not after what Justin and I went through." Then he added, in a whisper, "And I couldn't do it to you. Or us. *T'i voglio, Tonino. T'amo. Sempre.*"

I want you. I love you. Always.

"BYE-BYE!" Massimo shouted in English from his perch on Cary's shoulders. "Have a safe trip!"

John Redding waved back from his place in line at security.

"Will he come back, Cary?" Massi asked, once more speaking in Italian.

"Would you like that, Stinker?"

Cary looked up to see Massimo nodding happily. The kid was really getting too big for this, but Cary didn't mind that his shoulders would be sore later on—Cary knew it would be too soon that Massimo would be too big to carry. He'd savor this moment, as he'd done so many the past few weeks.

"Maybe. But we'll see him in July, remember?"

Massimo bent down so that his nose was pressed against Cary's face. "I wouldn't forget *that*! Papà says we're going to the top of the Empire State Building, and we'll go to a zoo in Central Park, and a big, *big* toy store— bigger than anything here in Italy." He continued on happily as they walked out of the terminal and into the bright sunshine of a spring day.

In the end, John had taken Cary's rejection better than Cary had expected. Maybe he had seen the determination in Cary's eyes, or maybe he was simply too tired to argue. Either way, John had not pressed the issue, although he had carefully avoided Antonio his last day in Milan. It had been a relief for Cary that Antonio had a meeting scheduled and couldn't come to the airport to see John off. It would be better, he told himself, if things had time to quiet down a bit between John and Antonio. Knowing Antonio as he did, Cary had no doubt the trip to New York in the summer would be fine.

It's good, thought Cary as he brushed away the sadness at having said goodbye to John. *It's all good.*

CHAPTER 24

THE MORE THINGS CHANGE

Milan, Italy—November

"*...TANTI auguri*, Massi, *Tanti auguri a te!*"

The sound of singing greeted Cary as he peered through the door of their apartment. From where he stood, he saw Francesca at the edge of the living room, and he put a single finger to his lips. She smiled and nodded ever so slightly to acknowledge him, then winked.

"Massi, caro, there's another gift for you," she said. Massimo's face lit up, and she pointed to the door. "It's there, but you have to go get it." She gave him a gentle push in the direction of the entrance.

"I don't see anything—"

"Happy birthday, Massi!" Cary shouted as he opened the door wide. Massimo ran up to him and jumped into his arms, causing Cary to stumble a bit. "Oh, good Lord, you're getting big!"

"Cary Papà! Papà said you were in Amsterdam until tomorrow night."

"I took an earlier flight. I didn't want to miss your eighth birthday."

Massimo got back on his feet and trotted happily back to the dining room, shouting, "Papà! Papà! Cary is home!"

"Welcome back," Antonio said, planting a kiss on Cary's lips and following Massimo back toward the table. Roberta had begun to cut the cake she'd baked for the occasion, a strawberry torte which made Cary's mouth water. "I'm glad you were able to make it."

"We wrapped up the recording last night. I pushed them a little. The engineer was pretty pissed until someone told him why I needed to leave this morning. Then he pushed them all harder. Turns out he's got a four-year-old daughter he doesn't get to see enough."

"Here's your cake, Cary!" Massimo pushed a plate into his hands.

"What? We don't get to give you your birthday present first?" Cary looked at Antonio and smiled. They had been planning this for months, and Cary had finally found what he'd been looking for in Amsterdam.

"But Papà already gave me a present." Massimo studied them both with suspicion.

"This gift is from both of us. Something your dad and I want you to have. Something really special." Cary turned and walked back out to the front hallway, where he had left his suitcase.

Two children dashed by them, nearly colliding with Antonio, who laughed and suggested, "Maybe we should go into your bedroom, Massi."

Massi's eyes widened. "It must be really, *really* special."

Cary nodded solemnly and winked at Antonio so Massimo would see. Massimo clapped his hands and was seated on the small bed in his room a few moments later, fidgeting in anticipation.

Cary set the oblong package down on the bed. The wrapping at the edges had begun to rip but had survived the airplane otherwise intact. Massimo didn't care; he tore into the wrapping with his usual enthusiasm and looked back up at the two men with a questioning look.

"Go ahead, Stinker," Cary prodded. "Open it."

"But, it looks like…," Massimo began.

"Open it, Massi. It's yours." Antonio took Cary's hand in his; the joy in those blue eyes made Cary's heart swell.

Massi ran his small hand tentatively over the case, pausing at the handle, then moving on to touch the closure in the center and the two silver latches on either side. He flipped one latch and then the next, then tried the center one. It was locked.

"Here, Stinker. You might need this." Cary handed Massimo a small key, which Massimo fit into the lock and turned, releasing the mechanism. He pushed the small button to the side of the lock, and the case opened with an audible *click*.

"Oh… oh… oh," Massimo mouthed as he lifted the red crushed velvet cover and gently held up the violin. "It's… it's so… cool!"

Massimo had been asking for a violin for more than a year, but seeing how delicately he handled the instrument now, Cary knew Antonio had been right when he'd said they should wait.

"Go ahead, Massi," he said. "You know what to do. Remember what Alex taught you."

Massimo nodded and put the violin back down, then retrieved the bow from its well, tightened it, then found the cake of rosin in one of the compartments on the bottom. He gingerly ran the horsehair over the rosin until Cary nodded; then he replaced the rosin and picked up the violin and put it under his chin. His eyes widened as he felt the instrument against his skin.

"It fits me!" he shouted. "Not big like Alex's."

"It's a half-size violin," Cary explained. He wouldn't tell Massimo it had taken him more than six months to track down a good European instrument. There had been plenty of inexpensive Chinese-made fiddles available, but he had wanted this to be special.

"Are you going to be my teacher?"

"It's not the same as a cello, so I wouldn't be very good at that. But we've got you a teacher."

"Alex?" Massimo asked brightly. "Is Alex going to teach me?"

Cary chuckled. "He'd probably like to, but you need lessons every week, and he's not in Milan often enough."

Massimo looked a bit crestfallen.

"But he's given us the name of a teacher here. Her name is Signora Riccardo. Your first lesson is this week."

Massimo put the violin and bow back down in the case, then flung his arms around Cary. "Thank you *so* much, Cary Papà!" A moment later, he did the same to Antonio. "This is the best birthday!" He then zoomed out of the bedroom to tell Francesca and Roberta and the other children about his gift.

"I still hate kids," Cary told Antonio.

"Right. You keep telling yourself that and maybe you'll believe it."

Late that same night, Cary slept with his face pressed against Antonio's back. The telephone rang, and Cary rolled over in the darkness to pick up the handset.

"Who is it?" mumbled Antonio, half-asleep.

"Not sure. US number." *It's about 3:00 a.m. here. That'd make it about 9:00 p.m. in the States.* They got a few of these calls, mostly for Cary— people who couldn't keep the time difference straight. "Hello?"

"Is this Cary Redding?" The voice on the other end of the line was unfamiliar.

"Yes. Who is this?"

"This is New York Presbyterian Hospital. We have you listed as an emergency contact for John Redding."

"What's wrong?" Antonio was now sitting up in bed, watching him with growing concern.

"Is he okay?"

"He's stable."

"*Stable?*" Cary choked out.

"He's had a heart attack, Mr. Redding."

Oh God….

THE roar of the engines was less pronounced here, in first class. Antonio had insisted he pay the extra money to upgrade. "You'll need to rest, caro. Once you get to New York, you'll want to be with him."

He reached into his small bag to find his iPod, thinking the music might help him sleep. His hand closed around something hard, and he pulled out a small metal airplane. *Massi.* He smiled, realizing Massimo had slipped it into the bag without him knowing.

He missed Massimo already. And Massi's father. Cary traveled all the time, but this was different. This time, he wasn't performing, although he had taken his cello.

The flight attendant stopped by to check on him. "Would you like some help with your seat?"

"Sure, thanks." He stood up as she converted his seat to a bed, then set out a sheet, pillow, and blanket.

Settled back in again a few minutes later, he stuck the earphones in and selected Alex's recording of Bach's unaccompanied violin works. The hard metal of the airplane poked him from where he'd put it in his pants pocket. He pulled it out and forced himself to close his eyes, still clutching the toy in his hand.

"MR. REDDING?" The woman who looked up from the nurse's station in the cardiac intensive care unit smiled reassuringly.

"Yes."

"Your father's in room five. He's doing fine. Dr. Sylvester will be by later on, and he can fill you in."

"Can I see him?"

"Of course. We've got a cot set up in the room, if you need to rest. My supervisor said you flew in from Milan this afternoon."

"Thanks," he told her. He had checked into the hotel to drop his bag and his cello off, take a quick shower, and change before coming to the hospital. Sleep was the last thing on his mind, but he guessed John wouldn't be going home for at least a few days.

"My name's Michelle. I'm your father's day nurse. Cathy is on the night shift."

"Thanks, Michelle. I appreciate your help."

She opened the door to a room a few yards from the nursing station. "Mr. Redding?" she said as they walked inside. "You have a visitor." Then she turned to Cary and added, "Press the call button if you need anything."

"Thanks."

Cary got his first look at John, lying in the bed, hooked up to half a dozen different devices and IV lines. An oxygen tube was taped below his nose, his face drawn and pale. The memory of Cary's mother's death resurfaced with the familiar surroundings, and Cary took a deep breath to counter his nausea. He was afraid, he realized. He had just gotten to know John again. He wasn't ready to lose him like he had lost her.

He's doing fine, he reminded himself. *This isn't the same.*

"Cary." John's face brightened. "I didn't expect to see you here."

"The hospital called." *When was it? Last night?* Cary's brain felt sluggish as he tried to take in the scene. "I caught the first flight out."

"You shouldn't have." John's face said otherwise; he was obviously pleased Cary had come.

"How are you feeling?" Cary sat down beside the bed.

"Better than yesterday," John said with a chuckle. "At least the elephant on my chest is gone."

"I'm glad. Have they told you how long they're going to keep you here?"

"Doc says if everything looks okay, I might be able to go home Friday. How long are you staying in town?"

"I've cleared my schedule for the next few weeks. Do you have someone who can help you out once you're released?"

"Nah. Don't worry. I'll be fine. Always have been."

"I'll help."

"Really? You'd do that? But what will Antonio say?"

"He understands." This time, Cary realized he felt no guilt. He had believed Antonio when he had said to take as much time as he needed to be with John. For once, he hadn't worried, either, that his partner would be angry or disappointed. He knew Antonio would be waiting for him when he returned home.

"ARE you John's son?"

"Cary Redding." Cary offered the doctor his hand as they stood in the doorway outside John's room. "Nice to meet you."

"I'm Frank Sylvester, your father's cardiologist. I've heard a great deal about you, and not just from your father. I heard you play at Carnegie Hall last year. I'm a bit of a fan."

"Thanks." Cary forced a smile. "So how's he doing?"

"Why don't we go somewhere a bit more private? The waiting room's empty."

Cary nodded and followed the doctor down the hallway.

"Please, have a seat," Frank Sylvester said, gesturing to the waiting room couch a few moments later and sitting down in a chair facing Cary. "Before I go into any detail," he continued, "I did want to let you know he's doing much better now that you're here. Depression is a real concern with patients like your father after a serious cardiac event."

"I have to admit I've been worried about him for a while. And when I got the call…."

"He's probably told you that we plan on releasing him Friday, assuming things continue to improve. But he's still pretty weak, and he'll need some help with cooking, cleaning—that sort of thing."

"I'm planning on staying for the foreseeable future. At least until he's doing well enough to be on his own again."

"That's great. He'll need the support."

"What's his prognosis?" Cary asked as he rubbed his eyes. "I mean, long-term?"

"That will depend entirely upon him." The doctor closed his clipboard and met Cary's eyes, then paused for a moment, as if considering how to broach the topic. "What do you know about his drinking?"

Cary let out a slow breath. "Only that he's probably been drinking for a long time. I didn't know him growing up. We only reconnected about a year ago. When I suggested he might need some help, he shut me down."

"The heart attack isn't unconnected to his drinking," the doctor explained. "His diagnosis is alcoholic cardiomyopathy. Basically what that means is that the alcohol has damaged the heart muscle, so it doesn't pump as efficiently. His heart's enlarged. I've prescribed some medications to reduce the stress on his heart, but unless he makes some serious lifestyle changes, his condition will only get worse."

Shit. "What can I do to help?"

"Not much, I'm afraid. Make sure he takes his meds. If he decides to enroll in a twelve-step program, be supportive."

"*If* he decides?"

"Mr. Redding, you and I both know that if he doesn't want to stop drinking, there's little anyone can do to stop him."

"But—"

"He expressed some interest in attending an Alcoholics Anonymous meeting once he's feeling up to it. Encourage him to do it. Sometimes an event like this is what it takes for someone to make the decision to change."

Cary's relief was tempered by the look of something approaching pity he saw in the cardiologist's eyes.

"You can't make him change, Mr. Redding. All you can do is give him support. Remember that. And if you're so inclined, you may want to catch an Al-Anon meeting. It might be helpful for you."

Cary nodded. It wasn't as if the man's words were a surprise to him— he and Antonio had discussed the same thing. He understood it. Or at least, he thought he did. "Thank you," he said at last. "I'll do my best."

"Feel free to contact me if you have any questions, and by all means, make sure he keeps his appointments so I can monitor his progress. We'll get those scheduled before you take him home."

Cary shook the doctor's hand, then watched him leave the room.

You can't change him if he doesn't want to change. He had understood that months ago, when John had left Milan. So why was it so difficult for him to accept?

CHAPTER 25

OUT OF THE BOX

"GOING to your AA meeting?" Cary asked, looking up from his cello. He'd been sitting in the middle of John's tiny one-bedroom apartment, working on some arpeggios, when John emerged from the bedroom.

"I'll be back after dinner. I told Tom we'd take some time after to shoot the breeze and grab something to eat."

"No problem. I'll clean up while you're out. Tell Tom I said hey."

"Will do." John grabbed his coat from off the hook and was out the front door moments later.

It's good that he likes his sponsor. And Tom will make sure he eats well.

Distracted, he decided to straighten up the apartment and finish his practicing later. He'd gotten four solid hours of playing in already and didn't feel as pressed to do more as he often did by midafternoon.

He and John had been living together in the apartment since John had been released from the hospital nearly two weeks before. Cary had hired a cleaning service to come in once a week, but as promised, he had been doing most of the cooking and day-to-day chores as John slowly recovered.

He had been pleasantly surprised when John announced he would be attending his first AA meeting the past weekend. Surprised and relieved. He had also said very little to John about it other than to tell him he was happy to hear it. They had not talked about John's alcoholism—John had made it clear the topic was off-limits—although John had proceeded to make a show of ridding the house of any remaining alcohol after he'd returned from the AA meeting.

It was while he was making the bed that Cary first noticed the shoebox on John's dresser. It was a battered old box with a peeling sticker on the side marked "Style: Darla, Size 8.5, Black." There was a drawing of a woman's shoe, high-heeled, next to the writing. On the top was a yellow sticky-note that read:

> *J-*
>
> *I was cleaning out the house the other day and found this. Looks like Janet wanted you to have this.*
> *-Charlene*

Charlene? It had to be from his aunt, his mother's sister. *Of course she would have known about John.* The realization angered him. Not that his relationship with his mother's only sibling was a close one—they saw each other occasionally at Justin's house over Christmas—but still, the knowledge that his aunt had known the truth of John's existence when her sister's own children had not....

Stop it. It's over and done with.

He took a deep breath and blew the air out from between his lips, trying to release the tension in his jaw and neck. He nearly opened the box, but he stopped himself. *This isn't yours,* he told himself as he went back to making John's bed, folding the corners as his mother had taught him years before. He found the monotony of the chore surprisingly comforting.

As he set the pillows back at the top of the bed, the box once more caught his eye. It hadn't been there before; he was sure of it. *He knew I'd be coming in here. Did he mean for me to see this?* He ran his fingers lightly over the lid of the box, read the note again, and lifted the lid with a tentative hand.

The box was filled with papers, photographs, and newspaper clippings, most of them yellowing at the edges. His lips parted as he once more considered whether he should be going through John's personal belongings without his express permission. In the end, his curiosity won out. He would apologize to John later and ask him about the box. What harm could he do by simply reading its contents?

He sat down on the bed and emptied the box onto the bedspread, taking care to keep the items in the same order in which he had found them. The first envelope he opened contained legal documents: a copy of his parents' marriage license and a copy of the divorce decree. A beginning and an end. Also inside was a faded old Polaroid photograph of his parents on their wedding day. His mother looked beautiful in her wedding gown, and John looked young and full of life in his tux. John's resemblance to Justin was even more striking in this photo than in real life. Cary could see himself in that youthful face, as well, and the realization was unsettling.

The next piece of folded paper was a copy of his own birth certificate. Inside the folds, another photograph, this time of him as a baby. Behind that, a photo of Justin, and a photograph of the two of them: Justin a bright-eyed five-year-old sitting next to Cary, who was wrapped in a blanket. Justin was clowning around for the camera, sticking his tongue out at baby Cary.

Cary smiled. He had seen the photo before, but it had been years ago, after his mother's death, when he and Justin had cleaned out the house to get it ready to sell. Seeing Justin in the photograph reminded him that he should take Antonio and Massimo to St. Louis to meet his brother and his family. *You just never know. Sometimes tomorrow is too long to wait.*

He continued to leaf through the contents of the box. Mostly, he found photos of himself and Justin as children—school portraits, and even a photograph of himself when he had just begun his cello studies at four years old. He studied each picture and tried to recall when and where it had been taken, with little success. After reviewing several dozen photographs, he came to a small manila envelope stuffed to bursting with the word "Cary" written across the front. It was his mother's writing—he recognized the neat script.

He opened the clasp and gently emptied the envelope's contents: newspaper clippings. *His* clippings. From the sheer number of them, he guessed his mother had saved every article, review, or mention of Cary Taylor Redding, from his first performance in the elementary school auditorium, to his Chicago Symphony debut as a young teen, to the last performance his mother had attended, shortly after her cancer diagnosis. Every last one of the clippings was cut neatly from the newspaper and pasted onto a piece of lined notebook paper. Not so surprising, really, from the woman who had promoted her son at every available opportunity. And yet there was more here than he had expected, for when he flipped the first article over to put it back on the pile, he realized there was writing on the back: "Cary Redding. Four years old."

Cary's first concert, his mother had written. *Mrs. Filmore told me he was "cute as a button" and "a real star." I worried he might be anxious, playing in front of more than just his cello studio, but he did a lovely job. I know it was only "Twinkle, Twinkle," but he was so poised. So confident.*

He turned to the next article, which was about a young musician contest he had won at the local performing arts center, and turned it over. "Cary Redding. Six years old."

Cary played the Mozart sonatina beautifully. There was a moment when I think he realized the contest wasn't so different than playing in our living room. He just knew what the music wanted, and he gave himself over to it.

He had no recollection of the concert—from the date on the note, he had been about six years old—but the words surprised him. More than that: he was stunned his mother would even write something like that about a concert. He had always seen her as detached and critical to a fault. And yet the praise and the pride in his mother's words were evident.

He continued to read until he had gone through nearly half of the clippings, each with a sentence or two written on the back. His mother had never kept a diary, Cary knew, and now he understood why: these articles, and the notes scribbled on the back, had been her surrogate.

It struck Cary as strange that not one of them was critical of him or of his playing. At least not until he found the next article, the *Chicago Tribune* article reviewing his Chicago Symphony debut. He had no interest in reading the article itself; he rarely read his reviews, let alone ones from when he had been Cary Taylor Redding, child prodigy. On the back of this particular review, his mother had written four paragraphs.

"Cary Redding. Fourteen years old."

The trip to Chicago flew by. Justin didn't want to come, even though he's on break from Wash U. He's doing well in school and has decided to major in electrical engineering. He seems to be well past the adolescent rebellion of a few years ago. Cary, on the other hand, seems barreling toward it.

The concert was lovely. Cary's playing was the best I've heard from him, although to be fair, John Fuchs's conducting makes everyone sound better. Afterward, Cary was sullen and wouldn't talk to the people who had gathered backstage. I did my best to smooth over any uncomfortable interactions, but I worry that Maestro Fuchs may have been left with less than a good impression.

Sometimes I wonder if we should be doing this, taking him from place to place so he can play. He seems to enjoy it, but then he complains that he's not home with Justin, playing ball in the backyard. And then someone like Maestro Fuchs tells me Cary is a true talent, and that he's following in the steps of the greats like Mstislav Rostropovich, Janos Starker, and Yo-Yo Ma. He says Cary will have a career not only now but when he's older. But he has to stick with it.

John was at the concert again. He's living near Chicago. I was tempted to confront him and ask where the support checks have been, but I didn't want him around Cary. I know I have to do what I have to do, but I worry someday Cary will think it was wrong of me to take some of the money he earns to pay for our expenses. I also worry Cary will learn to hate music because he works so hard. But I don't know what else to do. I need to know that when I'm gone, he'll be able to support himself. He's not like his brother, who's good in school. Without his music, what would he do?

For a moment, he just stared at the writing. He smiled inwardly at the knowledge that John Fuchs hadn't been at all deterred by whatever teenage attitude he had displayed at the concert; he had played many more times during the conductor's tenure with the Chicago Symphony. It also wasn't a surprise to read that his playing had helped feed their family; he had always known that, and he hadn't begrudged her for it. His mother had never hidden it from him. No, it was the rest of the note that surprised him.

John had been there. *Again?* He remembered John saying something about retirement accounts and the mortgage on the house. He wondered how often John *had* sent his mother money. He remembered nights when she had barely slept and the mornings after, when she had home-schooled him, and the dark circles under her eyes. *How old was she when she died?* Just a few years older than David Somers. *Forty-four?* Far too young, really. He hadn't thought of it at the time—he had been so young himself that she *seemed* old.

He leafed through more of the articles, scanning the notes on the backs. Here and there, his mother had mentioned their finances. He stopped when he got to an article from a concert in Madison, Wisconsin. *John met me backstage, and I realized he had been drinking. He told me three months earlier he had stopped and begged me to take him back. I just couldn't do that to my boys. I couldn't take the chance.*

Without reading the rest of the notes on the backs of the intervening articles, he skipped forward to the last one. Cary Redding. Nineteen years old. *Cary and I drove to Chicago. The new CSO conductor, David Somers, had heard Cary play in Boston and invited him to fill a guest spot on a modern music series. Charming man. I was sorry to hear he recently lost his wife.*

Cary remembered the trip well—the last one he and his mother took to one of his performances. He was already doing most of them on his own, but she insisted they drive up from St. Louis together. It was summer, and he was home from his second year at New England Conservatory of Music in Boston.

He drove; his mother was too exhausted from her first round of chemo to do the driving herself. He was surprised she'd found the energy to come at all. Maybe she knew this might be the last time she'd hear him perform.

I know Cary isn't fond of modern music, but however he felt about it, Maestro Somers was impressed. He's taken Cary under his wing, booking him next season and suggesting a European agent. It will be a challenge for Cary, keeping up with his studies at NEC and performing, but his professors have promised to work with him.

Cary told me something on the ride home. Something I had suspected for some time now. I didn't want to hear it. I tried to make him understand that his choices will leave him unhappy in the end. He didn't listen. It's not only that God tells us it's wrong, it's that his life will be so much more difficult. In the end, though, he's still my son.

Cary leaned back against the headboard and closed his eyes. He remembered the conversation as if it were yesterday. They had been listening to music, but the signal had faded and they had turned off the radio and driven in silence for quite some time.

Even now, he wasn't sure why he felt compelled to tell her. Did he want to start a fight with her? Probably. But there was more to it than that. He was tired of hiding it from her and tired of pretending to be interested when she called him in Boston to tell him about a friend of hers who had a daughter he should meet. He was tired of her trying to make his life "perfect." It was far from that. If she'd known that even at nineteen, he was cruising the clubs on weekends when he wasn't performing....

He still remembered the cornfields that lined the highway and how flat the road was. He could almost smell the manure, even now. He felt the guilt that always accompanied the memory of that conversation. Guilt at having hurt her, after all she had done for him.

"I need to tell you something, Mom."

"You've decided to take the gig in Paris in December?"

"No. I mean, yeah, but that's not what I wanted to tell you."

"Oh."

"What I wanted to tell you... is that... I'm... you know... gay."

She did not respond, and he wondered if she had heard him. Then he noticed her hands, which were now clasped tightly in her lap.

"I just thought you should know."

There was more silence, and she finally said, "Just because you haven't found a nice girl to date doesn't mean you're gay."

"There are plenty of nice girls, Mom. I'm just not interested in them."

"I'm sure you'll realize that—"

"*It's not a phase, Mom,*" he interrupted, gripping the steering wheel tightly and doing his best not to raise his voice to her. "*I'm not going to grow out of it. I've never wanted to be with a woman—not like that.*"

"*It's wrong, Cary. Whatever you think about it, it's wrong. God says it's—*"

"*I don't give a shit about what God says about it,*" he shouted.

"*You won't be happy living that way, Cary,*" she said. "*It's not natural. It's a sexual... perversion. It's sinful. An addiction.*"

"*I'm not a pervert, Mom. This is me. This is what I am.*"

"*How can you say that, Cary Taylor Redding? How can you risk everything we've worked so hard for?*"

"*Mom, I—*"

"*After all that I've done for you, you tell me this? Do you* want *to hurt me?*"

They hadn't spoken about it again for the rest of the trip. In fact, they hadn't spoken about it ever again, not even when Janet Redding lay dying in her hospital bed eight months later.

He drew in a long breath, then blew it out gently between his lips, as Aiden had taught him. *She understood,* he thought. *She didn't accept it—she* couldn't *accept it—but she understood.*

TWO hours later, his practicing finished, he lay on the couch, pulled his phone out of his pocket, and tapped it several times.

"*Pronto.*"

"Tonino?"

"How are you, caro?"

"I'm okay."

"How's John?"

"He seems to be doing well. He's meeting his AA sponsor. They're having dinner together."

"Massi's at his mother's. He wanted me to say hello for him. He asked when you're coming home."

Not soon enough.

"I told him you'll be back when your papà is feeling better."

Cary debated telling Antonio about the clippings and his mother's notes, but decided against it. He still wasn't sure what to think about it, and he wanted to talk to John first. There'd be time later, when he made sense of it.

"So how's Massi doing?"

"Great. He's been teaching me baseball." Antonio laughed. "I'm terrible at it, but I found a league for him. There are only a few kids, but they play on Sunday afternoons a few miles from the apartment. Some Americans, mostly Italians who like the sport. They're looking for coaches—Massi's already volunteered you."

"I can't wait. I thought I'd pick up another mitt while I'm here, maybe another bat. Looks like I need to get a mitt for you too."

"I think you need to teach me to catch first."

"I miss you," Cary said in a soft voice.

"It's only a few more weeks, and we'll be there with you."

"It's what's keeping me going. That, and my hand."

"Your... *hand*?" There was a moment of silence, then a chuckle and "Ah, I understand. What do you imagine when you use your hand?"

Cary closed his eyes. "You. Running my hands on your silk shirt, taking your nipples in between my fingers and rolling them around until I hear you moan." Christ, was he getting hard just saying it? He bit his lower lip as he slid his hand under the waistband of his sweatpants. "I could put my mouth on the fabric and bite at them, get your shirt wet."

Antonio's breath was audible through the phone. "And then what?" His voice was huskier than before, and Cary knew he was getting turned on as well.

"Then, when they're really hard, I'd unbutton your shirt. But I'd leave it on—I like the way the silk feels against my skin. And I'd lick and suck until you begged me for more."

"More. I like that."

Cary grasped his cock at the base and pulled up on it until his breath stuttered. "Then I'd unbutton your pants, and I'd scrape your ass with my fingernails. Then I'd take my finger and I'd tease you. I'd wet it and I'd rub it over your hole, not putting it inside."

"Do I have to beg you?"

"Beg me." *Oh fuck!* He could imagine Antonio's skin, imagine that tight opening.

"Put your finger inside of me. Please."

"I'd put my finger inside of you while I took your beautiful cock in my hand. I'd make it wet, and I'd slide my fist up and down, over the top. I'd tease your slit with my thumb."

"What then?"

Cary wondered if Antonio was stroking himself the same way he was. "I'd stick another finger in and stretch you so it hurt, just a little. But it'd feel so good you'd beg me to put another in."

"Please. Put another inside of me. Please."

"I'd put another in and keep stretching you, making you open to me. Then I'd make you lie down so I could see your ass better. And then I'd spread you wide so I could lick you."

"Oh God, Cary," Antonio growled. "You're going to make me come like this!"

Cary continued to rub and pull at himself. After nearly two years together, he still found few things sexier than hearing Antonio speak Italian. And *this* Italian—it didn't get better than this. "I'm going to lick your hole and suck until you can't stand it anymore. Then I'm going to stick my tongue inside of you and taste you. And when I do, I'm going to rub myself. Not too much. I don't want to come yet, because when I finish, I'm going to fuck you."

"Fuck me. Oh, caro, I want you to fuck me."

It wasn't often Antonio bottomed, mostly because Cary preferred it that way, but Cary could hear the raw need in Antonio's voice. Damn, but he wished he were there!

"I'm lubing you up. Now I'm pressing against you, inside of you, and—oh fuck—it feels so tight inside. Like you're swallowing me whole, and I could just stay there forever." He was close now, he could feel it, but he held back and imagined the way Antonio's muscular ass felt beneath his hands when he squeezed. "I'm squeezing hard. Can you feel my fingernails digging into your skin?"

"Yes. It hurts, and it feels so good." He heard Antonio breathe through the receiver.

"I want to hear you come first. I'm reaching around and grabbing your cock in my hand. It's wet now, and my hand is sliding up and down and squeezing it hard. And you're groaning." Antonio *was* groaning now, and Cary was sure he, too, had his hand on his erection and was stroking himself. It was so fucking sexy, he wasn't sure if he really *could* hold off until

Antonio came. "Come on, baby," he whispered into the phone. "Come for me. Let me hear you come."

Antonio's response was an incomprehensible growl and then a loud "Oh! Oh God, yes!"

Cary lost it, spurting all over his stomach and his hand, bucking up into his palm and crying, "Oh fuck!" He closed his eyes and imagined the look on Antonio's face—the peaceful, sated look Antonio got right after an orgasm. Cary grinned and sucked in a long, stuttering breath. "God, Tonino," he managed after a full minute had elapsed. "That was so fucking amazing."

"You could say that," came the response, a half chuckle, half gasp.

"I've never done that before."

"Could have fooled me. Not that I wouldn't rather have you in person, but I'm looking forward to your next trip now."

Cary laughed. "Damn, I love you. I miss the hell out of you."

"I miss you too."

"I'm coming home soon. Promise. John's ready to be back on his own again. The doctor says he's up to it, and I've hired a housekeeper to help for the next few months."

"We'll be here, waiting."

"I know."

And it means everything to me.

CHAPTER 26

REALITY BITES

THE apartment door opened and closed, waking Cary from his light sleep. He had fallen asleep on the couch, fully dressed. He sat up and the mattress springs creaked.

"Sorry I'm late." John glanced over at the couch. "We talked longer than I thought."

Cary reached over to turn on the small table lamp, which cast fuzzy shadows in the darkened apartment. Even from twenty feet away, he could smell the cigarettes and booze. "You've been drinking."

"Last time I checked," John answered, his words slurred, "it was legal to drink."

"But you know what the doctor said about—"

"Fuck the doctor. He's not the one who had tubes shoved into every goddamn orifice. Besides, a few drinks are good for the heart."

Cary wanted to protest, but he knew there was nothing he could say that would matter right now. *He's drunk, for shit's sake. You can't argue with a drunk.*

"You all judge me. You, your mother, that fucking ass-pirate you live with—"

"Shut the fuck up!" Cary balled his hands into fists at his side. "Don't you *dare* call him that!"

Cary knew the drill. He had done his reading. It was the alcohol talking. And John *wanted* him to argue with him. He had done it enough for himself—getting other people angry at him so he didn't have to feel angry with himself. He knew all of it, but to hear John call Antonio that.... *Breathe. Just breathe.*

"I won't shut up, not in *my* house." John tossed his jacket onto a nearby chair, and it slipped off, onto the floor. He made no attempt to retrieve it but stumbled into the apartment, toward his bedroom.

"John... I know you're scared, but—"

"Don't you fucking lecture me about what I'm feeling! I had enough of that bullshit with your mother. Why do you fucking think I left her? Always nagging me, telling me she was worried and crap."

"John, you were doing so well. What happened tonight?" Cary tried to keep the strain from his voice with moderate success.

"Nothing *happened*. I told you, there's no law against drinking." John stormed over to the couch and glared at him. "Why don't you call him? The high and mighty Signor Bianchi? Why don't you tell him what a piece of shit I am, and you two fags can gloat over how you were right."

Cary grabbed John by his arm and turned him around. "Look at me, you bastard," he snapped. "You can do whatever the fuck you want with your own life. Go drink yourself to death if you want. But don't you *ever* call me or Antonio that. *Ever!*"

I can't stay here. It was all he could do to stop himself from punching John. He took a deep breath and got up from the couch, avoiding John. He slipped on his shoes and grabbed his coat from off the rack.

"Where are you going?" John demanded, grabbing Cary's shirt and twisting the fabric. His face was red and bloated from the alcohol, and there was fury in his eyes.

"Out." Cary peeled John's hand off of him and pushed him away. He didn't owe a drunk any explanations. "Go sleep it off," he added as he stepped through the doorway. "Don't bother waiting up for me."

"Like I'd even bother for a piece of shit like—" The slamming door drowned out the rest of the tirade.

Cary wasn't sure how he had ended up in front of the bar. All he knew was that he had walked for a good hour into Brooklyn, and he had stopped here. It wasn't as if he hadn't seen the place before; of course he had. For as long as he had traveled on his own, he'd always made sure he knew where they were—those dark places that, in the daylight, retreated back into lines of brick and stucco buildings, waiting to come alive once evening fell.

But *he* noticed them. Even in the sunlight. Even now that he hadn't given in to that urge for more than two years.

He had passed the bar when he'd taken his morning run the day before. But until tonight, it had been just another gay bar on another dirty street. Now, he felt its call as surely as he still felt the anger that knotted his gut.

A pair of young men walked out the entrance, heads down, unspeaking. Headed where? The quiet alley a half a block away? An apartment? One of the warehouses or run-down parks near the waterfront?

Cary's feet were rooted to the ground, even as a voice in the back of his mind urged him onward. He wanted to forget the pain of his confrontation with John and escape into the dark, familiar warmth of the sex. It didn't seem to matter that, hours before, he had gotten off to the sound of Antonio's voice over the phone. In that moment, Cary realized that the thief—the undeserving usurper and the hallmark of his childhood—still lived and breathed beneath the adult man he had become.

He had known he couldn't change John, hadn't he? Or had he really believed that he could? No, he decided, he had *known* the truth, he just hadn't *believed* it. He twisted the ring on his right hand absentmindedly.

And how are you better than him? How is this different, really? Don't you need this—don't you want this—the way he craves his booze?

The realization hit him hard, and the chill accompanying it reached his bones and clawed at him.

You're standing here, wanting this so badly that you'd risk the only happiness you've ever known? The man who loves you? The sweet little kid who calls you his "Cary Papà?"

He looked down at the ring. His eyes burned with tears and the thief retreated.

"No," he whispered into the darkness. "I don't need this anymore."

He walked back the way he had come with hot tears on his cheeks.

His face was dry as he reached the bay a few minutes later and stopped to feel the icy wind against his face. The moon illuminated the water, and he could smell the salt on the air. The drone of traffic from the avenue mingled with the sound of the surf as the water lapped at the rocks. In summer, there had always been people walking on the paths by the water, but it was too cold now; even the homeless people who lived in the park were taking refuge in the subways and shelters. Still, the cold did Cary's mind good. It helped him to focus, to sort out the events of the day.

He walked over to the Ocean Avenue Bridge, then paused halfway across to lean on the railing and take a few deep breaths. *It's time to go home.* He'd known it for a few days now, and tonight had clinched it for him. Staying here was doing nothing for either of them.

He thought about his mother. *She was doing the best she could for us.* It was all anyone could do, right? *That's all you can do about John.* What other choice was there? Stay here, with him? *And leave behind the two most important people in your life? Nothing's really changed since you decided to stay in Milan.*

"Damn him." Something *had* changed. Somewhere along the line, he had come to love his father. In spite of everything. And it hurt like hell knowing he couldn't do anything more to help him.

Except be his son.

His anger would fade, and John would still be his father. Deeply flawed, like his son, but his father nonetheless.

Time to grow up, Cary Taylor Redding. Time to be a man and forgive.

"I'M SORRY," John Redding said as he sat and stared at his coffee the next morning. "I wish to hell I didn't remember what I said last night. I was a complete asshole."

Cary pressed his lips together in an effort to hide his emotional turmoil. "Thanks. I appreciate that."

They drank in silence. "The shoebox in your bedroom," Cary finally said, deciding he had nothing to lose. "You left it out for me to see, didn't you?"

John swallowed hard. "Yes." His voice crackled with emotion. "I want you to have it. She would have wanted you to have it."

"Thanks."

"It wasn't her fault. She never complained about how hard things were, but they were hard. I didn't make them any easier, either."

Cary stared down at his now empty coffee cup, noting the chip on the handle and rubbing his index finger over it distractedly. "I know. I wish I'd realized it earlier. We weren't exactly on good terms when she died."

"Charlene called to tell me when your mother passed. She said your mother was happy you were with her in the hospital."

"She did?"

John nodded. "She also told me your mother didn't take your coming out to her very well."

"You could say that."

"It was difficult for her. It still is for me. It's hard to let go of what you've been taught. But she loved you. *I* love you too," he added in an undertone.

Cary stood up and walked his cup over to the sink. He turned around and looked at John with a hard expression. "Saying you love someone is easy." Cary took a deep breath. He knew he needed to say this, but he didn't want to give in to his anger, either. And he was still *so* very angry with John.

"It's easy to say you were brought up to believe certain things and that it's hard to change. I believe you." *God knows I've changed.* "But what you said last night… I can't forget it. I don't think I ever will."

"Cary, I—"

"Let me finish, John," Cary interrupted. "I need you to hear this first."

John just nodded.

"It's fine to say you love someone," Cary said. "But it's not enough. You can talk all you like. You can tell me you always loved me and Justin…." He fought back tears of anger and hurt, taking a moment to regain his composure. "But you waited twenty-eight years to contact me.

"Twenty-eight years of dreaming what it would be like to have a father. Of imagining what it was like to feel loved. Wanted. And now you tell me you love me and that Mom did too." Cary was crying now, but he didn't care.

"It's not enough. I'm not sure it will ever be. So don't expect me to say those words to you. Because I can't. You *left* us. Even after Mom died, you waited. You waited because you were selfish. Because you were afraid. You weren't anyone's father until you felt like being one. But it doesn't work that way. It's not about you. It never was."

John too was crying, although he did not move from the table.

"Thing is, as angry as I am, I still want a father." Cary thought of the night before, and of the bar. They weren't so different, he and John. Where would he be without Antonio? He knew the answer: cruising the bars the same way his father drank. He was sure of it.

"I called Tom. We're going to talk this afternoon. I told him what happened last night." When Cary said nothing, John continued, "I can't promise anything."

"I don't expect you to." Cary sipped his coffee in silence for a minute or two.

"You're going home, aren't you?" No guilt this time, just a statement.

"Yeah. It's time. My flight leaves tonight." He took a deep breath, then said, "We'll be back here in March—we're bringing Massi along too." He didn't mention they would be visiting Justin afterward.

"You'd see me again, after what I did?" John's expression was hopeful.

"Yeah. I would." *I may be a complete idiot, though.* "But if you pull that kind of shit again with me…."

"I understand. That's fair."

CARY stood in the doorway of John's apartment a few hours later, cello and suitcase packed. "I'll see you in about a month, John. I'll be in touch about plans once I've had a chance to get settled back home."

John's smile seemed forced. "I'll be looking forward to it." He stepped closer to Cary and hesitated as if trying to figure out if he should embrace his son. It was Cary, however, who took the lead with an awkward hug.

"Take care of yourself… Dad." It was the first time he'd called John that.

John's eyes were watery as he hugged Cary. "Thanks, son. For everything."

THE cab dropped Cary off in front of the Milan apartment building around 9:00 a.m. He paused at the front door, key in hand, and took a deep breath. He had never been so happy to be home. After walking into the front hallway a moment later, wheeling his cello behind him, he quietly shut the door and took off his shoes. Sunday morning—Antonio would still be in bed.

He crept down the hallway to the bedroom. Much as he looked forward to seeing Massimo, he was relieved to see Massimo's room was empty. He wanted some time alone with Antonio before facing the eight-year-old whirlwind of a boy. The door to the master was slightly askew, and he tiptoed inside, pulled off his shirt and pants, and slid under the covers.

Antonio stirred and rolled over, his eyes opening slowly at first, then widening in surprise. "I'm dreaming." He offered Cary a gentle and heartfelt smile.

"Yep. You are." Cary took Antonio in his arms and gave him a tender kiss. "Just don't forget that the next time I piss you off when I leave my underwear on the bathroom floor."

He could feel Antonio's chuckle against his cheek. "It's good to have you home. The best surprise."

"Thought you might like it." Cary kissed him again.

"Have you checked your messages?"

"Not since I landed. Why?"

"Check them."

Cary laughed. "Must be something important. But I kind of had something else in mind."

"Check them," Antonio repeated.

"Okay, okay!" Cary reached for his phone, then tapped it several times and put it to his ear.

"Congratulations, Cary," came David Somers's voice. *"My agent called to tell me you've been nominated for Best Classical Instrumental Solo for our Brahms. You might want to book a pair of tickets to Los Angeles for the Grammys in February."*

Cary laid the phone down with a shaking hand, then turned and launched himself into Antonio's arms. "You up for a trip to LA in February?"

"Is there any question? Congratulations, caro. I'm so happy for you."

"Have I told you recently how much I love you, Tonino?"

"Not recently enough. No."

Cary sighed and kissed Antonio. "I love you." He paused for a moment, then asked with a crooked grin, "Still up for getting fucked into the sheets?"

"Is there any question about that, either?"

CHAPTER 27

THE ONLY THING CONSTANT IN LIFE

A WEEK later, Antonio was bent over a cutting board, slicing vegetables, when Cary got back from the post office, having mailed a birthday gift to one of his nephews. He was feeling pretty good about himself for remembering all of the boys' birthdays this year. Cary figured if Antonio could remember all of *his* nieces' and nephews' birthdays, the least he could do was handle his own three nephews'.

"You're home early," he said, grinning broadly and kissing Antonio on the cheek.

Antonio didn't turn around but grunted and kept chopping.

It was Roberta's night off, and Cary had actually been looking forward to cooking. Cary had discovered that he wasn't as terrible a chef as he had once thought, once he actually put some effort into it.

"I told you I'd take care of dinner tonight," Cary said as he put his hand over Antonio's to still the knife.

"Do you have something against my cooking?"

Cary debated how he should answer. The last dinner Antonio cooked had been an unmitigated disaster—a beef roast that had tasted only slightly better than the hockey puck hamburgers he remembered his mother cooking when he was a kid. When Antonio had struggled to chew the overcooked, dried-out meat, Cary had insisted that it was "a good first try" in an effort to reassure his partner. They had laughed about it later, Antonio admitting that perhaps he was better suited to choosing wines.

"Well...." Cary worked his arms around Antonio's waist and pressed his cheek against Antonio's back. "There *are* other things you're better at."

The muscles in Antonio's back tensed, and Cary realized that what he had meant as good-natured teasing wasn't going over at all as he had planned. "I'll never get any better at it if you never let me try," Antonio said, putting down the knife with such forcefulness that Cary nearly jumped at the clattering sound.

"I only meant—" Cary began, but Antonio pulled out of his embrace and stormed into the living room without a word.

Shit. Cary stood in silent shock. *What the hell just happened here?*

It wasn't as if they hadn't had their disagreements, even after John had left Milan. But those disagreements had been quickly resolved, and usually of Cary's own making. *He* was the one prone to snap at Antonio when he was nervous about a new piece or just antsy because he hadn't performed in a few weeks. Antonio had always been the calm one, reassuring him and gently pushing him to realize that the anxiety brewing beneath the surface was of Cary's own creation.

This was different.

He followed Antonio to the living room, where Antonio was seated on the couch, reading the newspaper. The newspaper he had already read that morning.

"Hey." Cary sat down next to Antonio, one leg casually crossed beneath him. "I'm sorry. I didn't mean—"

"Don't worry about it," Antonio interrupted. "It's nothing. I'm tired." His eyes never left the paper.

"Is something wrong?"

"Why do you ask?" Antonio's entire body seemed tense.

Cary took a deep breath and gathered his courage. "It's just that I've never seen you quite so tense. Well," he added after a moment's thought, "maybe once before. When John was here."

"This isn't about you, Cary. It's not always about *you*."

Antonio's words stung, but Cary did his best not to show it. Instead, he leaned over and kissed Antonio again. "What's wrong, Tonino? I know you. Something's wrong. I can feel it."

Antonio put down the newspaper but remained silent, as if debating how to broach the topic. Then, after a minute, he said, "Francesca called me today. She's thinking of interviewing for a job curating her own gallery."

"That's great news. She's been wanting to do that for years." But the look on Antonio's face told Cary that the news wasn't as wonderful as it sounded.

"The job's in London."

Cary's throat tightened. "Massi?" His voice was shaky, thin.

Antonio nodded.

"But you're his father."

"It's not that simple. We always agreed he would stay with her... that she would be the primary parent."

"But—" Cary began to protest.

"But nothing. I won't fight her on this." Antonio's words and his tone were unequivocal. "I always knew this might happen."

"But it's not fair."

Antonio managed a soft laugh, although Cary could see his body was still tense. "It's not about fair. It's about Massi and what's best for him."

"It's best for him to be near his father." It sounded so simple, but even as he spoke the words, Cary knew it wasn't so simple. This was Francesca's *dream.*

It's not as though Antonio won't be able to see Massi, either.

"Sometimes life gets in the way of what we want, Cary. You know that better than most. And it would also be good for Massi to see his mother do what she loves. London isn't so far that I couldn't see him every few weeks. And he could still come here over the holidays."

Cary wanted to protest that it wasn't the same—that visits over the holidays weren't the same as having Massi here, with them, or seeing him nearly every day. And then it struck him: *he* was horrified at the prospect of losing Massi. He, Cary Taylor Redding. The guy who used to say he hated kids.

It wasn't only that Massi thought of him as a second father. Cary thought of Massi as his son. His *own* son. The bratty kid who complained when he had to take a bath. The "little stinker" who interrupted him constantly. The same boy he tucked in at night. The one he kissed on the forehead.

I love him too.

Cary wanted to shout. To tell Antonio it was wrong—that he should fight for Massi. But he knew Antonio was right. Even if he knew in his heart that Francesca shouldn't leave, that it would be bad for Massi to be so far away from his father, he wouldn't say it. Instead, he reached for Antonio and drew him close.

This isn't the way I wanted it to be. He had longed for the day he would be able to comfort Antonio. And yet now he fought the urge to be comforted himself.

"It'll be all right," he whispered against Antonio's hair. "Whatever happens. You'll be there for Massi."

And I'll be here for you. I swear it.

CHAPTER

WISDOM OF OUR FATHERS

Milan, January

"MASSI," Cary called from the kitchen, "you need to finish cleaning your room before you can watch TV."

"Just ten more minutes and then I'll finish it!"

"Five minutes more, and if you don't get it done, no batting practice at the park."

"Okay."

Cary finished drying the remaining breakfast dishes and wiped down the counters. Roberta was visiting her son and his family in Rome, and with Antonio in Korea to wrap up a book deal for one of his clients, Cary had volunteered to do the housekeeping.

He had returned from a trip to the States only a week before. This time, Cary had gone alone and stopped in New York for two days to see John. Cary had stayed at John's apartment, and they had spent much of their time together, just talking. As always, John had been vague about his progress with AA. Cary had not pressed the issue. In the intervening weeks, Cary had found an Al-Anon meeting in Milan with Antonio's encouragement. He'd come to the uneasy conclusion that he wanted to stay in touch with John, but that until John fully came to terms with his addiction, he wouldn't invite John to Milan again. He knew the visit might never happen, and although it angered him to see John struggle, he knew he couldn't change his father.

"How's it coming?" He peered into Massimo's room and watched Massimo make his bed.

"I can't wait for Roberta to come home."

"No kidding." Cary chuckled and shook his head. "At least you haven't forgotten how to make your own bed."

Massimo turned around and stuck his tongue out at Cary, who promptly returned the gesture. "Roberta does it better."

"You do it pretty well too." He put his hand on Massimo's head and rocked him back and forth. *He's a good kid*, thought Cary, realizing Massimo had grown another two inches in the past few months. Sure, Massimo still ended up in their bed when he had a bad dream, and he had begun to talk back to Cary more than at first. Cary considered both of these behaviors an indication that Massimo had really come to see him as a father, and not just his father's boyfriend.

"Am I ever going to get a little brother or sister?" Massimo had asked the night before, as they ate dinner in front of the TV and watched a cheesy Disney movie about a family with ten children.

Cary hadn't known how to answer. "I don't know, Stinker," he said at last, trying to make his response sound offhanded. The truth was that he had wondered the same thing himself, in a vague, alternative-universe sort of way.

"Mamma and Marissa talk about it sometimes."

"They do?" Cary didn't let on that he remembered Francesca mentioning wanting another child and saying something about Antonio being unsure about it. But that was a long time ago. None of them were thinking about that now, not with the real possibility that Francesca might leave Milan.

"Yeah." A few more minutes passed, and Massimo added, "I think *you* should be the papà this time, Cary Papà."

Cary nearly choked on his pizza, and Massimo giggled.

"I know how they *did* it."

"How they… *did* it?" Cary coughed.

"Mamma told me all about artificial insemination." He grinned and added, "I know how babies are made, silly."

"Right," Cary managed as he took a long drink from his glass. His face grew hot, and he realized he was completely and utterly embarrassed. "That's good."

"So will you be the papà this time?"

"Wait a minute, Stinker! I never even said you were getting a little brother or sister."

"That's okay." Massimo's blue eyes met Cary's. "I can wait. But not too long, okay?"

"I don't...," he began. Then, realizing he had no hope of neatly extricating himself from this conversation, he finished, "Okay."

They hadn't discussed the topic again that night, but Cary had thought about it a few times since then. He had finally concluded he was deluding himself to think he could be a parent. Antonio was the only real father here. *And what the hell do you know about kids, anyhow?*

He brushed the thought away once more as he helped Massimo pull the bag with the baseball equipment down from the top shelf of his closet. In the end it was enough, he thought, just to focus on Massimo. More than enough. Especially now.

THE bat struck the ball, and Cary yelled, "Way to go, Massi!" in English at the top of his lungs. It flew over his head, high enough that it escaped his glove, and he chased down the hill after it at full speed. He climbed back up the hill a moment later and gave Massimo a bear hug.

"That was great! Best yet, Stinker. You're good at this." *All we need now is for baseball to become popular in Europe.* He laughed and clapped his hand on Massi's back. "All that practicing has been helping."

"Papà still can't catch."

Cary knew Massimo was a little embarrassed at the compliment. He had started to become more self-conscious. *More like an adult*, Cary thought wistfully.

"At least he can run fast." This had Massimo laughing and nodding his head.

The phone in Cary's pocket vibrated, and he pulled it out and tapped it without looking at the caller ID. "Hello?"

"Is this Mr. Redding?" The woman spoke in English, but he did not recognize her voice.

"Yes. How can I help you?"

"Mr. Redding, I'm afraid I have some very sad news...."

"CARY?"

"Marissa, I'm sorry to bother you. It's just that Tonino is out of town until Friday, and it's the middle of the night in Korea, and Roberta is in

Rome, and—" *You're babbling.* He couldn't help it. His mind was running on overdrive, and he didn't want to slow down enough to think about things.

"Cary," Francesca interrupted as she came to the door, "come on in. Massi, why don't you go help Marissa with dinner, okay?" Massimo nodded silently and followed Marissa into the kitchen.

Francesca put her hand on Cary's elbow and led him into the living room. "Are you all right? You look terrible. Have a seat."

Cary nodded and sat down on the couch. "I'm... we're fine. I'm sorry if I frightened you. It's just that Antonio's in Seoul. I left him a message, but he's probably sleeping, and...." He rubbed the bridge of his nose.

"What's the matter, Cary? What's wrong?"

"My father... he...." *Crap. Get it together!* He took a deep breath and then said in a tight voice, "He's dead."

"Oh, carino," Francesca said as she took him in her arms. "How terrible."

"There's no one to... take care of... you know... his... body. And with Antonio gone, I...." *Breathe. Just breathe. It's going to be okay.*

"We'll take care of Massi. Can you get a flight out tonight?"

Cary nodded.

"I'll get in touch with Tonino. He'll want to meet you there, I'm sure, and—"

"No. I can't ask him to do that. Just tell him to call me and not to worry."

"Okay. I'll let him know. We'll be fine here—you do what you need to do."

Cary stood up. "I haven't told Massi yet. I just... I just couldn't do it."

"We'll take care of it," she told him. "Please don't worry about us. Is there anything else I can do?"

"I'm fine. I'll pack a few things and call the travel agent about the flight. I can't thank you enough, Francesca."

"It's nothing, carino. It's what family is for, right?"

He managed a weak smile, and she hugged him. "Thanks. I'm really sorry I'm so... I don't know...."

"Don't apologize. Just do what you need to do. We'll take care of the rest, all right?"

"Okay."

CHAPTER 29

EVER AFTERS

THE sun was high in the sky, and the smell of exhaust from the cars on the Brooklyn-Queens Expressway mingled with the scent of freshly dug earth. It was unseasonably warm for early January, and the sounds of birds could be heard over the din of the traffic.

Half a dozen folding chairs were lined up on the grass in front of the gaping hole in the ground. Brass poles strung together with red velvet ties marked the four corners of the grave. It reminded Cary of a movie theater. It was a silly thought, but he imagined a popcorn machine and a pimply teenager chewing gum, waiting on patrons.

There hadn't been many people at John Redding's funeral: Tom and a few other men from AA; Silvia, the housekeeper Cary had hired; and a neighbor. They had all left more than an hour before, but Cary had stayed. He wasn't sure why, but he knew he wasn't ready to leave. Not yet.

"You're welcome to stay as long as you'd like," the attendant said in a low voice. "Someone will be by later on to finish up."

Cary nodded in reply.

Finish up. Dump the dirt over the coffin, smooth the ground. Plant some grass on the dirt, perhaps? *Another one bites the dust.* Another father gone. Another son left behind.

No. It's not like that. You got to know him, didn't you? He thought of Justin. It wasn't better to be left with what-ifs. He had called Justin, of course, but Justin had told him his father had died when he was a kid and that he didn't know John Redding. Cary understood and accepted his brother's perspective. Lord knew, it had taken him enough to come to terms with John himself; he could hardly sit in judgment.

He reached into his jacket pocket and withdrew a faded photograph he had found in John's wallet. It was the only photograph he had ever seen that showed his entire family. In the foreground sat his mother, holding him on her lap, wrapped in a yellow blanket. Behind her stood John, smiling, happy, his hand resting on Justin's shoulder. Ironic, he thought, that John had given him back his past. His pathetic dreamer of a father, who was incapable of even taking care of himself. His father, so flawed and damaged, much like the past he held in his hand.

He replaced the photograph and stood up, scooped up a handful of dirt, and walked over to the grave. The dirt was slightly damp in his palm as he squeezed it. Reaching out, he let it fall through his fingers, then brushed the remainder off with his other hand.

"Goodbye, Dad." Tears fell down his cheeks, and for once, he wasn't surprised he was crying. John had given him that, as well. Funny, he thought, that anyone would consider tears a gift. He sat back down again and allowed the tears to flow unimpeded as he rested his head in his hands.

Time passed, and he realized he must have dozed off. He awoke to the feel of a hand on his shoulder, squeezing gently. That, and a smaller hand, gripping his own.

"You... you came? Both of you?" He got up out of the chair and was immediately surrounded by Antonio's arms, and a second set of smaller ones around his waist.

"I wanted to be here for you. And Massi... he insisted on coming too. I would have called to let you know, but there was barely enough time for me to pick Massimo up and get back to the airport before our flight last night."

"Is John down there?" Massimo asked, peering down into the hole.

Cary thought of all the things people said at a time like this. *No, he's in our hearts*, or *No, he's with God now*, or even, *He's in a better place.* And maybe those things were true. Right now, though, they all felt like bullshit. "Yes," he said.

"Are you sad your papà's dead?" Massimo asked.

Antonio looked taken aback at Massimo's words, but Cary smiled back at him reassuringly. "It's all right," he mouthed, then squatted down next to Massimo and said, "Yes. I am sad."

"I would be too."

"Yeah?"

Massimo nodded. "If you or Papà died, I'd be very sad." Massimo hugged Cary so he fell backward onto the grass, chuckling. "I love you, Cary Papà. You're my papà too."

And what, thought Cary, *could you possibly say to that?* Oh, except "I love you too, Stinker."

BACK at the hotel later—Antonio had booked a suite and had Cary's things moved into it—they ordered room service for dinner. Afterward, Cary and Antonio sat on the couch while Massimo watched something on Cartoon Network.

"I'm so sorry you couldn't reach me. I tried to call you as soon as I got your message, but you must have already been on the plane."

"It's okay. Really. In a way, it was a good thing I couldn't reach you."

Antonio looked surprised.

"It's not a good thing that I couldn't talk to you then," Cary explained, "but it did force me to take charge of it on my own. Without your help. I needed to do it myself, and I know I wouldn't have realized it at the time."

Antonio flashed Cary a knowing smile.

"What?"

"You've changed since I met you, that's all."

"No kidding."

Let me see... from back-alley fucks to—what?—married life?

It was difficult to comprehend sometimes. Connor Taylor seemed like a bad movie.

"How are you doing?"

"I'm okay. Sad, but okay." He inhaled slowly as he gathered his thoughts. He was more than just sad, although he wasn't sure what else he felt. Whatever feelings his father's death had stirred in him, he would need time to sort through them. "I'm lucky that I had a second chance with him. And more than that—I had a second chance with my mom too."

"Your mom?"

"Yeah. It wasn't just the box of clippings. My dad helped me see her differently. I realized she was like the rest of us—doing the best she could for me and Justin." It had been something of a revelation, an epiphany of sorts, at his father's grave.

"You're not angry with her anymore?"

"No. Well, yes, maybe I still am. I'm not sure."

Cary shifted on the couch and ran a hand through his hair. It made him uncomfortable to realize that as angry as he had been that she hadn't understood *him*, years before, he hadn't tried to understand *her* until now, ten years after her death. Uncomfortable and sick at heart. For the first time, he was mourning *her* death.

"She still loved him," Cary added after a few minutes. "At the end. Even after everything. It's why she wanted him to have that box. She just couldn't tell him she loved him."

She couldn't tell me, either.

Antonio leaned over and kissed Cary on the lips. The unspoken meaning of the gesture was clear, but Antonio made a point of saying it aloud.

"I love you, Cary."

"Why haven't you had another child with Francesca and Marissa?" Cary asked later that night. The question had been dogging him for days now, since his conversation with Massimo over the movie—when had that been?—less than a week before. Strange, how time had seemed to run so slowly since the news of his father's death.

"Why do you ask?"

"Just curious. Massi said something to me the other night about wanting a little brother or sister."

Antonio chuckled. "Francesca asked me about it about a year before I met you. I just thought it was too much. I was working a lot, and it was hard enough just to find time to spend with Massi. I wanted to be a father to any new child the same way I'm a father to Massi, not just a sperm donor."

"And now?"

Cary could read the surprise in Antonio's face. Surprise, and something else—curiosity, perhaps? Hope, even?

"And now…. Why do you ask?"

"I've been thinking about things, I guess. How I like being a parent to Massi. Maybe I'm not as bad at it as I thought."

Did I just say that?

"You're a wonderful parent. You just don't see it."

"It's not like I had the greatest role models, though."

"Maybe not. But you're not your parents, Cary."

"I know."

"So you want to have a child?"

Cary pulled away and shook his head. "Wait a minute. I never said *I* wanted to have a child. Just that I've been thinking about being a parent."

"How is it that different? Thinking about it and wanting it?"

"I don't know."

"Think about it, then."

"Okay," Cary said, feeling a bit overwhelmed. "I-I'll think about it."

Holy crap. Is this really me? But he hadn't really needed to ask the question, had he? He had known the answer long before. He *had* changed. And now, more than ever, he was oh so grateful for it.

He did more than rescue you on that Milan street. He saved your fucked-up life.

CHAPTER 30

ACCEPTANCE SPEECHES

THE sound of a siren pierced the quiet of early morning, the bedroom window cracked open to the unseasonably warm weather. Cary awoke and realized that Antonio wasn't in bed next to him, and glanced at the clock—3:00 a.m. He had returned late from his gig in Rome and slid in beside Antonio without waking him.

Strange. It wasn't like Antonio to be up in the middle of the night. Not normally, at least. But then, nothing had been normal since Francesca had gone to England to interview for the gallery job a week before.

Francesca had returned from London full of hopeful enthusiasm. The gallery was small, but the money would be good enough for her and Marissa to buy an apartment in a nearby neighborhood. Massimo would have his own room. If she took the job—and last Cary had heard, she was still waiting to hear back from the gallery owner—Massi would be making regular trips back to Milan, and Antonio would be flying to London every other week to spend the weekend.

David Somers, who Cary decided really *was* richer than God, had volunteered his London apartment for whenever Cary and Antonio were in town. They would both go for visits, as long as Cary's performing schedule permitted, something Antonio had been more than pleased about.

And yet with all of the plans, both Antonio and Cary had been on edge. That Cary would be leaving for the Grammy Awards in less than two weeks only made it worse, for both of them. Cary struggled with the guilt of leaving Antonio, knowing what he might be going through if Francesca got the job, and Antonio, who'd originally planned on accompanying Cary, had decided to stay home instead to help Massi with the transition.

She hasn't gotten the offer yet, Cary reminded himself as he stared out the window. He slipped out of bed and pulled on a pair of sweats, then walked out into the living room.

Antonio was seated on the couch, his face in his hands. The realization that he was crying frightened Cary more than he could say. Had Francesca heard something?

"I missed you." He wrapped his arms around Antonio, holding his breath, afraid to ask.

"I'm glad you're home." Antonio turned his head into the crook of Cary's neck and sighed.

"Did Francesca hear?" Cary could barely speak the words.

"Yes."

Oh God.

"She got the job, didn't she?" Cary asked.

Antonio nodded silently.

Cary fought back tears of his own.

I need to be strong. For him and Massi.

"I'm so sorry, Tonino."

Antonio pulled out of Cary's embrace and looked at him, his eyes red, the dark circles of worry underneath more pronounced than they had been even the day before.

"No, caro," he said. Cary saw a glimmer of something in those eyes. Something he didn't understand.

"What?" Cary pressed. "She's leaving, isn't she?" He was losing the battle with his own tears now, but he didn't care.

"No." Antonio's voice was an undertone. "She's not."

"She... she's *staying*? Here? But you said she got the job. I don't understand."

Antonio took Cary's face in his hands and brushed the tear tracks away with his big thumbs. "She decided not to take the job." He smiled a tentative, hopeful smile.

"She's not...." Cary's mind refused to make the connection.

"She's staying. She decided she doesn't want to leave Italy. She doesn't want to leave Milan. She says she can't take him away from us."

"She's staying." It wasn't a question this time. "But if she's staying, why are you crying?"

Antonio's smile deepened, even through his tears. "Because I'm happy." He must have realized that it sounded strange, because he laughed outright. "And I'm scared too."

"Scared? Why are you scared?"

"Because I don't know what I would have done. I don't think I could have…." Antonio's voice trailed off, and his tears began anew.

"Shhh. Tonino. Mio caro. You would have been fine. *We* would have been fine." And in that moment, Cary *knew* it was true. They would be fine. Together, they would be fine.

When they were back in bed a few minutes later, Cary leaned over to kiss Antonio. "I love you, Tonino," he whispered as he ghosted his lips over Antonio's jaw.

Antonio was quiet as Cary drew back the covers and kissed a line down Antonio's neck. Cary pulled Antonio's T-shirt over his head, tossed it off the bed, and covered Antonio's bare chest with slow and sensual kisses.

Cary met Antonio's gaze. The raw emotions were still visible in Antonio's eyes. "I love you," Cary repeated, then took a pink nipple between his lips, tasting it and sucking until he felt Antonio's breath hitch.

Antonio's skin reflected the light from outside, and Cary marveled at the softness of it. He pressed his tongue down so he could trace the hard muscle beneath the warm flesh, then flicked his tongue about until Antonio let out a soft, shuddered sigh.

"I love you," Cary whispered again. "I love how you taste. How you feel."

He pulled off Antonio's pajama bottoms and, for a moment, just studied his lover's body. *He's so beautiful.* Cary took in the smooth skin, the muscled arms that felt so *damn* good clasped around him, the rugged jaw and the strong profile.

"I love you." Cary rolled Antonio over. Starting at his shoulders, Cary nipped, licked, and sucked, pausing from time to time to step back and admire his handiwork: the smooth skin had tiny marks he knew would be gone in the morning. Antonio groaned.

Cary smiled. He had grown to relish taking time to enjoy the feel of his lover's body beneath his hands and lips.

"I love you," he said again. This time he pressed his hands against Antonio's lower back, then kneaded the muscular ass. He moved downward, trailing his thumbs in the folds between buttocks and thighs, turning his hands inward so he brushed Antonio's sac ever so slightly.

"Caro." Antonio's voice was rough with need. *"Per favore...."*

Cary ignored this but continued his way all the way to Antonio's feet, which he massaged and licked until Antonio growled and turned around to pin Cary to the bed. Cary just grinned. He loved to push the usually patient Antonio until he lost control. This time, however, Antonio lubed up his fingers and stroked Cary's cock until it stood at attention.

"I thought I'd try another variation on your fucking me into the sheets," Antonio said as he lowered himself onto Cary.

"Oh fuck." Cary hissed as the heat of Antonio's body opened to him. The look on Antonio's face was one of pain and pleasure.

Cary reached up to grasp Antonio's waist, but Antonio just laughed and grabbed Cary's wrists, forcing them up over the pillow. He continued to hold on to Cary with one hand as he steadied himself with the other and moved up and down on Cary's shaft.

"Oh God... Tonino... you're wicked...."

"Tell me again, caro. Tell me you love me."

"I love you. What you do to me. How good you feel."

"Tell me you want me."

Cary swallowed hard, and tears burned in his eyes. "I want you. All of you. For as long as you'll have me."

"Forever?"

"Forever. Only you. *Sempre.*"

Antonio's face lit up with the words, and he pulled Cary up off the bed. His hands now free, Cary took Antonio's cock in his hand and stroked him in time with Antonio's movements.

"Ti amo, caro," Antonio said as Cary's body tensed with impending orgasm. *"Ti voglio. Sempre. Sempre,* caro."

Cary cried out as he came, clutching at Antonio's arms as his body shook and shuddered. Antonio came with Cary's name on his lips, spurting onto Cary's skin. Cary collapsed back onto the bed, and Antonio followed, clasping Cary against him and continuing to whisper his name.

"I love you, Tonino. Forever."

As the sun began to light the morning sky, Antonio's head lay against Cary's chest.

"What are you thinking?" Antonio asked.

"Just that you said that Francesca said she couldn't take him away from *us.*"

"Yes. That's what she said. Does it surprise you?"

"Yes. It does. I'm not his father."

"You're wrong, Cary. Haven't you realized it yet?" He paused and kissed Cary's bare chest. "You *are* Massi's father. A wonderful, loving father."

And for once, Cary didn't need Antonio to tell him it was true. Cary *knew* it for himself.

Los Angeles, February

"THE next award is for Best Classical Instrumental Solo." The presenter was a pop singer Cary recognized from a poster taped to the wall in his nephew's room. "And in case you all think I don't listen to classical"—he grinned at the audience, flashing them a set of brilliant white teeth—"my man Alex Bishop taught me a thing or two about it."

Cary glanced at Alex, seated to his left, and grinned. Cary gripped Antonio's left hand with his right as the presenter read the list of nominees.

"And Cary Redding, for his recording of the Brahms Double Concerto in A Minor, Opus 102." The presenter paused for effect, looking directly at Cary.

Cary's face felt hot as one of the cameramen swung about to capture him sitting in the audience. It still seemed strange that he had been nominated but Alex hadn't. Cary had told everyone who would listen that Alex was the "true master," and downplayed his own role in the project. Alex had responded by telling him in no uncertain terms that it had been *Cary's* performance that had made the recording such a success. Cary had brushed off the compliment and cracked a joke about violinists having smaller "instruments."

"And this year's winner of the Recording Academy's Grammy for Best Classical Instrumental Solo is… Cary Redding, for the Brahms Double Concerto in A Minor!"

Cary was sure he hadn't heard correctly. But when one of the ushers came from the side of the auditorium to escort him onto the stage, all he could do was follow with a quick look back at David, Alex, and Antonio, who, along with much of the crowd, were on their feet and applauding enthusiastically.

The bright lights stung his eyes after the relative darkness of the auditorium. He remembered how, years ago, his mother had taught him not to react outwardly to the multihued blur they left in their wake. Although he was no stranger to the lights or to large audiences, he felt almost naked without his cello as he stared out beyond the lights, holding the Grammy in his right hand. For a moment, he just stood there at the podium with a vague recollection of having been told to say something but keep it "brief."

Say something.

The irony that he, the man who always prepared for his appearances with something bordering on obsession, had not prepared a speech was hardly lost on him.

"Thanks to everyone who made this recording possible—the Chicago Symphony's musicians, my teachers, the people who encouraged me, my brother, Justin, my friends." His voice was strong and confident, despite the butterflies that danced in his belly and made his head spin.

"Thank you, David Somers, for having given me the opportunity to perform such amazing repertoire."

Thanks for your patience and unwavering friendship in spite of all my stupid shit.

"Thank you, Alex Bishop. For your friendship and your incredible fiddle playing. You made me sound good."

Thanks for listening and having faith in me.

Cary smiled. "Those are the easy ones. Some thank-yous are more complicated, but you know you still need to say them." He took a deep breath. "Thank you, Mom, for introducing me to the joy of music and for giving of yourself even when I didn't understand the gift."

Thanks, Dad, for helping me find the heart I had buried away.

"And my family. Massi and Tonino. Except I can't really thank you, can I? Because words seem so little to give you in return for what you've both given me. *Vi voglio bene.*" *I love you both.*

Thanks for giving me a life and a future. A home, a heart, an everything.

"Thank you."

AFTERWARD, Cary would remember none of the handshakes and congratulations backstage, the celebrities, the photographs or signing autographs. He was led past a gauntlet of admirers and curious onlookers, reporters, dignitaries. An hour later, exhausted and entirely overwhelmed, he was shown into a small sitting room, empty but for one person: the person he wanted to see most.

"Tonino."

"Caro." Antonio opened his arms, and they held each other for the longest time. At last, Antonio asked, "Are you happy?"

Cary nodded. "I hope you're not angry with me."

"Angry? Why would I be?"

"People will ask questions. About you... about what you mean to me."

"I've never hidden who I am. I'm proud to speak of my love for you."

In that instant, Cary understood something that he hadn't understood before. He knew what he wanted with a clarity that had until then eluded him.

"Tonino?"

"Hmm?"

Cary took a deep breath and released it, then pressed his head into Antonio's solid shoulder. "*Ti amo, Tonino. Molto.*"

"*Ti amo anche, Cary. Moltissimo.*" Antonio hugged him again, then pulled back so that Cary could see the expression on his face. Cary saw the love in Antonio's eyes—it was a palpable thing, warm and reassuring. How had he gotten so lucky?

"I want to have a child. With you."

Antonio's blue eyes grew wide. "You, you want to have a child?"

"Yes." Cary laughed.

"But how... I mean... why now?"

"I'm ready now."

"You're not afraid?"

"Are you kidding?" Cary laughed again. "I'm scared to death." He paused for a moment, then kissed Antonio lightly on the lips. "But I'm ready. So what do you think? Will you have a child with me?"

Antonio just smiled and kissed Cary tenderly, then drew him closer so that his lips were right beside Cary's ear, brushing the lobe and eliciting an audible sigh. Antonio took a deep breath, then whispered his answer. Cary smiled against Antonio's cheek.

Happy endings. Cue the fade-out.... No. Not an ending, Cary thought. *A beginning. A future. A life.*

In her last incarnation, SHIRA ANTHONY was a professional opera singer, performing roles in such operas as *Tosca*, *Pagliacci*, and *La Traviata*, among others. She's given up TV for evenings spent with her laptop, and she never goes anywhere without a pile of unread M/M romance on her Kindle.

Shira is married with two children and two insane dogs, and when she's not writing, she is usually in a courtroom trying to make the world safer for children. When she's not working, she can be found aboard a 30-foot catamaran at the Carolina coast with her favorite sexy captain at the wheel.

Shira can be found on Facebook, Goodreads, or on her website, http://www.shiraanthony.com. You can also contact her at shiraanthony@hotmail.com.

Romance from SHIRA ANTHONY

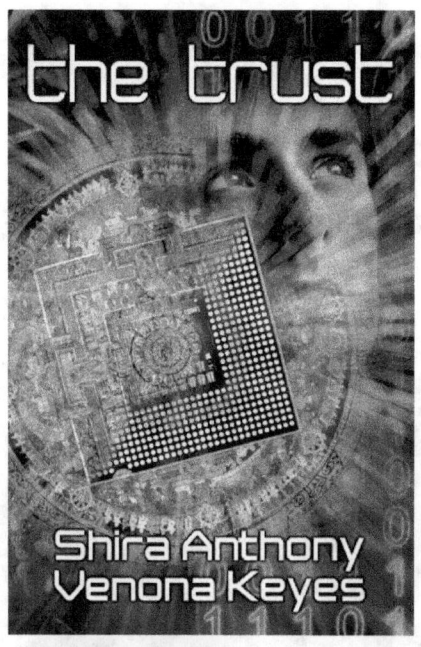

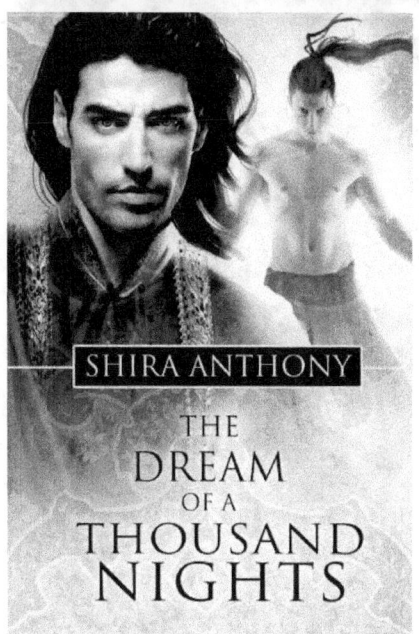

http://www.dreamspinnerpress.com